With a loud cry, Jesus breathed his last.
The curtain of the temple was torn in
two from top to bottom. And when the
centurion, who stood there in front of Jesus,
saw how he died, he said, "Surely
this man was the Son of God!"

—MARK 15:37–39 (NIV)

MYSTERIES & WONDERS *of the* BIBLE

Unveiled: Tamar's Story

MYSTERIES & WONDERS *of the* BIBLE

UNVEILED
TAMAR'S STORY

Roseanna M. White

A Gift from Guideposts

Thank you for your purchase! We want to express our gratitude for your support with a special gift just for you.

Dive into *Spirit Lifters*, a complimentary e-book that will fortify your faith, offering solace during challenging moments. Its 31 carefully selected scripture verses will soothe and uplift your soul.

Please use the QR code or go to **guideposts.org/ spiritlifters** to download.

Mysteries & Wonders of the Bible is a trademark of Guideposts.

Published by Guideposts
100 Reserve Road, Suite E200, Danbury, CT 06810
Guideposts.org

Cover and interior design by Müllerhaus
Cover illustration by Brian Call represented by Illustration Online LLC.
Typeset by Aptara, Inc.

ISBN 978-1-961126-88-6 (hardcover)
ISBN 978-1-961251-49-6 (softcover)
ISBN 978-1-961126-89-3 (epub)

Printed and bound in the United States of America
10 9 8 7 6 5 4 3 2 1

MYSTERIES & WONDERS *of the* BIBLE

UNVEILED
TAMAR'S STORY

To David and Rowyn,
Deanna and Candice and Betty, Bethany, and Cindy,
Pam and Steve, Danielle, Bonnie, and Caroline.
Thanks for being with me and cheering me on while
I wrote this on our wonderful P&P Retreat.
If only all books could be written at a beach house!

CAST OF CHARACTERS

Albus • soldier under Valerius

Bithnia • newest weaver, friend of Illana, follower of Jesus

Caeso • soldier under Valerius

Caiaphas • high priest of Israel from AD 18–36, of the Sadducee sect

Davorah • second-most-senior weaver

Felix • Valerius and Mariana's son, age 9 months

Gaius • beloved servant in the Marius house

Hannah • Levi's wife

Hinda • weaver

Illana • weaver

Jeremiah • Tamar's second eldest brother

Levi • Tamar's cousin

Livia • Valerius and Mariana's daughter, age 3

Mariana • Valerius's wife

Moshe • Tamar's eldest brother

Pontius Pilate • Roman governor of Judea, AD 26–37

Sarah • third-most-senior weaver, Tamar's close friend

Simon • Tamar's younger brother

Tamar • head weaver of the temple veil

Valerius Marius • Roman centurion, present at the foot of the cross and guarding the tomb

GLOSSARY OF TERMS

abba • Hebrew for father

Apollo • Roman god of the sun, music, healing, and prophecy, son of Jupiter

charoset • a sweet, dark-colored paste made of fruits and nuts; also known as apple clay

imma • Hebrew for mother

Jupiter • Roman king of the gods, god of the sky, also known as Zeus to the Greeks

mishkan • tabernacle, in Hebrew means "to dwell"

Pesach • Passover

tata • Latin for father

CHAPTER ONE

The girls chattered as they knelt before the huge loom in the weaving room. Tamar paced the floor along the length of the loom, watching every movement as fabric emerged from the intricately, perfectly woven cords. She barely heard their girlish talk, their voices blending with others that drifted through two wide windows. A nearly imperceptible breeze carried the aroma of onions and herbs from the market.

The scent almost distracted her. Last night the *Pesach* celebration had begun, and she'd eaten the first meal with her family. Her sisters and nieces would already be at work on the food for the second day of the weeklong feast, while she oversaw the last of the holy work they would do in the weaving room for the next week. No doubt her sisters-in-law were busy chopping vegetables and herbs and gathering eggs, while her cousin Levi, a priest in the temple, would be just as busy today as yesterday, slaughtering the lambs for the visitors to Jerusalem and for Gentiles who wished to celebrate with them. Levi, exhausted last night after the slaughtering for the resident Jews, had mused on how they might have to extend the Pesach sacrifices yet another day if the celebration grew any more.

Proof, they'd all agreed, that the Lord was at work in the world.

She jerked her attention back to the weaving room and the girls in her charge. Tamar smiled at their prattling voices, focusing on the fabric slowly growing on the cloth roll. She inspected the progress at each of the seventy-two rods with an expert eye to ensure every girl exerted the exact amount of tension needed. Their chatter quieted at her approach and began again as she moved along. She hid a smile. They weren't afraid of her, but they did respect her, especially the new girls—as they should for one who had served Adonai in such a sacred capacity for more than fifteen years.

Tamar halted, then dropped to her knees. A wayward thread protruded from the tightly woven cloth. She tugged lightly on the offending thread, and all conversation ceased.

"Did you not see this, Bithnia?" She looked at one of six girls who had joined the group two weeks before.

Bithnia's smooth brow puckered. She leaned across the taut rows of cords to examine the errant thread. "I…" She swallowed. "I did not notice. One of the strands must have frayed."

Tamar drew in a deep, calming breath.

"You *must* be more attentive." She controlled her tone but allowed a slight scold to creep in. She stood to look down on the girl. "One day this veil will guard the Most Holy Place. Adonai Himself ordained the design, and every strand *must* be perfect."

Bithnia rocked back on her heels, her head drooping forward. "Yes, Tamar. I…I was distracted."

"Distracted?" Tamar raised her voice to address the entire room. "This work is holy. We cannot become inattentive. This curtain is blessed. Sacred. It will safeguard the very presence of the Holy One. Who knows what would happen if the veil was imperfect?"

No one answered, the silence broken only by the sounds from the market.

Tamar bent, wrapped the strand around her fingers, and tore it from the woven fabric. She raised it, a scarlet thread to represent fire. When she knew she had everyone's attention, she released it. It fluttered downward and came to rest across the warp cords.

"Had we found it during the weave, we might have saved part of the veil. But now…" She drew in a deep breath and almost whispered, "Clear the loom and discard this imperfect fabric. We must begin again."

The girls raised a groan, and those around Bithnia glared at her. Tamar softened when the girl's features fell. She spoke again, loudly enough to be heard but this time with more compassion.

"Adonai knows we are not perfect." Again, the girls fell silent. Tamar gazed at the line of young weavers, each pair of eyes fixed on her. "That is the reason for the sin sacrifice, is it not?" The girls nodded, and Tamar smiled at Bithnia. "Did King Solomon not say, 'Two are better than one'? We help each—"

A commotion from outside interrupted her. A cacophony of angry cries filled the air. Not market shoppers. This sounded more like a mob. Tamar approached the closest of the windows and leaned out to look down the narrow lane.

To her left she saw only the shops and buildings lining the street until the road curved at the top of the hill. She turned her head to the right, toward the market, and her breath froze.

People packed the narrow lane, most walking backward to watch whatever followed. Their voices roared, some wailing, some shouting, some cursing. Beyond them, the metal helmets of Roman guards gleamed in the morning sunlight.

Tamar's stomach dropped. Another crucifixion.

She hurried to the door and threw it open then stepped onto the narrow stoop. Dimly aware that the girls crowded behind her or huddled around the windows, she stood as a barrier between them and the swiftly approaching crowd.

When their advance brought them to the shop, she extended her arms to protect her girls from the fury of the screaming mob.

They filed past, their garb identifying them as Jews. Probably pilgrims to Jerusalem, come to celebrate Pesach. But why were they so angry?

As the first wave passed, she heard the thudding of feet on the stone road. Through the crowd, she glimpsed a row of Roman soldiers, identifiable by their uniforms. And then...

Her stomach lurched. She'd seen crucifixions, but this man was barely recognizable as human, His face so disfigured from the beatings He had endured. Blood streamed from a crude circlet on His head, and even from this distance, she saw huge thorns digging into His skull. Just watching Him struggle to take His next step made her body ache.

"Who is that?" she whispered.

Tamar hardly knew that she had spoken until someone sniffled. She turned to find Bithnia standing beside her. Tears ran down the young woman's face.

"It is Jesus."

Work on the curtain progressed slowly. Tamar helped the girls remove the flawed fabric and drag it off to be discarded. They'd only been working on this veil for a few weeks, so the weight was manageable. Then they began the process of threading the tightly woven warp through each rod, attaching the weight stones, checking each cord's tension while ensuring that the twenty-four strands were firmly wound.

She was bent over the eighth rod when the light failed.

The room was enveloped in darkness. One young woman squealed in fear, and soon half the others joined in. Though she understood their fear—even experienced some herself—Tamar straightened and spoke firmly.

"Girls, control yourselves. Davorah, Hinda, Illana, bring lamps from the storeroom."

They hesitated only a moment before moving as one toward the back room.

Tamar addressed the rest of the weavers. "'Tis a terrible storm, no doubt. It will pass. We have lost too much time on this veil already. We cannot afford to waste any more." She forced a calm breath. "I know we all have Pesach meals waiting for us at home. Let us work quickly so we can join our families soon."

Though she heard several whimpers, Tamar ignored them and walked toward the door. She opened it and stepped outside.

The tall buildings that lined the street lay in deep darkness. It was around noon, but the sky was as dark as if it were midnight. She barely discerned the black clouds filling the sky. It seemed the sun had disappeared. From the marketplace came nervous voices, fear apparent in their cries.

She stepped back inside and turned to the seventy-two anxious women.

"As I said, a storm." She forced confidence. "Like all storms, it will pass."

The three returned from the storeroom. Tamar directed the placement and lighting of the lamps until the room glowed. The flickering lamplight soothed their nerves, and the sound of fearful sniffling disappeared. Work began again.

Hours passed. The girls worked diligently at preparing the loom for the new veil, Tamar inspecting every movement. At rod forty-two, Illana finished securing the warp and then moved to the next one.

Tamar stiffened. "Why are you overseeing two rods?" She surveyed the row of weavers and identified the missing girl. "Where is Bithnia?"

Illana bowed her head. "She left."

"Left?" Tamar drew a deep breath. One of the chosen weavers abandoned her post? "When did she leave? And why?"

Illana kept her head down. "When the sun darkened. She went to Golgotha."

The hill of crucifixions. The truth hit Tamar. "Bithnia follows Jesus."

It was not a question, but Illana answered anyway. "She does. She said she could not stay here while…" The girl swallowed and risked a glance at Tamar. "While her *Messiah* is dying."

Tamar gasped. Who hadn't heard of this Jesus, the one claiming to be the Son of God? She herself had been swept up in emotions a week before, when the carpenter rode into Jerusalem on a donkey.

But to desert your sacred post? To leave the others to carry on your task? It was unthinkable!

She started to say so, but the words never came.

A loud rumble interrupted her thoughts. Tamar covered her ears to drown out the sound, but it seemed to reverberate from the soles of her feet up through her body.

The vibration intensified. The earth shook until it tossed Tamar sideways. She grasped Illana for balance, but Illana had none, and together they tumbled to the ground. Fear gripped Tamar. She grabbed her knees and curled into a ball, praying for the tremors to cease.

Though the earthquake ceased after only a few seconds, it seemed to last a lifetime. The girls were still huddled around the room when Tamar stood, stretched, and drew in a breath of dusty-tasting air.

"Is anyone hurt?"

She allowed the girls a moment to take stock of themselves and their surroundings and to relax enough to answer her. She studied the frightened faces. This day had held enough turmoil. She was tempted to send them home.

But divine duty came first.

"Now," she said, "let us continue our work."

The girls released a sigh, but in it Tamar caught the tone of relief. These girls needed assurance that all was well and that she—Tamar—was in control.

They worked for perhaps half an hour.

Then the door burst open with a loud *bang*. The man standing in the doorway wore the garb of a priest.

Tamar looked closer and gasped. This man was none other than High Priest Caiaphas.

She halted her inspection of the loom and knelt. In the fifteen years she had been overseeing the weaving of the holy veil, the high priest had never visited the weaving room. Why would he now? Did his presence have something to do with the darkness and terrifying earthquake?

"Where is Tamar?" His voice held suppressed rage.

"I…" The word was weak with fear. She cleared her throat. "I am Tamar."

The high priest paced forward.

"You will come with me, woman." He gripped her arm and dragged her toward the door.

"I—" Tamar gasped with pain. "Of course. Where are we—"

Caiaphas trampled the carefully strung cords and the holy threads and pulled her behind him. Tamar cast a helpless last glance at her girls' terrified expressions before he dragged her through the door and down the lane.

Tamar struggled to match his pace, but she was no match for the high priest's long legs. Merchants stared, their compassionate gazes turning to judgment when they recognized her captor.

The temple was not far, by design. Three hundred priests were needed to transport each perfectly completed veil. The high priest dragged Tamar the short distance in a few minutes.

"My lord, where are you taking me?" Tamar's teeth were clenched in fear.

"Hush, woman," Caiaphas spat, and Tamar fell silent.

They entered the holy temple through the Beautiful Gate. They passed through the gate into the Court of the Women, and still, Caiaphas dragged her forward.

When they reached the Gate of Nicanor, which separated the Court of the Women from the Court of Israel and the Court of Priests, she dug her heels in.

"I cannot enter the Court of Priests," she gasped.

Caiaphas turned a gaze on her that froze the breath in her chest. "Do not speak to me, you sinful woman."

Such anger, such accusation, in his eyes. Tamar shrank from his fury and shut her eyes as he dragged her forward.

Then he released her. She wavered on her feet. Terrified of divine retribution for entering a forbidden area, Tamar stood statue-like, afraid to look, to move. She heard the sound of a door sliding open and smelled the incense.

"Look, woman!" Caiaphas's voice ground out, fury clear in his words. "Look what you have done!"

Though she could barely breathe, Tamar raised her head and opened her eyes.

What she saw stunned her.

The curtain—the one she had overseen and finished not a month past—lay before her, ripped in two from top to bottom.

She closed her eyes and shook her head. No. Impossible. The veil was a handsbreadth thick and untearable.

Yet there it was. Torn in two. And beyond it...

Tamar collapsed prostrate to the floor. *No!* No one could look upon the Holy of Holies and live.

Caiaphas's voice cut through her horror. "You have done this. You have exposed the Lord to the world!"

No! The veil was perfect. I saw every strand woven into place!

But the words would not come. Once again, she peeked at the torn veil and beyond. The Holy of Holies, the dwelling place of God Himself, uncovered to the world.

What had she done?

CHAPTER TWO

The world was in chaos, and in the wake of it, Valerius wanted both to run home and make certain his family was safe and to stand still, his gaze on the man who hung lifeless before him. His heart had already sprinted toward the Roman sector of Jerusalem, toward his precious Mariana and their two children.

Had the quake shaken their home as it had this hill? What if the walls had come crumbling down around them, over them? What if they were injured—or worse? His gaze searched the road toward the city, but other than clouds of dust filling the lightening sky, he saw no obvious destruction. Even so, his feet itched to run.

But duty held him rooted to the ground on this hill the locals called Golgotha, the Place of the Skull. Duty…and wonder, all focused on the man who now hung lifeless from the middle of the three crosses. He knew the man—Jesus of Nazareth. Knew Him better than he was generally comfortable admitting. He had followed His teachings for the last two years, albeit mostly in secret.

Surely the time for secrecy was over. Nature itself had responded to this man—darkness covering the world as He suffered, the very earth shaking in protest as He breathed His last. But…He *had* breathed His last. Died. What did that mean?

"Surely this is the Son of God." Valerius had spoken the words aloud a few minutes ago, as he fought to keep on his feet on the bucking landscape. They'd been aimed at Longinus, at the observers gathered, at his own confused heart.

He was still learning who God was, had been learning it ever since he and his wife first moved to Judea so he could accept this post as centurion. They'd been here seven years already—long enough to see zealots rise and fall, to crush rebellions, to become dreadfully familiar with the hatred leveled at him by most Jews he passed, simply because he was Roman.

"Pagan dogs," they called him and his soldiers. He could understand that. The Romans were the conquerors, the ones who had stolen the Jews' right to enforce their own laws, who kept them carefully pinned under the rule of Rome.

But they spat the same words at his wife and the two little ones who had been born here, who had never even seen their homeland, and *that* was unacceptable. People could call him anything they wanted. But sweet little Livia? Precious baby Felix? They were innocents. Roman by birth, yes, but Judea was the only home they knew. He and Mariana were raising them to worship the one true God.

The attitude wasn't so different from the very ones in which the Romans held the Jews—disdain. That was why it had taken several years for him to realize that this God of the Jews was different from the gods of Rome, despite how alike His followers were to anyone else in their hatred and bitterness. To realize that the One they claimed was the sole Creator of the whole world and all who had ever dwelled within it was, by that very definition, *his* God too, if he chose to accept Him.

A God not of a city, not of a nation, but of the world. A God not of thunder or rain, of fertility or harvest, of war or music, but of *all*. A God who willed peace and harmony. A God who *loved* His creation.

Loved *him*. It hadn't been fathomable when he began to study the ways of this people from his first post in Capernaum. Gods didn't love mankind. Some were generous, some treated humanity kindly, but *love* was what men were to give to them, expecting nothing in return but favor now and then. Mostly, people just prayed against the evils of misfortune and pain and poverty. Gods used men as nothing more than pieces on a game board, acting out their own desires and whims, which could change with the tide.

This God—the God of the Jews—was something different.

That was when he had declared his own war—a war on the prejudice of both sides. He had defied all expectations of his Roman upbringing and begun to seek out the devout Jews in Capernaum, where he'd been stationed before this recent promotion to Jerusalem. He'd asked for instruction in the way of the Lord, and he had even used some of his family's legacy to build a much-needed synagogue.

It had won him friends there in Capernaum. Friends he missed every day, and certainly every week when he tried to learn more about God. Gentiles were allowed into the outermost court of the temple, yes, but no farther. In Jerusalem, none of the priests or scribes seemed to have any interest in speaking with and instructing the handful of Gentiles who collected in that court every Sabbath.

Longinus stepped to his side, his spear still dripping with the blood and water of the supposed heretic. His hand, clutching the wooden shaft, trembled. "I owe you an apology, Valerius," he said. His gaze too was locked on the man whose death he'd just confirmed.

On another day, Valerius might have smiled. Of all the Romans in Judea, of all the centurions he served with in the legion, Longinus was the one he counted as his closest friend, yes, even when they'd lived twenty miles apart and saw each other only rarely. But that didn't mean Longinus had understood as Valerius stopped offering sacrifices to Jupiter and Apollo. Certainly not as he'd begun to follow the teachings of the unassuming Rabbi from a random backwater.

Valerius had tried for the last year, after his promotion to Jerusalem, to get his friend to see what his own heart insisted—the man was more than a teacher.

Teachers do not heal the blind.

Teachers do not cast out demons.

Teachers do not raise the dead.

"Son of God." This time, as the words fell from Valerius's lips, they were more prayer than statement.

"I thought…I thought I would grant you *prophet*, at some point. The Jewish definition of one, that is. Certainly not an oracle like the ones we know. But the very earth does not lurch at the death of a prophet." His friend wiped at his eyes, blinked a few times. "But I do not even know what that phrase means—*Son of God*. How does this one God have a son? How *could* He if He is so unlike Roman gods? If He does not have affairs with human women as Jupiter or Apollo did in the days of the heroes, how could a son even be conceived?"

"I do not know." Valerius had been struggling with that ever since Jesus had actually paused to hear his request, sent through those hard-won friends in Capernaum. Since He had granted him the healing that Gaius had so desperately needed. Since He had praised Valerius's faith as greater than what He could find in Israel.

Valerius had known, as he'd rushed home after his messengers returned from intercepting the Teacher and found Gaius not only out of danger but on his feet, laughing with Mariana and playing with Livia, that *prophet* wasn't a strong enough word either. He'd read the accounts of the Jewish prophets. They too had saved people from death, yes. But not by a mere word from miles away.

He hadn't known, then, what to call Jesus. Even now, the words that sounded right from his lips carried more mystery than answer. "I do not know," he said again, "but I intend to learn."

Longinus shook his head. "How? You have been learning their ways for years already, studying under whatever rabbi will allow you to. You have said it yourself—they have no more answers than anyone else about the things this man taught."

Valerius was Roman, from the heart of the empire, the heart of education. He knew how to discover what he needed to know, once he'd landed upon the questions that he should ask. He would simply do what he'd done before when he wanted to learn about God.

He'd go straight to the people who should know and demonstrate that he was their friend.

"His disciples will have the answers." He turned to the small knot of them under the Rabbi's cross, though that only made him frown. The man had a dozen core disciples, and hundreds of others who followed Him too, wherever He went. Yet the only ones beneath the cross were a few women and one young man.

He couldn't just stride up and ask the mourners for a lesson. One of the weeping women was Jesus's mother, he was all but certain. He couldn't intrude on her grief like that—he could only imagine how his own mother would feel if she'd witnessed his execution.

Broken. Distraught. Undone. Certainly not ready to answer theological questions from a stranger.

His determination leaked out in a sigh. "Another day. We had better see to the other two as quickly as we can. I want to get home and make certain everyone is all right."

Crucifixions were certainly not enjoyable, but he'd volunteered to oversee this one when he learned that the rebel Barabbas had been released and the Teacher offered up in his place. Valerius had known very well that it was jealousy from the religious leaders of the Jews that had led to this, nothing more. The Teacher, the man so much more than a teacher, had been guilty of no crime against either Rome or Judea. Valerius had wanted to be sure someone was present to deal respectfully with Him—and with the others too, for that matter. The label *criminal* did not mean the men weren't still men deserving of that last consideration.

The legs of the two convicts flanking Jesus had already been broken, and without that meager support, life hadn't lingered long. Valerius waved a few of his soldiers over to help him lower each of the crosses and remove the men from the beams.

Relief and panic warred in his blood when he heard a familiar voice call out, "Master!"

He spun, gaze finding Gaius easily as the old man ran through the dwindling crowd. Trusting that his men would carry out his orders, Valerius strode toward the servant who had been with his family all his life, who was more father than servant. Who would be dead now, if not for Jesus's gracious word of healing. "Gaius."

Gaius had seemed younger since his healing too. He ran forward with the vitality of youth, not limping slowly as he'd done two years ago. His face still revealed his age, but it was uncreased with pain or panic, which allowed Valerius to relax the knot of his shoulders.

Gaius smiled. "We knew you would be worried. Mistress bade me run to assure you that we are well. The only loss in the earthquake was that old vase you always hated anyway."

Valerius breathed a relieved laugh. "No loss at all, then—and thank you. I was indeed anxious."

"Of course." Then Gaius's face darkened as he looked beyond Valerius, toward the central cross even now being lowered. The weeping from the women at Jesus's feet grew louder as one of them begged to be allowed to hold her son. "It is true, then. I hoped, when the gossip reached us midday, that they were mistaken."

"If only they had been." Valerius's voice sounded heavy to his ears, as heavy as it felt in his throat. Never before had he followed a teacher who met such a fate, but he was now one of thousands of people who would have to face the most horrible of questions.

What was one to do when one's leader was executed? Try to keep His teachings alive after Him? Or admit that His enemies had won and slink back into whatever else life had to offer? Forget all Jesus had taught?

But Valerius *couldn't* forget. How could he, when Gaius stood beside him, healed and whole?

Regret twisted his stomach. He hadn't even met Jesus face-to-face to request the healing—he'd been too ashamed, too afraid that the great Rabbi would refuse to see him because he was Roman. In that moment, when he'd considered striking out to intercept Him, it hadn't mattered that he'd made friends with as many of the Jews as he could, that he'd funded the building of a synagogue, that he'd learned as much as possible about the Lord God.

He'd been certain of his own unworthiness. Absolutely certain that Jesus would refuse him if he dared to ask for something as unheard of as His presence in a Roman household.

Gaius's face twisted in pain. "It should have been me."

"Pardon?" Frowning, Valerius followed his friend's gaze to the limp figure now being held by one of the women.

"*I* should have died. I have lived my life, I am an old man. A sinner. So many things I have done that I regret! Yet the Lord spared me, through one word from Jesus. How, then...*how*? How is He the one who has died, while I still walk the earth? It is not fair. It is not right. He has never done anything wrong."

Valerius sighed and reached out to clap a hand on Gaius's shoulder. He hoped it conveyed encouragement, though if it did, it was only by the grace of God. Heaven knew he had nothing to offer. "I know exactly how you feel. And yet here we are, left to sort out what it all means."

"Sir?" one of his men called to him, arm lifted in a bid for his attention.

Valerius nodded his acknowledgment, squeezed Gaius's shoulder, and then let go. "You had better get home. Please assure Mariana that I am well and that I will be home as soon as I can get away."

Gaius's mouth curved in a small, sad smile. "You know very well what the mistress will say to that, Master."

Despite it all, a chuckle warmed his throat. He'd been wary, he could admit it, when his family arranged the marriage to a woman so much younger than he, a woman who, upon first glance at her lovely face, seemed ill-suited to be the wife of a centurion. But he had relented, because it was what one did.

It had taken mere weeks for him to realize how wrong his first impression of Mariana had been. She was in fact the perfect centurion's wife. Far from resenting the time his duties demanded, she was the first to encourage him to be the best, most attentive officer he could be. To care for his men, for his tasks, for his superiors. Yet he couldn't suspect her of simply wanting him out of the house and her company, because she always welcomed him home with the warmest of affection and excitement.

In those few weeks, his wariness had melted into a love he'd never expected to feel. Now, eight years into their marriage, he indeed did know what his beloved wife would say—to any duty, but especially this one, that involved the care of the Teacher in whom they'd both put their trust.

"She will say that I should stay as long as I am needed to ensure the Teacher is given every respect, even now. Especially now."

Gaius nodded. "Livia will not be as quite as understanding, of course."

This time his chuckle was brighter, as the image of his small, demanding daughter filled his mind's eye. Demanding, but only of their presence. That was all she ever wanted—the people she loved best to surround her. "True."

Gaius stepped away. "I will assure them you are well too. And confirm the sad truth about the Teacher. If you need anything else, Master—"

"I will not hesitate to send someone with a message. Thank you, Gaius." As his old friend hurried away, back to the Roman quarter, Valerius strode toward the men patiently awaiting his instruction.

The strange darkness had faded into a dull gray light, yes, but he couldn't shake the feeling that it was still there. Surrounding them. Consuming them. A thick, suffocating darkness that snuffed out all the light. It closed in again when Gaius left, seeming to settle on Valerius's shoulders and wrap its fingers around his throat.

His gaze tracked to the man in whom he'd put so much hope.

The Son of God. *Dead.*

Where did that leave the rest of them?

CHAPTER THREE

A t some point, the high priest's words had turned to little more than crashing cymbals and echoing gongs in Tamar's ears. The cool stone of the temple floor was hard beneath her knees, but she'd stopped feeling that ages ago too.

Time had stopped. Reason had fled. Nothing made sense any longer.

She still knelt where Caiaphas had thrown her, where one heavy edge of the torn curtain was close enough that she was able to reach tentative, knowledgeable fingers toward it.

She'd overseen this veil. She'd studied every single thread, time and time again. She'd examined every inch created with skill and expertise. She'd smiled with satisfaction at the holy work her girls had accomplished when the three hundred priests carried it from the workshop to the temple just a month ago, ready to install it here.

Never had she expected to see it again—because no woman and few men were ever allowed this close to the Holy of Holies. She'd expected that it, like the veils before it, would serve its time and that before the first signs of wear could even be seen, a new veil would take its place.

Preserving perfection, always, as was right and just. If so much as a thread unraveled as it hung, it would be an offense to the Lord. It was why they always had a new veil underway. They took no chances.

Yet her fingers trailed now over countless broken threads. Every single thread in this line, broken. Snapped. Not frayed as if pulled apart by force, but sliced evenly, as if with some enormous sword.

It made no sense at all. Fabric this thick was impenetrable to anything but fire—even blades couldn't cut it through in a single slice. No earthquake had ever wrought such damage to a veil before. How could it have done so this time?

It couldn't have. *Couldn't have.* That was the trouble.

Her fingers played with the cut end of a gold thread that had once been part of a tree in the scene of paradise so carefully woven into the curtain. Now it was nothing. Uncreated. A reminder not of the perfection of the Lord but of destruction.

She started, a squeak of protest slipping through her lips, when hard fingers gripped her arms and yanked her back to her feet. It took a moment for her eyes to refocus, to see the angry face of the high priest instead of the snapped threads.

"Well?" he demanded, the fury in his eyes unabated by however many minutes or hours or days or years she'd been on that floor. "What excuse do you give, woman?"

Her throat was so dry she didn't know if she could speak, even if she had words to offer. Which she didn't.

In the weaving room, she knew her place. She could lead with confidence. She'd always been so certain of her every action and the reason behind it. In her family's homes, she could slip into her place too—doting aunt, loving sister, beloved cousin. Blend in. Do whatever was expected of her without ever being more than one of the crowd. Respected because of her position, but therefore also a step removed.

Here though? Now? With the high priest fuming at her? She had no words.

His hands apparently meant to shake some out of her. "Speak!"

She had to swallow first, and even then the sounds that emerged were so faint they should scarcely be called words. "It…it is impossible."

Caiaphas pushed her away with a sound of disgust. "And yet there it is. Your handwork, mutilated. Will you tell me it is the fault of the earthquake, though such a thing has never hurt a veil in all the history of Israel? Since the first veil protected the ark in the *mishkan*, this has never happened!"

"I know it has never happened. And no, I would not tell you that."

"How, then? What man is strong enough to rip the veil in two?"

She shook her head. "No man. Only God could do this."

He sneered. "This is not the work of God—this is the failure of *you*, you and those useless women you employ. And you will pay for it!"

"What?" That pulled her out of the haze so sharply she felt the jolt from head to toe. He couldn't be serious, could he? If he held them accountable, what punishment could even be prescribed? Would they simply be dismissed…or would he have them executed for such an affront against the Lord? "No!"

"My lord—I beg your pardon. A moment of your time."

Tamar couldn't tear her gaze away from the high priest long enough to see who had dared to interrupt his diatribe, nor could she quite believe it when Caiaphas turned toward the newcomer, smoothing out his features.

A reprieve, if only for a moment. But she hadn't any idea what to do with it. A few extra minutes would give her no miraculous words to explain away the impossible nor to offer an explanation that would prove this disaster wasn't her fault.

What if it is?

The words slithered through her mind and lodged in her heart. No…it couldn't be. Could it?

"Tamar. *Tamar.*"

She blinked, the familiarity of the voice breaking through her new stupor and pulling her gaze to the right. Her cousin was there, dressed in his priestly vestments, motioning urgently for her to join him.

Her feet obeyed him before her mind had given them a recognizable command, and she was more than a little surprised to find herself at his side a moment later. "Levi." The syllables emerged as a weak whisper. He'd always been one of her favorite cousins—and it was to him she owed her position. He'd vouched for her skill in weaving twenty years ago, when she was little more than a child and he first began serving in the temple.

Was he in danger now too because of her failure? Would the blame extend its stain backward to him?

His fingers curled around her upper arm, yet even as they exerted pressure that allowed no argument, they were infinitely gentler than Caiaphas's had been. "Come with me. Now." He darted a glance over his shoulder and propelled her quickly away from the Holy of Holies, out of the Holy Place altogether, and toward the outer courts. "He has been in a rage all day—one would think he'd be satisfied over his victory at having the Rabbi executed, but instead…" Levi shook his head, expression dark.

"Did you...were you...?" She darted a glance back too. Not at the high priest—at the failure for which he blamed her. "Did you see it happen?"

Levi shook his head and led her down a corridor she hadn't even spotted until he pulled her into it. "We *heard* it—everyone, all through the temple. It echoed like thunder, shook the complex in a way different from the quake. Or so it seemed. We knew something had happened. Though we never could have guessed *that*."

"It is my fault." She spoke the words so quietly that even she could scarcely hear them over the sound of their sandals against the floor. They tasted like bile on her tongue. They weighed like stone on her heart.

Levi sent her a hard look. "Do not be ridiculous. No *person* is responsible for that, and I will not stand by while you bear the punishment for it. I do not know what crime against Rome he would fabricate as an excuse to turn you over to them or if he would settle for a punishment we are permitted to dole out ourselves, but Caiaphas has been breathing threats of death, and I won't let that happen."

"I deserve it."

"You do not!" He bit the words off, kept them quiet enough that they didn't echo in the corridor. Nor could they lodge in her heart. "You oversaw the weaving of a perfect veil, just like the four you oversaw before it. This is not your fault."

"It must be." The world tilted, shook, and for a moment she thought the earthquake had started up again—but no, it was only her own body betraying her, trembling in her cousin's hand. "There must have been some flaw I failed to see."

Levi pulled her around a corner but then halted, gazing down at her with an almost feverish look in his eyes, so intense was it. "And what of the other weavers, then? Is it their fault too? Should Caiaphas punish all of them?"

"No!" Tamar pulled away from his grip at that suggestion, the clouds before her eyes clearing. Those women and girls—Caiaphas couldn't punish them all, could he?

But what if he tried? Even if he didn't execute them—*that* was surely beyond what Rome would allow, even if he somehow convinced the governor that a crime had been committed—what if they were dismissed? So many of them were widows or daughters of widowed mothers. Weaving was one of the only things they could do to make an honest living, and the temple employment was the only such position with constant work and reliable pay.

Levi leaned close. "You are not responsible only for the veil, Tamar. You are responsible for the seventy-two women who weave it."

She lifted her chin. "I know I am."

"So protect them now by protecting yourself. You must disappear—just for a few days, until Caiaphas's rage has cooled. He will see reason soon enough and will realize that this is the fault of no human. He will relent on his harsher threats, but he may still think it his duty to dismiss them all. When that happens, you must still be alive to protect them."

A shiver coursed through her. "Of course." She could agree easily to that much. But... "Do you really think he would have me killed?"

Levi's mouth pressed into a hard line, and he pulled her forward again. "I would not have thought so. But he just had a man executed for teachings he did not like, because they reflect poorly on him and the rest of the Sadducees. He will not want to be remembered as the high priest under whom the Holy of Holies was compromised. He will reason that swift action against some other culprit will salvage his reputation and legacy."

Her stomach felt as though she'd swallowed a rock. "What am I to do?" The words emerged as little more than a whisper.

Levi cast another glance over his shoulder and then hurried her through a doorway and into the gathering dusk outside. "Hide. Just for a few days. Do not return home to the family. That will be the first place he looks. Rent a room somewhere." He pulled something from around his neck and pressed it into her hands.

His money purse. She felt the jangle of coins inside it as she slipped it obediently over her head and let it settle under her tunic.

Levi scanned the crowds around them. "Meet me at Iocav's stall on the first day of the week, at noon. I will let you know then where we stand."

She nodded and then reached out to clutch his arm when he went to move away. "Levi, will you be in trouble too? For vouching for me?"

Her cousin's lips twitched into a sad smile. "He would not dare. If he tries to blame me, every Pharisee in Jerusalem will be ready to go to war with his sect."

That eased one concern, anyway. She let her fingers fall away and squared her shoulders, knowing she had to give her cousin a brave face, assurance that she wouldn't squander this gift of freedom he was risking too much to provide her. She nodded and took a step backward. "Noon on the first day. Go with God, Levi—and assure everyone that I am well."

They would worry when she didn't show up for the Pesach celebration, when she didn't come home for the night, even. Her brothers and their wives, sisters of her heart, their mother with her age-dimmed eyes, the other cousins who would join them for much of the weeklong celebration. Her nieces and nephews would pout when she wasn't there to play the games she had promised them.

Would Levi tell them the truth, or would it be safer for them all to simply think she'd accepted an invitation from one of the other weavers?

The others! She spun, darting through the crowds toward the weaving room. What if Caiaphas turned on them when he realized she'd slipped through his fingers? She had to warn them all, and quickly.

Rather than retracing the direct path the high priest had pulled her along a few short minutes ago—the light in the sky assured her she hadn't been gone long at all—she hurried along the back way and ducked into the door that opened into the storeroom. When she burst into the cavernous weaving room, she found the women still there, huddled in groups, fingers still and fear on their faces.

"Tamar!" Illana spotted her first and surged away from the group of women who always sat nearest her, her hands outstretched. "What happened?"

Tamar let the younger woman grip her fingers and gave them a squeeze in return. "The veil ripped in two during the earthquake."

She intended to go on, but the instant reaction of shock was too great. Gasps and disbelief and confusion sounded through the room. Tamar had to reclaim her fingers so she could lift a hand to silence them. "We are being blamed, and the high priest is enraged. My cousin advises us to return quickly to our homes and stay out of sight. If guards come, do not lie, but try to avoid them if you can."

As she spoke, she strode to the shelf where their records were kept and snatched up the scroll that contained the list of her workers and their families and where in the city they lived. There was no way Caiaphas would know who all seventy-two of these women were, nor where to find them. So long as they weren't *here*, they ought to be safe enough, if she could keep this list out of his hands.

Spinning back around, she saw that the women still stood in their knots, eyes large in fear. Tamar tried to summon a reassuring smile, but when that failed, she settled for the calm authority she always utilized here. It settled over her like a comfortable shawl, even now, when all else shook and quaked. "Go! Enjoy your Pesach, and I will see you when the festival concludes."

The command broke through the shell of stillness and sent them into action. Once moving, they made quick work of gathering their things and rushing out into the street.

All but Illana's group, who moved toward her instead. Hinda stepped forward this time. "What about you, Tamar? They will not take the time to question each of us, I daresay, but *you...*"

Tamar held herself tall and still, silently thanking the Lord that the tremors that had seized her in the temple had gone, leaving her with at least an imitation of her usual composure. "On my cousin's advice, I will stay out of sight during the Sabbath and let the high priest calm down."

"But where will you go?" Davorah asked, concern etching new lines into her face. They'd been serving here together for seventeen years. Davorah was a few years her elder but had come to the room two years after Tamar, after her husband died. The woman had always been too quiet for Tamar to feel as though she knew her well, but many years of shared space had nevertheless formed a bond. She was the second-most senior weaver here, dependable and steady.

Davorah had been here so long that she could well be the next one questioned. Tamar squeezed the woman's shoulder and summoned a small smile. "Do not worry for me. I will be fine. Go, enjoy the celebration with your family."

"But—"

"Guards are coming!" Hinda had moved to the door but now darted into the room, panic on her face.

"Go!" Davorah pushed Tamar toward Illana and then turned to intercept Hinda. "We will keep them occupied in the front. You two go out the back."

Before Tamar could make any objections, Illana had pulled her forcibly into the storeroom and, from there, out into the alleyway again. There were no guards here, at least. With daylight fading, they couldn't pursue her for long. The Sabbath would forbid it.

Of course, that meant she didn't have long to find a hiding place either.

Illana slipped her vibrant blue-and-yellow head covering off and pulled Tamar's pale blue one off too, switching them. Tamar frowned, but Illana smiled. "They have already seen you today. They will be looking for your clothing, the headscarf especially, from behind."

She was right, of course. But Tamar knew how proud Illana was of the beautiful scarf she'd woven for herself, its bold colors and intricate pattern a testament to her skill at both the dye vat and the loom. "I will return it to you after the festival."

"I know." Illana positioned Tamar's blue cloth over her own dark curls and smiled. "Stay safe, my friend. I will beseech the Lord for His protection for you."

"Thank you." At the end of the alley, Tamar nodded to Illana on her way to her family home and then darted across the main thoroughfare toward another alley. She tucked the scroll out of sight in her sash and granted herself one look over her shoulder.

No guards were chasing her down.

But where could she go? Her cousin could instruct her to rent a room all he liked, but that wouldn't make any *available*. It was Pesach! Jerusalem was teeming with pilgrims. Every bed in every inn had been taken at this point, she knew. She'd heard the disgruntled complaints of the visitors in the markets over the last few days, whole caravans of people who would have to camp outside the city because there was no room left within it.

Her chest went tight. She had family with room enough. Her immediate family with whom she lived, yes, but even beyond them. Other cousins, several who had tried to convince her over the years to stay with them, at least for a holiday week. Part of her yearned to let her feet follow those familiar paths. To knock on Sarai's door, or Zipporah's.

But she couldn't. Caiaphas would know to look for her at any of her relatives' houses, and she had no idea what danger she would put them in if she were found beneath their roof.

No. No, her only option was to act like one more pilgrim. She would go outside the city. Find a group of travelers big enough that their size would offer safety and anonymity.

It was the best plan she could devise at the moment. Perhaps, if she claimed to have been separated from her family and unable to rejoin them—true enough, in its way—someone would even welcome her to their fire and their meal. She had Levi's money, so she could offer to pay for whatever she ate. Most families she knew would refuse such offers in favor of hospitality, but at least she knew she had the coins.

Setting her feet on a street that would lead her to the nearest gate, she kept her pace quick enough to guarantee she'd have time to exit the walls before darkness fell and brought the Sabbath with it. Not so quick that she'd garner any attention. Everyone was hustling to get where they needed to go in the remaining minutes of daylight.

Then, finally, she was outside the walls. Jerusalem was at her back, the last golden rays of the sunset rimming the hills before her with gold. She was one of many people hurrying through the gate, even while others hurried to get in.

"Tamar?"

She jumped at the voice, even as she registered its familiar tones. No one out here was supposed to know her. But it was only Bithnia, heading back into the city from wherever she'd run off to.

The crucifixion. Oh, gracious. *The crucifixion.* Tamar's gaze flew past the young woman, to the hill of Golgotha. No crosses still stretched into the sky, but the normally empty area was alive with people, many of them coming down the road toward the city.

She should have chosen another gate, any other gate.

Bithnia edged closer, and her red-rimmed, puffy eyes were visible in the fading light. "Were you looking for me? I apologize for leaving my post. I know it is inexcusable, and I understand if you are going to dismiss me. I—"

"You are forgiven." Perhaps on a normal day, Tamar would not have been so quick to offer a second chance. But this had proven to be anything but a normal day. She pulled the girl out of the way of the others hurrying by in both directions. "In fact, I daresay I will be in no position to chastise you after this." In as few words as possible, she whispered what had happened to the veil and how Caiaphas was putting the blame squarely at her feet.

Bithnia's swollen eyes went wide. "You? But you have done nothing wrong!"

It was sweet of the girl to be so firmly on her side, when all Tamar had ever been to her was a stern authority figure. It brought the tired start of a smile to her lips. "I appreciate your support. But it will no doubt be in your best interest to keep your distance from me. Go, return to your family. Although..." Now she frowned. "If they question you..." What to do now? She couldn't ask Bithnia to lie for her. That would be sinful.

She'd simply have to change her plan so that Bithnia could honestly claim not to know where she was.

The young woman straightened. "No. I will not turn my back on someone in need. I will help you, Tamar."

Tamar's brows lifted. She could make her plan work. She didn't need this girl's help. Did she?

But if the guards questioned the pilgrims, no one would have any reason to protect her. Perhaps it was foolish to think she could rely on anonymity. Perhaps the Lord had crossed her path with Bithnia's now for just this reason.

She let out a long breath and met the girl's gaze again. "What did you have in mind?"

Bithnia offered a wobbly smile. "I know where you can hide."

CHAPTER FOUR

Valerius strode into the governor's palace with a nod of greeting to the soldiers guarding the entrance. They all knew him by sight, of course, so they let him pass with a salute with no command to halt and wait to be announced to the governor.

Pilate would be waiting for him. He'd been insistent this morning that Valerius report as soon as the crucifixions were complete. There had been trouble in the governor's eyes, more than Valerius had ever seen in them before—and he'd known Pilate long before they ended up in Jerusalem at the same time. Their families had been friends in Rome for generations. Pontius was nearly a decade his senior, so they'd never been friends exactly, but he and Valerius's eldest brother had been close when they were boys.

It was still strange sometimes to realize that Julius's old chum was now the highest-ranking Roman in Judea. The first time he'd walked in here on official business and seen the familiar, if older, face above the official's striped toga, he'd nearly laughed at the incongruity of it all.

At this point, however, Valerius had grown accustomed to answering to him, and Pilate, in turn, always seemed relieved to see a face he knew he could trust. Valerius didn't envy him the constant turmoil that politics inevitably brought with it. Pilate would have to worry every day of his career about who wanted to discredit him, who wanted to betray him, who would sell his soul for a chance at what Pilate had won.

Give him the certainty of the military any day. Valerius far preferred climbing the ranks in an orderly, well-organized fashion rather than elbowing and clawing his way to the top of something. He had been a good soldier from a good family, and so he had been given command of a hundred. In another year or two, he would be recommended for promotion to a prefect. If he served well there, perhaps he would eventually become a tribune or even a legate. But that was years in the future. Today, he would serve to the best of his ability exactly where he was, not scrabble for more.

He'd expected the hall to be calm if busy, filled with officials going about their tasks as Pilate closed his court proceedings for the day and everyone prepared to either join him for the evening meal or, if not invited to do so, go to their own homes for it.

Instead, he stepped into the great hall and raised his eyebrows. The space was alive with people, all of them vying for attention in a clamor that had the governor clearly frazzled. Even though he knew Pilate was waiting for him, he wasn't about to elbow his way through the crowd of what looked like wealthy Jewish men. He opted for moving to the side of the room and making his way toward the front along the wall.

Snatches of their demands found his ears above the babble of the rest of them.

"...is not deserving of such an honor!"

"What if the zealots steal His body away? It would..."

"...offensive! He is *not* our king!"

As Valerius watched, Pilate's face hardened degree by degree from overwhelmed to finished. Valerius knew the look well. It was the same expression Pilate had worn as a lad when the crush of younger siblings and friends and cousins wanted attention. At first he would indulge them, but long before Julius ever brushed them aside, Pontius would stand up, stony-faced, and declare the game over. The younger ones would scamper away, crestfallen. Because once Pontius declared the fun over, it was *over*.

He ought to have realized then that his brother's friend was destined for politics.

Tracking Pilate's expression with every step, Valerius fought a twitch of his lips. He could see the last ounce of patience draining away. Watch the frazzle turn to authority. Watch the tired man remember that he had the power to shut down every argument.

Did any of those hapless men realize how precarious their situations became the moment he rose from his seat? "Silence."

He didn't bellow it. He didn't have to. There was something about the way he stood, back straight, jaw set, his exhaustion only lending credence to the work he'd done that day. He raised a hand.

The gaggle went quiet.

"Am I correct in assuming that you are all here about Jesus of Nazareth?" A silent chorus of nods. Pilate scanned the crowd, something in his face relaxing when he spotted Valerius, now at the front of the room. He waved him forward, and the crowd who had been pressing close to Pilate's seat retreated a few steps to make room for him.

The governor lifted his brows as Valerius clapped a hand on his shoulder and gave a quick kneel of respect. He was ordering him to rise before he'd even completed the gesture, and he pitched his voice low. "Well? It is over, I assume?"

Valerius nodded. "All three convicts are dead. Jesus expired in the second before the earthquake—the others upon our breaking of their legs."

Something flashed in Pilate's eyes at the mention of the earthquake—or perhaps of the timing of it with the Teacher's death. He nodded. "The bodies?"

"Two of the three had family to come forward to collect the bodies. The third will be buried among the poor."

One of the men in the crowd was either brave, determined, or stupid. He stepped forward, face flushed red. "I demand to know where the blasphemer has been taken. He had no family property in Judea for His mother to have buried Him."

Pilate cut a gaze toward the man, irritation ticking in his jaw. "As I already told you, Caiaphas, a man from Arimathea came forward an hour ago and offered use of a tomb. I imagine he has gone to meet the mourners with the body and show them the way."

Caiaphas...the high priest? Valerius frowned. He had spotted the high priest from a distance a few times but never close enough to see his face clearly. All he knew about the man was that he was of the sect that denied the possibility of a resurrection of either body or soul, which pitted him against teachers like Jesus and the Pharisees. But he knew from Pilate that the governor and high priest had had many occasions to work together over their shared years of service, and generally they were congenial.

That didn't seem to be the case today.

The man dared to take another step toward Pilate, face stern. "Unacceptable. I demand to know where this tomb is."

Pilate sighed. "And why is that of any interest to you?"

"Because His disciples are sure to know, of course! And we fear they will steal away the body and then claim the criminal rose from the dead."

Pilate blinked at him. "I beg your pardon. Rose from the dead?"

Caiaphas waved a hand. "Ridiculous, as well you know. But He made claims about rebuilding the temple of His body in three days."

Was that amusement in Pilate's eyes? "I am afraid even I do not have power over the dead. If the man wishes to rise, I cannot stop Him."

The priest's face flushed red. "It is deception and theft we wish you to prevent, my lord. If His disciples are permitted to steal the corpse away and then propagate such a myth, then He will cause even more damage than He already has."

Pilate sighed. "You want a guard for the tomb, is that it?"

Caiaphas nodded.

"You have one." He cut a gaze to Valerius. "You will see to it?"

Valerius nodded too, his mind already racing through his list of soldiers and how best to divide them into shifts over the next several days. He'd hoped to go straight home from the palace, but he would need to stop by headquarters first and dole out the new assignments.

Ah, well. Mariana *had* told him via Gaius to see to his duties.

He angled his body away, ready to see to the task the moment Pilate dismissed him. But instead of giving him the nod of permission, the governor raised a finger. "A moment, if you please, Valerius." He said it quietly, in a tone that said he wished to discuss a personal matter, not give a command that could be issued before the crowd.

Then he returned his attention to the others and made quick work of dismissing them.

Valerius stepped back to the wall behind Pilate's chair until the last of the men had cleared the room, then edged forward again as his old friend sat with another sigh in the governor's seat. He rubbed at his temples. "What a day."

"Indeed." Valerius kept his feet planted in military stance, knowing that, if he dared to relax, his superior would see his impatience. He made himself smile. "I do not envy you your role in all of it, Pontius."

Pilate huffed a laugh. "Nor should you." He lowered his hand but stared up at the ornate ceiling instead of looking over at Valerius. "I have had to do many things in my career that were distasteful. No doubt I have sentenced innocent men to death before. But this one… this one was different. When He gazed into my eyes, I could have sworn He saw all the way to my soul." He blinked and refocused his gaze on Valerius. "Do you think that mad?"

Valerius shook his head. "Far from it, my lord."

"Claudia was tormented by dreams of Him last night," he said of his wife.

Valerius startled a bit. "I did not know she knew of Him."

"She did not—not to speak of. But she sent me a note during His trial telling me to have nothing to do with His death." He held out his hands, staring at them as if expecting to see the man's blood staining them. "She was inconsolable when I admitted to her midday that my hands were tied, that He was even then being crucified. And when the earthquake hit…I sent for Mariana and the children—I did not know what else to do. No one brings her comfort like your family."

Valerius had to fight a frown. That messenger must have come after Gaius was dispatched to find him, perhaps even crossed paths with Gaius. "I am certain Mariana was happy to lend any comfort she could."

Now the governor looked nearly sheepish. "I believe my wife insisted that your family stay the night with her. You know how she loves playing with the children."

Which meant that if Valerius went home, it would be to an empty house. He fought back a sigh. "Yes, of course I do. They bring joy wherever they go." Hence why he could use a dose of it himself. He needed to take his wife into his arms and hold her tight until the scent of her perfume chased away the stench of death and hatred. He needed to tickle his daughter until her laughter chased away the echo of screams. He needed to cradle his son until he could believe there was hope and a future.

"You are welcome to come with me now, of course. To dine with us."

But not to stay, because Mariana and the children would be in Claudia's quarters all night, and he was certainly not welcome there. If Claudia decided to dine in her rooms—which she usually did if she was distraught enough to need Mariana's soothing presence— then it would be only him and the governor reclining at the table, and he'd see his family only for a moment, long enough to greet them and leave again.

Even a moment together was nearly enough to tempt him to undergo a dinner he didn't feel up for. But he shook his head. "I thank you, my lord, for the generous invitation. But I had better see to this guard, and I do not wish to hold up your repast."

Pilate's nod said it was what he expected and that he wasn't sorry for it. "Very well. I thank *you*, Valerius, for the company of your family." His face went soft. "You know how Claudia has hated this place. Your wife's arrival in Jerusalem has proven the sweetest balm this last year."

That was Mariana, without question—the sweetest balm. Valerius couldn't help but smile at that. "She is happy to have a friend in Claudia too. You know I do not begrudge Claudia her company. At least"—here he grinned, gratified to see it light a bit of good humor back in Pilate's eyes as well—"as long as she doesn't keep her from home *too* long."

"I will make certain your family is escorted home in the morning."

In which case, Valerius might just assign himself the night shift of the guard. He didn't need to, of course—he didn't need to take any shifts. But he led his men best when they saw he wasn't afraid to serve alongside them. He always took a shift of whatever duty he gave out, assuming he had such leisure. Not always the first, but often. Not always at night, but sometimes.

Tonight he would. Why not? There was nothing to return home to and, frankly, he wanted to make certain the Teacher was laid to rest with the respect due Him.

He didn't share the priest's fear that His disciples would steal Him away—but he wouldn't put it past the Rabbi's enemies to try something to discredit Him even further. But they wouldn't succeed any more than a thief would.

Not on his watch. Not as long as his men were there after him, either. "Where will I find the tomb that was donated?"

Pilate motioned toward a scribe hovering near the exit. "Titus will give you the information. Thank you, Valerius."

"It is a pleasure to serve, my lord." He genuflected again and then strode from the court, the scribe falling in beside him as he went.

CHAPTER FIVE

Tamar let Bithnia pull her into the unfamiliar garden, looking this way and that in search of some familiar landmark...or people she needed to avoid. She saw only the rose-tinted stones glowing in the sunset and the birds roosting on olive branches for the night. Her ears heard only the whisper of the wind through those same branches and the skittering of the small stones their sandals sent tumbling down the path.

She'd lived in Jerusalem all her life and had explored much of the countryside around it, but she'd never been to this garden before. Its beauty made her wonder why that was. Surely someone should have told her of this place of lovely tranquility before.

Regardless, she was grateful to Bithnia for introducing her to it now. It would be the perfect place to hide herself away during the Sabbath, and perhaps she would even emerge more at peace. This felt like the sort of place where she might hear the still, small voice of the Lord reminding her of His precepts.

Bithnia drew her to a halt, cast a glance around that looked far from settled, and motioned at one of many openings cut into the rock of the hillside. "There. That is where you can hide. No one will bother you, I promise."

Tamar nodded, taking one step toward the cave but then stopping. She would search it more when Bithnia had gone, but it seemed rude to do so now.

She and her siblings and cousins had explored many a cave in the region when they were children, and she had fun-filled memories of their adventures. For a while, an uncle had owned a cave outside the city, which he'd used for the family livestock. Some distant relatives had even made their homes in similar caves throughout the years. "Does this belong to your family?" she asked Bithnia in a hush.

Whispering seemed more than necessary—it seemed *right* out here in this quiet place.

Bithnia hesitated a second and then nodded. "That one, yes. But not the others. You will no doubt see or hear a few people coming and going, but if you stay in there, no one will bother you." The young woman looked again toward the cave but then angled her body to the path. "I will bring you food and water as soon as I can."

Tamar frowned. She didn't know exactly how far they'd walked to reach this garden of caves, nor what side of the city Bithnia called home, but it seemed likely that this place was more than a Sabbath day's journey away—certainly if one added up the distance to and from. "You need not worry about it. You cannot come this far on the Sabbath, and afterward I can simply leave. I am certain I can find a stream somewhere nearby for water, and I can go a day without food."

A strange, determined look took possession of Bithnia's face. "It is not unlawful to do good on the Sabbath, Tamar, and feeding the hungry, giving drink to the thirsty, is certainly good. I grant that I will not be able to make the journey in the darkness, but I will be back first thing in the morning."

The rumbling of Tamar's stomach and the dryness of her mouth told her not to argue. But the band around her chest that insisted this was displeasing to the Lord was stronger. It had to be stronger. If simple hunger or thirst was an excuse to break the Law, then they were no better than the heathens. "No. I refuse to be responsible for causing you to sin. I thank you for showing me this place, but hurry back to the city before Sabbath begins—and then stay there until it is over. I will be well."

Bithnia's expression didn't waver. "Twenty minutes after first light. I will be here with *charoset* and unleavened bread, with cheese and grapes. And enough water to see you through."

Tamar opened her mouth to argue again, but the young woman didn't tarry to hear it. She was already scrambling back down the path, far more quickly than they'd ascended it. Tamar huffed out a breath and relented.

She would pray that Bithnia felt the conviction of the Lord during the night and would relent from her determination to sin. She would find a stream or a well to see her through and resign herself to a rumbling stomach. If Bithnia did show up in the morning, she would chide her and refuse to partake of what she brought.

If she could not teach the girl with words, she would teach her with her example. "'Not a sin to do good on the Sabbath,'" she muttered as she turned back toward the cave. A slippery slope, that claim. Couldn't one say *anything* was good, then, and make an excuse to do it? Then before long, one wouldn't honor the Sabbath at all, nor keep it holy.

While she still had light enough, she scouted the garden, her frown growing deeper as she looked about. It was a lovely spot, yes, but there were no streams or wells nearby. Most of the caves were sealed with large stones, which was odd. Clearly no one else lived here, despite the convenience of its nearness to the city.

It made no sense. Caves like this one, in such a prime location, ought to be teeming with life. There ought to be animals braying from some of them, families laughing in others. There ought to be cook fires crackling, the smell of roasting lamb wafting her way even now as families prepared their meals.

She returned to Bithnia's cave, her mind drifting back to the city, where her own family would be celebrating this week of most sacred remembrances. She could almost hear the familiar laughter of her nieces and nephews, the musical voices of her siblings and their spouses.

Her heart squeezed painfully as she stepped into the black interior of the cave and tried to make out any shapes or features in the darkness.

She'd never been away from her family during Pesach, not for more than a necessary shift at the loom. Tonight, she'd expected to be nestled in with the little ones, telling them the stories not just of the first Passover—that story had been told already last night—but also their own family stories of Pesachs past. The ones that would make them laugh, make them cry, make them feel the connection to the family members they would never meet, who had gone to the bosom of Abraham decades ago.

Would someone else tell the stories in her stead? Or would they go untold without her there to begin the remembering?

Her eyes had adjusted to the darkness enough that she could make out several shelves carved into the wall, one at the perfect height for her to sit or lie down on. She looked for a darkened ring on the floor to indicate where past fires had burned, but there wasn't light enough to make out anything like that. At the back, the darkness seemed even deeper, making her wonder if this first chamber led into another. She wasn't about to investigate, not without light to guide her.

There were no pieces of pottery stashed in the corners though. No shards to indicate some had been there before and had broken. No other shelves were carved into the walls for storage, nor troughs for animals. Only the rows of stacked stone shelves, long enough that she could make one into a bed. Nothing else.

Voices intruded on the silence, too hushed for her to make out words, but startling enough that she slipped quickly and soundlessly nearer to her cave's opening.

They won't be coming here, she chanted to herself, over and again. This was Bithnia's family's cave, and she wouldn't have brought Tamar here if there were any chance she'd be discovered. That had to be true. It *must* be, because she needed it to be.

Careful to stay in the cloaking darkness, she edged as close to the opening as she dared. The last glow of sunset still clung to the hilltop, though it wouldn't last long. Whoever was climbing that path was in grave danger of being caught out after Sabbath.

She frowned anew when the figures took on form enough to make it clear they were primarily women. One man led the group. He was older than Tamar by at least a decade, making him perhaps fifty years old. He was motioning toward another cave nearby. "This way," he said, his voice husky and quiet. "Are you certain I cannot help you carry Him?"

Women crowded behind him, something large and long in their arms. "No, please," one of them said. "It is our honor. And we are already unclean. But you, Joseph..."

Unclean. Carry *Him*. A limp form in their arms...

A *human* form—a man! And if carrying him could make one unclean...

Tamar had to press a hand to her mouth to hold back a horrified gasp. A corpse. Those women were carrying a *corpse* into the neighboring cave. Which meant...which meant...

Revulsion twisted her stomach, forcing her to her knees. A tomb. Bithnia had led her to a *tomb* to hide her! Never mind that it had clearly never been used, never mind that it meant fewer people to discover her than if this had been a place of the living.

This was a place of the dead. Where, when people did approach, it was with the unclean bodies of the deceased.

What if she'd stumbled into an old, unsealed tomb where the dead rested? She could have touched something without realizing it. She could have become unclean during this holiest week of the year.

The hard stone beneath her shot pain into her knees. What a disaster that could have been. No doubt on the first day of the week she would have to offer some sort of defense to the Sanhedrin, something to convince them that neither she nor her weavers were to blame for the tearing of the veil. How could she do that if she was ceremonially unclean?

It took her a long moment to realize that the heat surging through her veins was anger. How could Bithnia have been so foolish? So shortsighted? Didn't she realize what could have happened? How it could have impacted them *all*?

Bithnia could have at least warned her. Told her what this garden was, so that she'd know not to wander beyond this one unused cave tomb. Why had the girl remained silent on this crucial bit of information?

With the next thud of her pulse, the anger grew. Shifted. Bithnia, despite that oversight, had at least tried to help. Caiaphas was the one truly to blame. The high priest was supposed to lead their people in spiritual matters, be the one who, above all other men in Israel, could be trusted to be wise and loving, to represent God before men.

How dare he stoop so low? Succumb to prejudice and hatred? Cast blame on hapless artisans only trying to honor the Lord and make a living for their families? What kind of shepherd treated his sheep so?

Beyond that, why hadn't Levi considered how impossible renting a room would be? He should have made a better plan than thrusting a few coins at her. He should have advised more specifically her on where to go. Why had he left her to come up with a plan alone?

But also, what of her brothers? Were Moshe and Jeremiah and Simon even bothering to look for her, or had they merely shrugged when their cousins told them she wasn't coming home, and left it at that? She certainly didn't hear anyone calling her name out there.

Her family probably wouldn't even miss her, not really. They would note her absence, but it would be easily filled. They wouldn't worry for more than a minute or two. Levi's assurances would soothe them, and no one would spare a thought to wonder where she was now, whether she had food or water, where she would sleep.

No one else would spend the night on a cold stone bed meant for a dead man, absent so much as a blanket or a dipper of water. No one else would suffer a rumbling stomach tonight—no, they'd all be feasting, while she shivered, hollow-bellied, in the night.

It wasn't fair, wasn't just, and the very fact of that made the anger burn brighter, fiercer, hotter.

Then, all at once, it went out. Her eyes slid closed, leaving her in deeper darkness. *Forgive me.* She sent the plea heavenward, even though it seemed to bounce back at her off the stone ceiling. She oughtn't get angry with any of her friends and family for not being able to do more—this situation was beyond their control. Caiaphas was the high priest, the anointed of the Lord. How dare she think she had any right to stand in judgment of him? He was the appointed leader of their people, not her. He was the one with spiritual authority, and he'd done such a good job thus far that already his term had outlasted any other in recent history.

If he said she was guilty…then she was guilty.

A new pang, a new squeeze of pain hit her. But before she could do more than acknowledge it, the voices from outside grew louder again, and she shrank farther into the shadows.

The women were insisting they should stay, to see to the body more completely. The man was insisting they couldn't, that they must hurry back to Bethany before they lost the last of the light. One of the women assured another that they would be prepared to come with the first light of dawn on the first day of the week.

Then their voices were trailing off, along with their footsteps. They were leaving, and though it didn't sound as if it was by the same path they'd come up, they didn't pass in front of Tamar's hiding place.

Dragging in a long breath, she rearranged herself against the cold stone wall and let her eyes slide closed again. She was so thirsty—probably more so than if she wasn't keenly aware that she wouldn't drink until tomorrow, and that was assuming that Bithnia did come back.

If she did, perhaps Tamar would let herself indulge in that much of the provisions. Just water. The food she would still refuse out of principle.

Though would it matter, if she didn't refuse it all?

These thoughts were going to give her a headache if she didn't find a way to silence them. It promised to be a long, trying Sabbath.

More noises interrupted her brooding—heavier steps than those that had come before, but from the same direction, coming up the same path. Voices, but these too were different. Three of them, all the deeper tones of men. Speaking not in the familiar cadences of Greek or Aramaic, but in Latin.

This couldn't be good. She opened her eyes again, but it made little difference—darkness had cloaked the landscape and covered the opening to the tomb. But it eased away as the voices grew nearer, light flickering and dancing in time to the torches she glimpsed in the hands of the men.

Romans, yes. But not just any Romans. Roman *soldiers*. One wore the uniform of a centurion, the other two of regular soldiers. The two lower-ranking ones were joking, laughing between themselves, while the centurion led the way to the tomb the women and man had vacated moments earlier.

Careful to keep out of the torchlight, Tamar repositioned herself so she had a better view. Her pulse quickened, palms going damp. *They are not here for me*, she told herself. They were heading toward that one particular tomb, though she had no idea why. They weren't so much as looking around to see what else was in the vicinity.

Not yet, anyway. Though surely they would. They were Roman soldiers, after all. Renowned for their thoroughness and skill. How was she supposed to hide from them if they looked in here?

The centurion jammed his torch into a crevice so that it lit the scene without being held and then motioned toward a large stone chiseled into a circle. He gave a command in Latin. She knew little of the language, but the few words she could pick out matched their next actions. They were sealing the tomb.

The soldiers went about it cheerfully, grunting with the effort but still laughing under their breath at whatever their private joke was. The centurion watched and gave directions, halting them once the stone was in place.

Maybe that was all they'd come here for. Unburdened by the rules of Sabbath, they could perform the tasks the Jewish family that had just been here could not.

Reasonable...almost. But *why* would they do it? The Romans weren't known for going out of their way to assist the Jews in their chores and tasks. Quite the contrary—they were known for pressing Jewish citizens into helping them with *their* chores, forcing them to carry their burdens while they walked. There was even a law saying how far they could force someone to help them—one mile.

Her second brother, Jeremiah, had been forced to carry a Roman's burdens for a mile just a year ago, and thinking about it now brought his seething countenance back into her mind.

"Humiliating!" he had declared. *"Not just because I had to bear the load of our oppressors but because the very act stated that* his

business was so much more important than mine. I lost hours! He forced me to go in the opposite direction of where I needed to, so I had to double back. I wanted to spit at his feet when he finally released me."

He hadn't, of course. That would have been asking for punishment. But her family had been even more careful to avoid any Roman they saw after that. The lesson had hit hard. Romans cared for no one and nothing but themselves.

So why, then, were they here? Was the body in that tomb one that needed to be sealed away? Perhaps it was a person who had some sort of contagious disease…or perhaps it was one of the criminals executed that day. That would concern the Romans, perhaps.

Her musings went heavy and sank into her stomach when, rather than pick up his torch again, the centurion settled onto one of the many rocks in the garden and pulled forward a sack he'd been carrying. He opened it up and took out what appeared to be rations. He offered portions to each of his men, who had claimed rocks of their own.

This wasn't the behavior of a trio soon to make their way back to the city and their duties within it. This was the behavior of men who meant to stay right where they were for long hours.

Had she dared to, she would have groaned. As if it wasn't bad enough that she had to spend the next day and a half in a tomb, she'd have to spend it with Romans but a few feet away. Could things get any worse?

CHAPTER SIX

Valerius had long ago abandoned the hard surface of the rock he'd sat on to eat and now stood near the sealed tomb. They'd heated the wax while they ate and poured it around the stone once it was pliable enough, creating a seal. It certainly wouldn't keep out anyone determined to get in, but it would indicate if the tomb's rock was rolled away.

He'd glanced inside only once, when they first arrived, before he'd instructed his men to put the stone in place. Verified that the body of Jesus was there, laid out on a stone shelf carved into the empty tomb. His torchlight had cast the prone figure in sharp relief, making the white of the carefully positioned shroud that covered His body shine bright against the darkness of the stone.

His throat had gone so tight, he hadn't been sure he could eat a bite. But he'd made himself—not because he was hungry but because he would need the energy to stay awake and alert tonight.

Albus and Caeso were still in good spirits, laughing about some story they'd heard in the barracks that day. Valerius didn't bother asking them to tell it to him so he could share in the joke. He had no desire to laugh. No desire to treat this task like any other. But he didn't chide them either. He knew these men. He knew that the moment anyone else approached, their levity would fall away and they'd snap to attention, all senses focused and alert. They were two of his best men, on and off the battlefield.

Even so, their laughter grated against his sorrow, and it took effort not to keep looking at that sealed tomb.

It wasn't just a body in there. Wasn't just a condemned criminal who had been executed. It was *Jesus*. The man whose teaching had made Valerius dare to believe that there was more to this life than accruing wealth and doing prescribed actions and praying it was enough to please some capricious, selfish god. Jesus had made him believe in the possibility of miracles, of healing…of forgiveness.

Repent! For the kingdom of God is at hand.

That was the message His precursor had preached and which He had picked up. *Repent.*

Valerius used the bottom of his sandal to nudge an annoying stone out of the way and then replanted his foot. His gaze cut through the shadows, looking for anything out of place. Any movement. Any sign that someone was trying even now to sneak up and steal away the body.

He almost wished someone would. Not because he fancied arresting Jesus's disciples but because he needed to meet them. Talk to them. *I have repented*, he would tell them. *I turned from my sin. I know that Jesus was the Son of God. But now He is gone…and I do not know what to do.*

Before, even just a few days before, it had seemed simple. He would listen to whatever sermons the Rabbi gave in the vicinity of Jerusalem. He would go home and write down all the instruction he could remember. He would study those commands and insights every day, whenever he had the chance. He would talk them over with

Mariana. They would, together, attempt to shape their lives around the words.

It had never felt as though they were doing enough, true. But he'd had a sense, deep in his spirit, that trusting Jesus, trusting that His words were truth, was the most important thing.

What did that mean now, when He was gone? When He would give no more instruction? When He would shine no more light on truth? How could Valerius trust a dead man to help him? To wash him clean of his sins? To somehow, maybe, possibly make a way to the Father?

He had claimed that—Valerius had those words inked onto a scroll too. He'd promised that He was the way to God. He was the path. That whoever followed Him would meet the Lord.

Did that mean following Him to the grave? Did it mean simply following His words still, though His lips had gone silent?

His fingers went tight around the shaft of his spear, and he prayed that something, someone would break through the darkness. Someone who, rather than slinking away again in fear when he spotted three Roman soldiers guarding the tomb, would approach anyway. Would know, as Jesus had always seemed to, what he was thinking. The questions spiraling through his mind.

I know He was the Son of God. But then why did He die?

The heroes of legend, the supposed sons of the Greek and Roman gods—Heracles, Achilles, Aeneas—gave him no insights here. Theirs were always stories of great triumph, great strength, great victories… and then tragic and heroic death when some other great hero or monster overwhelmed their godlike strength and feasted on their human nature.

Jesus was like none of those stories though. His was not a tale of adventurous quests, inhuman physical strength, or conquering armies led by His charm and powers of intimidation. No, His was a tale of profound wisdom. A heart that loved beyond human limitations. Mercy that stretched beyond the borders of His own country and people.

He was not a demigod. Not a legend. Not a warrior.

He was something more. Something different. Something Valerius had only just been beginning to understand, and now everything he'd thought he knew seemed useless.

Because Jesus, the Son of God, the one who claimed to be the way to the Father, was gone.

Albus and Caeso settled into silence, as they always did after the first hour of a night watch. They took up their positions on the paths leading away from this newly carved tomb, their torches crackling from the holders they'd jammed into crevices or the ground itself, the orange light shouldering the darkness away from their little triangle.

Valerius drew a long, slow breath into his lungs. He wanted the quiet to be soothing, but it wasn't. He doubted that anything really would be. It seemed that the longer he stood here, nothing but a stone separating him from the man he'd never allowed himself to meet face-to-face, the more grief filled his heart.

He had known, when he sent his friends to beseech Jesus on his behalf, to beg Him to heal Gaius with a word, that he was unworthy to approach Him himself. He'd known it down to his bones. He'd always been content to be just one person in the crowd, unassuming. He had *needed* to be that, to feel, if only for an hour, like one of many. Like the rest of the seekers needing His touch, His words.

Now, though, he regretted all of those decisions. He regretted that the first time the Lord had looked him in the eyes, it was on Golgotha, when Valerius was there as one of His executioners.

The eyes had cast no blame upon him. He had even whispered a prayer that God would forgive His tormentors.

But would He? How could He? The whole world ought to be punished for allowing this to happen—and maybe it had been. Maybe that was what the earthquake, the darkness had been about. Maybe, because they'd treated His Son so poorly, God would remove His hand of protection from all of humanity now.

Maybe this night wasn't just a vigil to keep anyone from stealing the corpse of a master teacher. Maybe it was one of the last nights that the world would even exist. Maybe God would pour out His wrath upon them all after this.

As if they could hear his thoughts, Albus and Caeso both shifted uneasily, clearly sensing something out of the ordinary. Something that wasn't right. Valerius renewed his vigil as well, straining to see beyond the ring of firelight, to hear something more than the rustle of the wind in the trees.

But there was no wind. It was still, far more still than usual, making the cloaks they'd donned nearly unnecessary in the temperate spring evening. He pulled his torch from where he'd set it and stepped forward. "I am going to check the rest of the garden." His voice came out low, quiet, more murmur than anything. His men both gave a quick nod, on alert for anyone or anything that approached.

He hadn't expected this assignment to require much by way of action. Their role was simply to stand here and dissuade any vandals or thieves, and hence he hadn't ordered his men to sweep the whole area as soon as they arrived. They didn't need to chase off any actual mourners at other tombs, and with night and the Sabbath falling, no one had been in sight anyway. But perhaps he should have been more thorough, because he could swear he felt someone watching him.

Nonsense, probably. Just the unease of the day and all the questions stampeding through his mind.

He started along the path, moving first to the nearest tomb, which was unused, given its mouth gaping open, no rock even in place to roll over it. A quick peek inside, a flash of his torch from the left to right, and he stepped out again. The tomb, as he'd assumed it would be, was empty. Not so much as a jar of spices or a burial cloth to hint at its impending use. It looked as though it might have a rear chamber too, but he saw no point in examining it, given the utter silence. This was newly hewn, quite possibly not even purchased yet. He did pause and listen for a moment, but he heard no breathing, no shuffling, nothing to indicate any thieves lurking within.

He ducked out again, continuing his search through the rest of the garden of tombs. He found three other open, empty caves that held no one, either living or dead, and saw no one on the paths, not even the usual small, scurrying animals. Not until he returned to his post did he hear anything to make his shoulders knot.

He stopped between his two comrades, all their gazes on the path by which they'd arrived. Footsteps, several pairs of them, intruded upon their awareness and grew louder with each passing second. He tensed because his training had taught him to, even as his mind insisted that thieves wouldn't walk so boldly up the path.

Nor, he was certain, would they be carrying torches of their own, but the light from both torches and lamps soon broke through the night.

He frowned as the men—four of them—came into view. They were dressed in the garb of temple guards, unarmed thanks to Roman laws prohibiting them from carrying any weapons, but well trained nevertheless. He thought he recognized one of them from his visits to the Court of the Gentiles, but he couldn't be certain about that in the night, and out of context.

Valerius did not need to call out the order to stop. The men seemed to expect them to be there and greeted them with raised hands, but they halted just outside the Romans' torchlight circle. One of the four eased a half step beyond his compatriots. "Good Sabbath."

A strange greeting from men who were breaking it—and to Romans who they had to know weren't observing it. As much as Valerius might like to, his superiors weren't willing to entertain such things. "Good evening," he said in reply. Had the high priest decided that he couldn't trust Romans to guard the Rabbi's tomb? Had he sent his own men instead?

If so, why had he bothered beseeching Pilate for a guard instead of using the priests usually stationed at the temple?

He didn't ask though. He waited for them to state their business.

He didn't have to wait for long. The one who greeted them continued. "We are looking for a fugitive—a woman. She is about this tall," he said, indicating his shoulder. "Pretty enough, between thirty-five and forty years of age. She was last seen wearing a dark brown tunic with a pale blue headscarf. Have you seen anyone meeting that description here?"

Valerius, Caeso, and Albus all shook their heads. Valerius asked, "What is she wanted for? Is she dangerous?" Unusual as it was to come across a violent female fugitive, it happened now and then.

But to be sought by the temple guard? Her crime had to be religious, not violent. Though he couldn't think what would be so dire that these men would break—or at least risk breaking—Sabbath rules about the distance one could travel in search of her.

The man shook his head. "No, no, nothing like that. She is head of the temple weavers—the ones who weave the veil."

"The veil" could only mean one thing—the wall-thick curtain that separated the Holy Place from the Holy of Holies. The veil that physically separated God from man.

A veil he had felt all his life, even if he'd never set his physical eyes on it. As a Roman, he wasn't even allowed that far. He was kept always on the outside. Apart. Separated not just from God but from His chosen people too.

Perhaps his frown looked darker than he meant it to, because the newcomers eased back a step. "And what has this weaver done to warrant such an unusually timed search by the priests who guard the temple?"

The leader lifted his chin a degree. "She has provided a defective veil for service to the Lord—a sacrilege."

"Defective?" His frown pulled deeper. "How could it be defective?" He had heard stories about the awe-inspiring curtain that took seventy-two women three years to weave. He had even glimpsed part of the procession a month ago when the newest one was installed. It was so massive that three hundred men were needed to transport it.

Had someone found a thread out of place? Frayed? A mistake in the pattern?

Was that worthy of being hunted down in the dead of night by priest-guards?

Silence stretched until it crackled. The priest seemed reluctant to say what had been found wrong with the veil, but Valerius could tell from the sounds of shifting beside him that both his men had moved into more intimidating stances, silently shouting, *Answer him or you won't pass by here.*

The leader cleared his throat, glanced at his companions, and finally heaved out a breath. "It tore during the earthquake."

Tore? A cloth of that size and weight? "By 'tore,' do you mean a little rip or...?"

"In two." He gritted it out between clenched teeth.

The silence pulsed again. Valerius was careful to keep his shock away from his face, to call on every last bit of Stoic training he'd received at his father's knee. It was unthinkable enough that a wall woven of cloth, one so carefully crafted, could be ripped in two by any force.

But the earthquake? The one that had shaken the city in the very moment that Jesus cried out to heaven? The moment He gave up His life? *That* earthquake had torn apart the veil separating man from God?

His insides went hollow. It couldn't be. Could it? Yet if it was... if it had truly happened...

"Why is the weaver being blamed? An earthquake is an act of God, not of a woman—or even seventy-two of them."

The priest started, clearly surprised that Valerius knew even that much about the weaving. Then he squared his shoulders, met Valerius's gaze.

Yet Valerius could have sworn the man was no more convinced than Valerious was by his reasons for being here as he said, "There must have been some fault in the fabric for it to rip like that. How could it have happened otherwise? The high priest wishes for her to be held responsible."

How, exactly, would a woman be expected to take such responsibility? He couldn't imagine there was any fine that could be paid. Did the high priest mean to imprison her? Or, worse, send her to the Roman courts for execution as he had Jesus?

He could have asked. Instead he said, "And you think this woman is hiding here, among the dead?"

The priest shook his head. "Unlikely, I grant you. But we have been scouring all gates leading out of the city, and someone reported seeing a couple of women huddled outside the nearest gate, one of whom could have been Tamar."

Tamar. Clearly, she didn't think she was responsible for the rip. "Did she escape your authorities?"

The priests exchanged a look, and if he wasn't mistaken, two of them fought back a grin. "She has a cousin in the temple. We think he must have helped her slip out while the high priest was distracted with other business. We have yet to find him either, though, to question him."

Sounded like a wise family. Valerius nodded, but he didn't move out of their path. "I just searched the entire garden a few minutes before you came. There is no one hiding here, neither woman nor man. But if she comes this way, we will, of course, detain her." At least for a moment, long enough to ask her if she'd seen this ripped veil with her own eyes. If it could be true.

What it meant.

The priests nodded, looking more relieved than inclined to argue. The leader lifted a hand again. "Thank you. We will bother you no longer, then."

They turned and moved back down the path, leaving Valerius and his comrades to their circle of light and unanswered questions.

Albus slid up to Valerius's side. "Please fill us in on what this means, my lord," he said. "Why should a woman be arrested for this, even if there was a fault in the fabric?"

She shouldn't be—but Valerius couldn't admit that out loud. Couldn't admit that if something had ripped the veil in two, then it had to have been the very hand of God.

He couldn't say any of that. Because to speak it would be to hope that the impossible had happened. That God had torn down the divide. That they could *all* approach Him.

But to hope in that was too much to consider on top of everything else today. If that hope turned to dust as so many hopes did, he didn't know if he would survive the resulting despair.

To his men, he said, "Only perfection is allowed in the temple of God. No blemish can be excused."

Albus screwed up his face. "Seems like a rather demanding deity."

Perhaps, if one looked at it only that way. But God knew they all sinned. He knew they were imperfect. It was why they had to offer

Him the best in recompense. Only perfection could wash away the stain of imperfection. Only the pure could sanctify the defiled.

Only the worthy could forgive the unworthy.

He turned back to the sealed cave. Inside lay a man who had been worthy. Pure. Perfect. If He was gone now, where did that leave the rest of them? If the veil was gone as well, what was left to protect them from the wrath of God?

CHAPTER SEVEN

The cold of the spring night wasn't what caused her trembling. Tamar couldn't convince herself it was. It had begun well before the temperatures dropped, the moment she heard the centurion announce he was going to check the rest of the garden and its tombs. She'd known he would find her, but she couldn't just let him, without even trying to hide. So she'd felt her way into the deeper darkness, toward what had appeared to be a rear chamber.

It was. Without light, she couldn't say how big it was or how deep it went, and she'd been afraid to walk too far into it lest she get turned around and never find her way out again—foolish, probably. This was a garden of tombs, not a system of caves that would connect to others...right?

She hadn't been willing to risk it, especially as the trembling took her over. She'd heard the stranger's footfalls, deliberate and heavy. She'd seen the light of his torch stretch to the end of the main chamber and light the opening of this corridor or second chamber she was in.

He would come back here. Of course he would. He was a Roman soldier, thorough and determined. Tamar held her breath and prayed he wouldn't hear the pounding of her heart.

But then the light had vanished, and the sound of his steps had tracked his retreat. She hadn't dared to relax, nor to creep out into the main chamber again, not until she heard his return many minutes later, heard him bypass her tomb again, heard the confrontation—if one could call it that—with the temple guard.

She'd stayed hidden away in this chamber darker than shadows while they spoke, but she had no trouble hearing their words. Their voices carried through the garden and seemed to echo their way to her.

Only once the temple guard left did she dare to inch her way back into the main chamber, after first stashing both the list of weavers and her cousin's money pouch in the rear chamber, in a carved-out nook she'd found. The Romans were unlikely to search the tombs again. As long as she stayed quiet, she would be all right. Probably. Perhaps for safety she ought to have remained in the deeper darkness, but she just couldn't. At least in the main chamber, moonlight spilled through the opening, along with the dull, flickering gleam from the torches at the next tomb over.

Before she'd realized what this place was, she'd thought that she'd use the hewn shelf as a bed. It would be hard, but no harder than the floor, and at least it would be off the ground. But now, knowing that it was a slab intended for a corpse? She settled onto the floor across from it instead, trying to ignore the chill that threatened to make her shivers even worse.

She listened, her brows knit, as the Romans talked in low tones about the temple guards' search, their words in Greek now rather than Latin, making it easy for her to understand them. Why would they look to one of their own for an explanation of it? She was fairly certain it was the voice of the centurion who answered, who said, *"Only perfection is allowed in the temple of God. No blemish can be excused,*" as if he actually knew the Law and held it in reverence. As if he understood.

Her lips curled away from her teeth in a silent snarl. He was a Roman. What did he know of the covenant between God and man? Nothing. If these pagans had any reverence for covenants at all, they wouldn't be in her land. They'd have respected the treaty struck between Judas Maccabeus and their own senate nearly two hundred years ago.

But they could all see now how little that friendship had meant. The Romans cared nothing for peace, and their word carried no more weight than a feather. This centurion spoke of perfection? He couldn't possibly know the meaning of the term.

She knew, though, and just as she knew it was beyond her as a mere human, she'd worked so hard to attain it—first in her work and then in life outside the weaving room. Her eyes burned, but she drew in a long breath and willed the tears away. She didn't dare cry. Crying would make her nose run, and a sniffle was certain to get the attention of the Romans.

No, she must stay silent. No crying, no sniffling, no gasping for breath. *Hold yourself together, Tamar,* she silently demanded.

But though the tears retreated, the thoughts didn't. Every time she closed her eyes, she saw again the tapestry underway on the loom, the one they'd removed amid groans. She saw that single thread, dangling and broken.

Imperfection. One strand of imperfection, and it had ruined three weeks of work. Only weeks, not years, but even so.

She ought to have caught it sooner. *Bithnia* ought to have. Earlier, and they could have salvaged their work. Tamar closed her eyes, shutting out what little light reached her, yet still she saw that thread. *Imperfection.*

Only perfection is allowed in the temple of God. No, the Roman couldn't know what that meant. Nevertheless, his words were true. Had there been imperfection in the veil that had ripped? Had the earthquake been God rejecting it?

A new shudder, more severe than the underlying trembles, coursed through her. She didn't know how else to explain it. But she'd gone over every fraction of an inch of that veil before it was deemed acceptable for its task. She had looked for any frays, any weaknesses, any flaws, any mistakes. She had been fully prepared, if necessary, to declare it unworthy and cast it aside, to start over from the very beginning.

But there had been none. Nothing. She was sure of it. She was certain, not just because *she* had gone over it but because others had too. Some of the women and then some of the priests. They had all agreed.

The veil had been perfect, suitable for its holy purpose. She could still remember the feeling that had surged through her when it received approval—the same feeling she got each time a new veil was carried from the weaving room and into the temple.

She had felt...*clean.* Worthy. Suitable. She had looked at the women surrounding her and thought with satisfaction that this holy work had made them all a bit holier. That by bending day after day over the rods, tracing the lines of colored thread with their gazes, they had sloughed off a bit of their imperfect natures and eased a step or two closer to the divine. They had done good work for the Lord, and in turn, He would smile upon them.

What, then, did this disaster mean? Was the high priest right— was it a condemnation of her?

She closed her eyes, barely hearing the occasional words the Romans exchanged. They'd drifted back into Latin, and though she knew a few words, she was by no means fluent. Most of what they said floated right past her, as incomprehensible as the whole day had been.

Her fingers knotted in the length of bold colors in the head scarf Illana had lent her. If Tamar was guilty of sin serious enough to have warranted such a dramatic action, what of the other women? Was Illana guilty too—for helping Tamar, if for no other reason? Was Bithnia? Would God pour more judgment out upon them? What about Levi and their family?

Stories from sacred Scripture crowded her mind. Stories of the earth opening and swallowing whole families for the sins of their patriarchs. The women and children hadn't been spared when the sons of Korah rebelled against Moses. Had they all been guilty? Or was the association enough to condemn them?

Another bone-jarring shiver coursed through her. If she had been sinful enough to warrant this very overt chastisement from the Lord, what chances did her family have of surviving His wrath?

"Forgive me." She put no breath behind the words, simply moved her lips and tilted her head toward heaven. She knew, because the Psalms told her so, that no matter where she was, the Lord was there. He could hear her.

Before today, that had felt like a comfort. Just now, it seemed more a threat. She could hide from the priests in this tomb, but she couldn't hide from God. If He was the one out to punish her, there would be no escape.

"Forgive me," she mouthed again. They felt like only words though. Words couldn't be enough. For forgiveness, she'd need to bring an offering to the temple and confess to the priests what she'd done. She had to make recompense. Blood needed to be spilled so that she had a visual, visceral reminder of the cost of sin.

She didn't even know what she'd done wrong. The curtain had torn, yes. Did that mean she'd overlooked a flaw, failed in her duties as head weaver? Or did it point instead to some other, deeper sin, as Caiaphas had indicated when he'd called her a sinful woman?

Had she put something before the Lord? Worshiped Him in a displeasing way? Had she treated His name too casually? Dishonored her parents or family? Accused someone falsely? Coveted what wasn't hers?

What—*what* had she done to warrant this? She made mistakes, yes. Of course she did. She had snapped at her family members, sighed over some of her father's edicts over the years, and lied more than once in her life. Perhaps sometimes she was too harsh a taskmaster in the weaving room. But for the most part, she did everything she was told. Obeyed every law and encouraged others to do the same. Her family belonged to the Pharisees and worked always to preserve the importance of the Law, so that Israel would never again find itself torn apart, its people sent into exile.

As if mocking that thought, a burst of laughter came from where the Romans stood guard. She frowned. Her people hadn't been led away captive again, but they were held captive nonetheless, despite the work of the Sanhedrin to keep Israel obedient to the Law and the Prophets. Her father had always said it was not a punishment for sin but rather setting the stage for the promised Messiah to come and deliver them once and for all.

But what if he was wrong? What if the Lord was displeased with them? What if the veil hadn't torn just because of Tamar's sin but because of everyone's?

What if it was God's way of saying He would commune with them no more?

"No. No." Again, her words had no voice, only desperation. Suddenly aware of how cold her hands had grown, she knotted them in the fabric of her garment and wished for the comforts of home. Her room, her bed, her blankets. Her family, crowded around, laughing and telling stories. Warm food, spiced drink.

But she had none of that. None of them. She sat in a tomb, more alone than she'd ever been in her life. No family gathered around her, no friends…and if even God had turned His face away from her, from them all perhaps, then what did that leave her?

In the darkness, she could easily call up the image of that now-ruined tapestry. After studying it for so many hours, she knew every thread, every weave, every image. Sometimes she wished she'd been there when the children of Israel first left Egypt, when the first veil was woven for the mishkan. They had the instructions Moses had given them, of course, so she knew that the original veil was made of threads of scarlet, purple, blue, and gold. According to the stories, it had been striped, though that wasn't specified in Scripture.

When Solomon built the first temple, however, the veil took on new life, and that had set the stage for the centuries thereafter too. The veils she and her weavers created still used the same colors as the original, with all their significance, but they weren't simple stripes any longer. As Solomon had instructed, they wove the Garden of Eden into their veils. The Tree of Life, the Tree of the Knowledge of Good and Evil, even the cherubim guarding the entrance with their flaming swords.

The veil wasn't just a masterpiece of craftsmanship. It was a masterpiece of artistry as well. A beautiful reminder of the last time God and man walked together in perfect harmony. A reminder of the perfection they had forfeited, but which they must strive always to regain. A reminder of the God who created them to be holy as He was holy.

Exhaustion rolled over her, and Tamar let it urge her down to the cold, damp floor. She didn't expect to sleep. It was bound to be the most uncomfortable night she'd spent in many years, given the solid stone she'd call her bed. But if she could doze even a bit, it would pass the time. Maybe things would be clearer in the morning. If she could get enough sleep to put it all in perspective, anyway.

But she didn't want to sleep too soundly, regardless. She didn't want to risk making a noise or not hearing it if the soldiers made another round of searches. She really should forgo the small bit of comfort given to her by moonlight and flickering torches and sleep in that rear chamber. That would be wise. She would get up and move in a few minutes...after she'd dozed for just a bit.

When she next blinked her eyes open, the light had changed from fire-kissed black to soft gray. Tamar had no moment of confusion—the hard ground beneath her made it clear from the first moment of regained consciousness that yesterday had been no nightmare. Which was why it was all the stranger that dawn had come already and brought with it a sound at once familiar and far too foreign to this place.

A child's laugh.

At home, that would mean nieces or nephews, and she would have the luxury of smiling at the morning greeting, scooping them into her arms, and starting her day with a hug to warm her. Here, though? A child's laugh had no place in an empty tomb.

Yet there it was again, from right beside her, and little fingers reached out to pat her cheek too.

Maybe she *was* dreaming—now, if not before.

A small voice whispered, "Why are you sleeping here? Do you not have a bed?"

Tamar turned her head enough to see little toes peeking out of well-crafted sandals, a tunic of fine linen pulled up a bit to reveal small legs, bent in a crouch. She sat up as quickly as her aching muscles allowed.

The little girl didn't move, just kept crouching there, smiling at her. "Good morning," the girl said. "Mango?" She held out a bag with dried strips of the fruit in it.

All logic said Tamar should refuse the offer of food from a child she'd never seen before, especially when she was supposed to be hiding here in this tomb. But maybe it was a sister or cousin of Bithnia's? Had she been sent here to bring her food?

Odd—the girl couldn't be more than four. But perhaps she'd come *with* Bithnia and had simply beaten her into the cave?

Regardless, Tamar's stomach was hollow, and she reached out, with a careful smile, for a slice of mango. "Thank you," she said. She answered in Greek, because that was what the girl had spoken. Though now that she thought about it, that made her frown. If this was a relative of Bithnia's, Aramaic would have been her instinct.

She had forgotten her determination to refuse any food that caused her friend to break the Sabbath, which she didn't even realize until she'd taken her first bite of it.

"Livia?" Another voice broke the stillness of the morning now, feminine but much older than the child's. "Where have you gone, sweet one?" It was amusement in the woman's voice, not panic or frustration.

Instead of noting that, she should have been trying to sort out how to escape the situation. Because amused or not, the voice wasn't Bithnia's.

Tamar got as far as her knees before the soft light of dawn from the cave's opening was half eclipsed by the figure. The woman looked perhaps thirty years old, and the baby boy on her hip could be no more than one.

The stranger didn't scream. Didn't shout for her daughter to get away from the madwoman sleeping in a tomb. She didn't react much at all to spotting her little girl crouching beside a total stranger in the oddest of situations.

But Tamar did. Because the woman wore a *stola* over her tunic— a stola! She was Roman. Surely that made her the worst person in the world to happen upon her.

CHAPTER EIGHT

Valerius nodded his greeting to the next shift of his men, not objecting when the two who had been on duty with him all night approached their friends and settled in for what looked to be a few minutes of jesting and chatting before the new arrivals took up their positions. Had it been a more public, higher-risk situation, they wouldn't have dared to be so informal.

But it was a tomb, and no one was trying to steal the body. No one would, he was all but certain. He didn't mind at all if his men indulged in a few minutes of conversation before Caeso and Albus went to find their beds and their three friends settled in for a day of watching birds flit and clouds roll by. Nothing else was likely to happen.

Yet he heard footsteps coming from behind him, which had him wheeling around, hand gripping the shaft of his spear. Then his shoulders relaxed. He recognized the sound of the steps, especially in conjunction with each other. Gaius, Mariana, and the happy, light skip of Livia.

He smiled when he heard Livia skipping off with a laugh, no doubt leaving her mother and Gaius behind, just as she always did. He hadn't expected his family to come and find him at the end of his shift—frankly, he was surprised that Claudia had relinquished them so early in the morning. But he wasn't surprised, either. Mariana loved to "catch him" at his work, and it wouldn't have been difficult for them to procure directions to the garden from Pilate.

"Livia?" Mariana's voice met his ears as he spotted her and Gaius both cresting the hill, emerging from the morning's mist. He could hear his daughter laughing, though it had an echoing quality. She must have found one of the empty tombs and decided to explore. After darting a look over his shoulder to reassure himself that no would-be thieves would be able to approach from the other path, given the knot of soldiers, he strode toward his family.

Mariana ducked into the neighboring tomb, but Gaius had spotted Valerius and approached with a muted morning smile and a lifted hand. "Morning, Master."

"Good morning." Valerius stopped beside Gaius. "You all are out early."

Gaius shrugged. "The lady Claudia awoke early but in better spirits, so when Livia said she wanted to come find you, we were sent on our way." He motioned to a bag slung over his shoulder. "With breakfast, if you are hungry. And various other gifts, as she so loves to do."

He chuckled at the truth of that. Yes, Pontius and his wife were in a higher position at this point, but that wasn't why Claudia showered Mariana and the children with gifts. It was simply what she loved to do for those she loved. Rarely did they spend time together that wasn't punctuated with the gift of a new garment or manuscript or pair of earrings, a toy for each of the children, a treat to eat, or even an exotic bloom or spice she'd discovered in the markets.

The only rule they'd had to impose was that she refrain from sharing any idols—a rule resulting from a rather disastrous exchange six months ago. Claudia had been so excited to have found a silver statue of Minerva bedecked with jewels—all the more so because she had noticed the lack of idols in their home and thought it an oversight or unwillingness to spend money on them. It was the first gift Mariana had refused, and it had taken an hour-long explanation filled with tears—Claudia's—to smooth things over.

Breakfast, on the other hand, was never unwelcome. Valerius stepped closer to Gaius, eyes on the bag. "And what did our friend send for us to eat this morning?"

Gaius chuckled. "Livia is already eating the dried mango she sent. I believe there is also fresh bread, some cheese, smoked meat of some kind, and I do not know what else."

Valerius was hungry enough after being awake all night to ask Gaius to unload the bag then and there, but before he could suggest a breakfast in the garden—never mind that the garden was filled with tombs—Mariana stepped into view again. Felix was on her hip, and he clapped and gurgled his excitement upon spotting Valerius.

His wife, however, had a strange look on her face. He didn't have words to describe it, except that it wasn't one he'd seen there before. Not her usual expression of joy at seeing him after a longer-than-usual absence, not the relief she sometimes wore when it had been a hectic day with the children. "My love," she said, voice so very even that it brought him to attention as high emotion wouldn't have, "could you come here for a moment?" The gaze she flicked past him, toward his men, communicated in a heartbeat that she meant *alone.*

He nodded, curiosity surging. He'd heard Livia laughing from in there, so nothing alarming could be underway. But then, their daughter was in that stage where she sometimes decided to do something utterly incomprehensible to the rest of them. For all he knew, Liv had decided that they ought to eat in the tomb, using the shelf for a table. Or she could have decided to play Egyptian mummy again and stripped off her clothes so she could better wind her mother's scarves around herself and pretend she was a pharaoh.

He'd learned that when it came to his imaginative daughter, he ought never to assume anything.

Turning back to his men, he called out, "I will see you later. My family has joined me." A motion toward Mariana, carrying Felix, was all it took for the soldiers to call out their greetings and nod him on his way. Though they were on friendly terms with his family, they also respected that Valerius and his wife and children didn't always want a crowd of soldiers tagging along on their every outing. When Mariana and the little ones showed up, the men kept their distance unless asked not to.

He'd made it clear this was one of those times for distance. Whatever mischief his daughter was making in that tomb would be kept to their family. Valerius moved along the path toward the unused tomb, Gaius keeping pace half a step behind him.

Mariana moved back into the cave as they drew near, her voice echoing strangely in the space and barely making its way to him. "I promise you, everything will be well. No one will hurt you."

Valerius's brows drew together. Who was she talking to? Not Livia—that wasn't the voice she used with Liv, and their daughter never needed that kind of encouragement. It sounded more like the tone she took with Claudia when the governor's wife was distressed and Mariana was trying to calm her.

He cast a glance at Gaius. Was this concern, whatever it was, one they'd brought with them? But his manservant shrugged, looking every bit as clueless as Valerius was.

Though dawn spread ever-brighter wings over the landscape, it didn't stretch beyond the mouth of the cave. He stepped inside, blinking a few times to let his eyes adjust to the dimmer light.

His frown only deepened. Mariana and Livia and Felix weren't the only ones inside the tomb. Another woman stood there as well. A Jewish woman, judging from her dress. She wore a utilitarian tunic in dark brown, the head covering of bold blue and yellow the only splash of color. She looked as if she was somewhere between him and Mariana in age, and clearly she had been here all night. She looked as though she'd just woken up, and the shadows under her eyes testified to poor sleep.

He sucked in a breath. The headscarf didn't match the description the temple guards had given last night, but everything else did. Dozens of questions flooded his mind—when she'd arrived, how he'd missed her, why his family was now trying to soothe her—but the only one to make it past his lips was, "Are you the weaver? The one blamed for the tearing of the veil? Tamar?"

The woman drew back a step but lifted her chin, fear warring with pride. She reached to tuck a lock of stray hair behind her ear and righted the headscarf while she was at it.

"The what?" Mariana spun from the woman to him, her brows lifted. "What veil?"

"The temple veil. It ripped in the earthquake." He held out his hands for Felix, who was leaning toward him with enthusiasm, oblivious to anything else.

The woman seemed to relax a degree as he took his son in his arms. Perhaps she assumed that if his hands were occupied with a baby, he couldn't arrest her.

He let his lips quirk up. He could always call his men to do the arresting if he had any intention of doing so. But frankly, he felt no inclination to do the priests' job for them, especially when it could be no crime wrought by a human that resulted in that tearing. Caiaphas was just looking for someone to blame.

After witnessing the high priest's last tragic success at that, he wasn't about to aid in any other unjust punishments.

Mariana's eyes had gone wide. "The temple veil *ripped*?" She turned her confusion back on the stranger. "How could that be? I thought it was thick as a wall."

"It is." The woman sighed, her hands falling to her sides. If she had intended to lie to them, she apparently gave up the thought. "And yes. I am Tamar, the head weaver."

"Lovely to meet you, Tamar." Mariana sounded genuine as she said it, and she reached out, now that her arms were free, to make a calming gesture. "And please, be at ease. We are no threat to you. Isn't that right, my love?"

It was more a command than a question, which made his smile grow. Mariana took hospitality and friendship very seriously. "Quite right." He moved his gaze to the weaver. "I do not know what it means, that the veil tore in two—but I know it could only have been the hand of God that accomplished it. I will not turn you in."

"You will not?" It was her turn to frown as she darted her gaze from Livia, who had woven her little hand through Tamar's as if they were longtime friends, to Mariana, to him, and then beyond him. "Is it not your duty?"

He lifted a brow. "My duty is to Rome. Not to Caiaphas. I was given no official instruction to look for you, and I have no desire to assist your priests in an unjust arrest. My role in the garden is solely to ensure no one steals the body of Jesus of Nazareth."

"Oh." Tamar blinked several times, presumably to let this new vision settle before her eyes and in her mind. A Roman family, yes. A centurion, yes. But not a threat. That must be unexpected. Then she frowned anew. "The Teacher is entombed here? But why would anyone try to steal his body?"

Valerius explained in a few brief sentences, and as he spoke, he motioned Gaius in with his head, the nod toward the bag all the instruction the old man needed. Grinning, he began unloading the food that Claudia had sent with them.

It took only a second for Mariana to catch on. The moment he stopped talking, before Tamar could ask any questions, she said, "I promised Livia we'd eat here in the garden when we found her father. Will you join us? I admit I am famished, but Claudia sent us with far too much food, as always."

Tamar watched the food being set out with interest, but not too much. She had likely missed her evening meal, but no more than that. She would be hungry but far from starving, and many of the Jews fasted weekly anyway, so she might have been accustomed to skipping meals.

Even so, she *had* to be hungry—yet she edged away a step, pasted a smile on her lips, and shook her head. "I do thank you, but no. A friend of mine is coming any moment, and I promised her we would eat together."

Truth? A lie? He wasn't certain. But something unequivocally true struck him, and he silently cursed himself for not remembering it a moment sooner.

No Jew would eat with Romans. Pagans. Uncircumcised heathen to their way of thinking. Never mind that his family believed in the one true God. She wouldn't know that and likely wouldn't care, regardless. They were, to her eyes, unclean. Breaking bread with them would make *her* unclean.

Frankly, he was a bit surprised she consented to Livia holding her hand.

The rebuff was too familiar to sting him, but his family dealt less frequently with the Jews. They lived in an area with other Romans, surrounded always by friends who thought them odd for eschewing the gods of Rome but who welcomed them nonetheless. Perhaps it was foolish to want to protect his family from this truth and to protect the stranger from having to explain it.

If so, then he was a fool, but he nodded and said, "We understand. Your friend will have gone to much trouble to assist you, and you would not want to rebuff her efforts. But perhaps we could leave some food with you to eat later, in case she brings only enough for one meal? Only what you would like." Some of the meat was, he suspected, pork, so that was out of the question. But the bread and cheese and dried fruit ought to be acceptable to her.

Perhaps she knew what he was about. Perhaps it confused her, and that was why a furrow creased her brow.

Mariana, who could usually follow his logic like no one else, scowled at him. Livia pouted and wrapped her arms around Tamar's. "But I want her to share our breakfast, *Tata*."

He crouched down, Felix giggling in his ear at the change in altitude. "And that is generous and gracious of you, sweet one. To your credit. But your new friend Tamar has made a promise. And what does the Lord teach us about our promises?"

Her lip stuck out, but she muttered, "Let our yes be yes and our no be no."

"That is right." He gave Livia a warm smile and held out an arm. She pouted one moment more, arms still wrapped around the stranger's, then let go and hurried forward for the hug she always wanted whenever he arrived home. Hoisting her onto the hip opposite the one her brother occupied, he stood again.

Tamar's frown only deepened. "You teach your child the ways of the God of Israel?" Her tone was likely only incredulous, but it sounded nearly accusing. Scoffing.

Mariana's chin ticked up. "We teach our children the ways of the one true God, who promised that through Abraham *all* nations of the world would be blessed. The God who inspired the psalmist to charge the people of Israel with proclaiming the Lord's glory to all peoples."

Tamar's face softened, likely from a silent command to herself rather than actual relaxation. Even so, he appreciated the smile she sent his wife. "Forgive me for sounding as I did. I am only surprised. But also glad to hear the Lord has stirred your hearts." She sucked in a breath and turned her gaze back to him. "And that is why your men asked you for clarification on the veil last night? Because you have been taught in our ways."

Valerius nodded, trying not to be yet another person frowning as her words answered a question of his.

She'd been in this tomb all night, likely since before he arrived. His gaze flicked to the rear of the chamber, to the darker section that he had suspected led to another room. She must have been hiding in there when he searched the place.

Had he been more thorough, he would have found her. He would have shouted, because it was what his training told him to do, and his men would have rushed up, and they wouldn't have given any thought to rousting her from her place and forcing her on her way. He probably would have assumed she was exactly what Caiaphas feared—part of a group set on stealing away the body of Jesus. Why else would she be hiding in the neighboring tomb after dark on the Sabbath?

It must have been the Lord's hand that guided him onward, preserving her secrecy. Which meant that the Lord had wanted her to remain hidden. Protected.

He drew in a deep breath and put Livia back down when she wiggled for her freedom. He had learned over his years of study that this true God, as true master of all creation, guided His people where He wanted them to go. Valerius was no expert at listening for His voice. He was no prophet, no judge of old. But he was certain God had led him to John the Baptizer five years ago and to that sermon of Jesus's at the start of His ministry, and he was certain now that their paths had crossed with Tamar's for a reason. To protect her.

He turned to Gaius. "Will you keep an eye out for her friend? And perhaps brace her for what she will find here? I do not want my men to give her a hard time."

Gaius agreed without any hesitation and ducked out of the cave again.

"It is her family's tomb," Tamar said, a bit of defensiveness creeping back into her tone. "She has every right to be here."

He granted that with a tilt of his head. "You are absolutely right. However, if my men see her walking toward Jesus's tomb, they will ask her for more information about why she is here, and then they will ask her *why* she is visiting an empty tomb on a Sabbath day. Questions I daresay neither of you would like to have to answer."

Tamar's breath gusted out. "I should simply leave. It is not safe to remain here."

"Do you have somewhere to go?" Mariana eased closer to her again, face open and bright once more. "We can escort you. Make certain you arrive safely."

The opening of Tamar's mouth produced no sound, and then it closed again. She shook her head. "No. Nowhere. I cannot risk putting my family in danger."

His wife looked as though she would like to cry over the injustice of it. "How horrible for you—and for your family. Do you have a husband? Children who are missing you?"

Though she shook her head, a smile curved Tamar's lips at the mention of children. "No, I live with my family. My brothers and their wives and children. They will be missing me, but only as their doting aunt."

Mariana sighed, the sound interrupted by voices from outside. Quiet ones, but enough to pique everyone's interest. Gaius's voice he knew, of course. The feminine one who answered him must be Tamar's friend, because her face lit up when she heard it.

Then, from where he'd left his men, "You there! Your business?"

Gaius laughed. "It is only *our* business, Master Albus."

Had it been just any servant dismissing a soldier, it wouldn't have gone so well. But all his men knew that Valerius trusted Gaius implicitly. In turn, they did too. Albus no doubt waved them on without another thought.

A moment later, Gaius reentered the cave, a young woman with him. She appeared to be perhaps sixteen, dressed simply, with a parcel in her hands that no doubt contained food for Tamar.

The young woman's eyes went wide when she spotted them. "Tamar? Are you all right?"

Valerius looked back to Tamar in time to see a strange thing happen. In the blink of an eye, she went from an uncertain and even frightened woman who didn't know what to make of them to reassuring certainty, shared in the form of a smile and an outstretched hand. Almost like when Mariana played hostess, but not quite.

It was something more than that. It was, he realized, the fact that Tamar was accustomed to being the one in authority when it came to the younger woman. She was accustomed to being the one to *give* support and encouragement and direction, not to receive it. It slid over her like a garment, banking the fires of worry in her eyes and replacing it with practiced calm.

He already knew she was the head weaver. He would have been willing to wager this newcomer was another weaver in her crew.

"All is well, Bithnia," Tamar said, her voice soothing and cool. "It seems we have found a few new...friends."

Bithnia's expression didn't exactly relax. If anything, her frown intensified as her gaze lingered on Valerius's uniform. "I did not realize when I brought you here that there would be Romans guarding..." The girl stopped, and her nostrils flared. "I did not realize they would bring the Rabbi here. Perhaps I should have—I knew Joseph of Arimathea owned the neighboring tomb, that it was unused, and that he follows Jesus."

Valerius exchanged a glance with Mariana. He knew well that if he spoke to the girl, who had been careful not to lift her gaze above his cloak pin, she would recoil. But his wife might be able to get away with speaking to her.

Mariana shifted closer to Bithnia, her smile compelling and her eyes bright. "Do you perchance know this Joseph was a follower of the Lord because *you* are?"

He hid his smile in the kiss he pressed to his son's head. By calling Him "the Lord" instead of by name or even "the Teacher," she'd made it clear where she stood, which invited Bithnia to turn a wide-eyed but no longer confounded gaze on her. In fact, something nearly joyful bubbled up in the young woman's face. "Are you too?"

Mariana nodded enthusiastically, motioning toward him and Gaius. "For a while now. My husband heard Him teach nearly three years ago and told me all about what He said. His lessons resonated deep within us. And then, not long before my husband was transferred from Capernaum to Jerusalem, our dear Gaius fell deathly ill." At the memory, tears flooded her eyes, even as her smile beamed sunshine. "Valerius sent emissaries to the Lord, to beg Him but to say a word for Gaius. We knew that was all it would take to heal him."

Bithnia's expression shifted to one of awe. "I heard a story about that. I did not realize...that was you?" She turned to face Valerius.

Tamar sucked in a breath, clearly surprised that a Jewish maiden would dare to talk to a Roman man directly. *She* had, but that had been in answer to his questions.

Valerius nodded, feeling again the same emotions that had swamped him when Gaius lay burning up with fever, his breaths so shallow, his form so haggard and wasted. He'd seen such fevers before. He'd known that his friend would die by the next day.

He'd known that Jesus was his only hope, but that he, a sinful Roman, was so very unworthy of hosting the Lord under his roof.

Yet Jesus had had mercy. He had commended his faith.

He had healed Gaius.

Even now, gratitude and amazement overwhelmed him. "There is much I do not know about the Law and the Prophets, about the one true God. But I stood beneath the cross of my Lord yesterday. I watched the earth tremble as His soul separated from His body. I know that Jesus is the Son of God. I am just not exactly certain what that means."

Bithnia let out a shuddering breath. "We were waiting for a Savior."

"Someone to free you from Rome? Another Maccabeus?" The words slipped out before he could think to stop them—words that emerged dry and sardonic. How many times had he heard that refrain?

He could understand it. No people wanted to be under the heel of another. But it was the way humanity worked, it seemed. Someone must rule. Someone must submit. Someone must serve. Someone must be served.

Bithnia's shrug looked more like confusion than apology. "Many think so, of course. But one thing I learned following Jesus was that it is not Rome that holds me captive—it is my sinful nature. A free Israel will not make us true children of God. Only a free soul will do that." Her face fell back into confusion. "But...now He is gone. I do not know...I do not know what we will do now."

Mariana stepped closer, reaching out without quite touching Bithnia. "Moses is gone too, is he not? As are Elijah, Elisha, Isaiah. And yet their teachings are no less important. Their words are no less valid. They still point the way to God."

Love swelled up in his chest, nearly taking him off guard. He knew, of course, that his family had chosen him a wonderful bride. But these last years, as they followed the Teacher, it seemed new wisdom had found her.

He could only pray perhaps she'd have an idea of how to sort out the more pressing issue. They still needed to find a way for Tamar to remain safe while the high priest was trying to blame her for an act of God.

CHAPTER NINE

Tamar sat on the shelf meant for the dead, still not sure how she'd ended up here. One moment she'd been listening with a strange band of pressure around her chest as Bithnia and the Roman woman spoke of following the teachings of Jesus, and in the next moment they'd somehow decided that the best way to assure Tamar's safety was to learn why, exactly, Caiaphas had decided she was the one to blame.

"There will be gossip at the temple," Bithnia had pointed out. "When they gather for the Sabbath teaching, word will spread."

"You are right, of course." This wasn't something the priests could keep secret, especially given that they'd been searching openly for Tamar. "But Bithnia, neither of us dare show our faces at the temple today."

"On the contrary," Mariana said. Her eyes had been dancing in a way that made it clear where little Livia, who had once again claimed Tamar's hand, got her enthusiasm for life. "You just cannot show them the face they expect to see. But arrive with a different face—or rather, a different mode of dress altogether—and they will look right past you. Trust me."

Her gesture toward her own clothing made clear what she meant. A moment later she'd unfurled another Roman tunic and stola from her bag. A gift, she'd claimed, from Claudia, the governor's wife.

Bithnia's eyes had bulged. Tamar's throat had gone tight. Her family was by no means poor—but neither were they rich enough that she'd ever even considered draping herself with silk. It didn't seem right, somehow. Granted, there was no law against silk, nor one that stated she must wear only the largely shapeless garment she usually did. But shouldn't there be? Shouldn't there be *some* prohibition against wearing clothes not your own so that no one would recognize you?

Yet she'd found herself pushed into the back chamber, the cool silk as smooth as water in her hands. She'd fumbled putting the long tunic on, knowing it had looked blue in the faint morning light stretching into the main chamber, but seeing nothing but darkness in the rear.

Vision hadn't been required to flinch at how the silk draped and clung in ways wool never did. She'd been grateful for the stola to put on over it, even if she'd had no idea of how to fasten it. Mariana had made quick work of that the moment Tamar emerged again, beaming a smile so full of gratitude and joy that Tamar had sealed her lips against the objection she'd intended to make.

It was the gratitude that had silenced Tamar. There was no reason in the world for this rich Roman woman to want to help her—a perfect stranger, a Jew, wanted for a crime against heaven. Yet she was clearly *grateful* for the chance to help.

Hence why Tamar sat now on the stone table, letting Mariana first brush through and then style her long hair in the Roman fashion while Tamar ate some of the unleavened bread, apple clay, and cheese Bithnia had brought her. It seemed she had to walk farther than she ought to today anyway, she might as well have sustenance for it. She cast a longing glance toward Illana's yellow-and-blue patterned head covering, but she couldn't wear it with this Roman attire. If she was going to attempt to remain invisible as a Roman—which it seemed she was—then she must not give herself away with something so obvious.

Perhaps Mariana had read her mind somehow, because as she finished with whatever braided vanity she'd been doing, she smiled and said, "I know your people consider us immodest, but our clothing is also meant to demonstrate our morality. The stola is worn by married women over our tunic to signal propriety, as are the *vittae*." She indicated the long bands of fine wool she was using to secure Tamar's hair in place. Then she pulled the last item from the bag the governor's wife had sent with her—another length of cloth that matched the set of clothes Tamar now wore. "Now the *palla*. Perhaps you have noticed. We wear them like shawls most of the time, but the moment we enter the temple complex, we will draw them up over our heads."

Relief washed over Tamar as Mariana draped the new piece of cloth around her. "Oh good." She didn't know how she'd managed to set foot on temple grounds with her head bare. It would have been too disrespectful. But honestly, she'd never studied what Roman women wore. Whenever she'd seen one in Jerusalem, she'd looked the other way, just as her father had taught her to do.

Bithnia swayed into view, the baby having somehow ended up on her hip while Tamar was facing away to give Mariana access to her hair. "I suppose even Roman gods demand such respect?"

Mariana hesitated, strange clouds settling on her face. "It is less respect than fear of a curse falling upon us if we are not protected by something. The evil eye. The men will also lift their togas over their heads when they offer prayer or sacrifice, lest a curse land upon them."

Bithnia frowned. "They really think a bit of wool will protect them from a curse?"

Mariana spread her hands wide, shrugged. "Respect…fear—they are not so different in appearance sometimes. I have noticed that many of our practices have similarities to yours but different reasons to explain them. I have often thought that the similarities point to our common origins. We are all descended from Noah and his sons, are we not? But the differences demonstrate the time and forgetfulness of the many generations separating us. We have clung to certain things without knowing why, and so we write our own explanations for them. The kernel of truth is there, just as it is in the very world God created. We simply have to peel back the layers to find it."

Tamar darted a glance toward the centurion to see what he thought of his wife's opinions, but she had to look away again when she saw the expression of open affection and pride on his face. It was one she knew well, the same one *Abba* had reserved for *Imma*. That her brothers reserved for their wives. It showed her the truth of Mariana's words.

Different as they were, God had created them all. He'd created them for the same purpose—to love. One another and Him. Perhaps Romans failed at the latter most of the time…but so did plenty of Jews. Certainly the whole of mankind failed at the former more often than they succeeded.

How strange and sad it was, that the thing most fundamental to humanity—love—was also their greatest failing.

"There." Mariana made one last adjustment to the palla and stepped away, her smile soft but strong. It reminded Tamar suddenly of her mother's touch, which had always paired those same qualities.

Her throat went tight again. Not so different. Yet so very different.

Little Livia bounced on her toes, clapping. "You look beautiful!" she proclaimed. Lifting her own skirts, she twirled around. "Someday I am going to wear pretty things like that too."

Her mother laughed. "You need no silk to make you beautiful, my little love. Only your bright smile and your love of the Lord."

Another pang shot through her. Her mother had said similar things countless times to Tamar and her sisters, whenever they focused on the exterior instead of the interior.

"Now." Mariana crouched down, pulled her daughter into a hug, and then nudged her toward her father. "You go with Tata and Felix back to the house so Tata can rest. I will go with our new friend Tamar to see what we can learn."

Had anyone asked Tamar yesterday if a Roman centurion would ever consent to such an arrangement, she'd have scoffed. They were military machines, weren't they? Monsters. They cared only for torment and power and might.

Yet Valerius took the baby back from Bithnia with a smile, held out a hand for his daughter, and looked to the old slave, Gaius. "Stay with them."

Gaius nodded. "Of course, Master."

Tamar sought some excuse, some objection, but she didn't know what to say that wouldn't offend these people, and that was the last thing she wanted to do right now. They were still Roman, yes. But not pagan. That counted for something, didn't it?

Bithnia stepped closer to Tamar, her face an uncompromising mask. "I will come too."

"No." Tamar used the same tone of voice she did in the work-shop, the one that didn't ask for agreement but rather brooked no argument. "It is too dangerous. If you are recognized—"

"I will follow behind the two of you with my head down, like a slave. No one will even glance at me when I am in your shadow. You know they will not."

Tamar opened her mouth to argue again but stopped. Bithnia was right. The moment a Jew spotted a family of Romans, they looked away. They didn't pause to wonder which unfortunate Jew had been forced into their service. She ought to be glad, relieved to have a friend along. It took her a long moment to identify why she still wanted to argue.

Tamar had decided when her betrothed died, well before she reached marrying age, that she would never marry. She would serve the Lord in the temple instead, serve Him with the skill of her hands. She had worked diligently all these years not only to prove her devotion to God but also to deserve the position she now held.

Bithnia, Illana, the other weavers—they were the family she'd built, rather than one from her womb. They were her daughters. She wanted to send Bithnia home to safety just as Mariana was doing with Livia.

Yet this young woman had already risked much to help Tamar, and Tamar must honor that too. She must grant that every daughter had the right to choose to protect her family. She must be grateful and honored that Bithnia chose to do so when she'd not even been in the weaving room a full month. She must accept it with humbleness of heart.

Why was that so difficult?

She made her lips turn up. "Thank you, Bithnia. There are no words to express how grateful I am for all your help. I am in your debt." And that, perhaps, was the rub. She wanted to be in no one's debt. She wanted to have to rely on no one. She wanted to be the one others relied on.

That, however, didn't seem to be her lot just now.

Moments later, their whole group was stepping out into the morning light. They turned immediately away from the knot of Roman soldiers, though not before she saw that their numbers had dropped from the five voices she'd heard when Livia found her back down to three. They'd gone silent, settling into their useless watch again.

She glanced away quickly, but then Mariana looped their arms together and leaned in. "You will want to check that impulse while you are dressed like a wealthy married Roman woman. Modesty is expected, yes, but those men are beneath the status you are wearing. Do not glance away as if the sight of them burns your eyes."

Tamar forced a smile. "You cannot know how odd this is to me."

"Perhaps not exactly, but do you think it has been easy to move to a hostile land, where the locals look at me as though I am a monster? To give birth to my children here, where I have to send for a Roman midwife because no Jewish woman will help me? Do you think it is easy to explain to one of the only friends I have here that I have decided not to serve her gods?" Mariana shook her head, and the morning light gilded her face with gold. "You are a woman with more authority than most, beloved and respected by your community. For the first time in your life, you are experiencing disdain—but for something not your fault. It is a trial, yes. But it will soon be over. Your family will welcome you home the moment you return. Some of us do not have that promise."

Tamar frowned at the pretty young Roman. "Your family won't welcome you when you return to Rome?"

It took Tamar a beat to recognize the look Mariana sent her—a look *no one* ever sent her, at least not recently. A look that accused her of being naive. "We made our choice to follow the Lord and the teachings of Jesus knowing full well it would mean being cut off from our families when they learn of it. We will, of course, try to persuade them of the truth of the one true God when we eventually return to Rome. But it is more likely that we will never be accepted by them again. We will never be fully accepted by the Jews, either, thanks to our Roman birth. So we will likely never be accepted by anyone."

Tamar turned her face forward under the guise of watching her step as they followed the path winding its way back down toward Jerusalem. She didn't like the questions Mariana's story raised in her mind.

She'd never had to choose God over family. Serving God was *part* of her family, something that bound them together. Would she have chosen it still, had it torn them apart? Would she choose service to the Lord over her parents, her siblings, her nieces and nephews? Would she choose it if it meant losing them all forever?

"I admire you," Bithnia said from behind them, softly. "You and your husband have made a brave choice. I know that God will reward you for it—in heaven, if not on earth."

By instinct, Tamar bristled. Heaven was for *them*. For the children of Abraham. It was the place where Abraham and Isaac and Jacob waited to welcome them. Didn't Bithnia fear she'd be struck down for daring to extend the welcome to anyone else?

But there had been many converts to Judaism throughout history. God would probably welcome them too…wouldn't He?

It was far too early in the day after far too uncomfortable a night to make any sense of such questions.

Bithnia went on. "I heard Jesus promise that He is the way to the Father. That whoever believes in Him will live forever in heaven. I have been clinging to that. My family are mostly Sadducees. They believe there is nothing beyond our life on earth. They claim that this is all the Scriptures promise, that if we honor God here, we will be rewarded with long life and wealth. But that always felt so… empty."

Tamar glanced back at her young friend. She'd known, of course, that the women under her direction came from all sorts of Jewish families. Some from Pharisees, like her own. Others from Sadducees. Others from less prominent sects, or sects within the main ones. She made no effort to differentiate. In the weaving room, the only thing that mattered was that they served the Lord with diligence and respect. Theological differences were to be left at the door.

She'd had no idea that Bithnia was raised to believe only in the here and now. She'd had no idea that she longed for more. Tamar's brother Jeremiah, the second eldest of her brothers, would have grinned and said this girl had better marry a Pharisee so she could embrace the hope of a resurrected life with the Lord.

Bithnia, it seemed, had sought that comfort in a different way. Not in a husband who would let her believe as her soul yearned to do. But in a Teacher who promised it to all who would listen.

She shifted, wishing she could pull her arm from Mariana's without causing offense. The Rabbi had caused a considerable stir in the region, she knew that. She'd only heard Him preach once, and it had struck her as sound enough teaching. Perhaps that was why, a week ago, she'd let herself get caught up in the excitement when He returned to Jerusalem, riding a donkey as if He were a prince arriving with a message of peace.

Still, she hadn't been able to argue with her eldest brother when he insisted Jesus was guilty of sacrilege either. How could she, hearing statements like the one Bithnia had just shared?

No man should claim to be the pathway to God. No man could be. Anyone who thought he was such a pathway, who thereby set himself equal to God, was at best a madman, and at worse a criminal deserving the death Caiaphas had arranged. Such heretics *had* to be eliminated, lest they drag all of Israel down. That was the lesson her people had learned through centuries and millennia of oppression.

When they turned from God, when they let people—their own or their pagan neighbors—lead them astray, they paid the price. They lost the favor of God.

Heretic. It wasn't a word to be taken lightly, and the mere whisper of it had been enough to make her and the rest of her family present in that crowd a week ago shake their heads and slink away from any further mention of Jesus of Nazareth. He'd said nothing sacrilegious in the single sermon she'd heard, but if He was going about saying things like *that*, then He was a danger to them all.

But she didn't much fancy siding with Caiaphas on anything just now. Which made her insides a muddle.

Mariana and Bithnia were still talking, Bithnia having asked Mariana what the Roman view was on the afterlife. Tamar paid little attention as Mariana described bathing in the River Lethe, which removed human memory, and then being ushered into one of the various places in the underworld, determined by how virtuous a life one lived on earth. She didn't chime in as Bithnia explained the Hebrew understanding of Sheol, which wasn't so dissimilar. It was all the Sadducees would ever grant—that departed souls gathered in a place deep down, but that it was what the very word meant: hollow. It was an empty place. Not one of comfort, nor of reward. No paradise. Just...there. A gray place, a place of shadows and emptiness.

She much preferred her own sect's insistence that God would raise the faithful in the last day. That He would even grant access to His presence beforehand to those who lived virtuously. Elijah, after all, hadn't been caught up in a chariot of fire just to be delivered to nothingness, had he? Moses's body hadn't been buried by the hand of God Himself, only for his soul to be consigned to nothingness. David, who had chased after God's own heart and found it, claimed in his psalms that God lifted the soul from the deepest Sheol to dwell in His presence.

They reached the end of the garden path, their feet once more on the plain that would lead directly to the city. Tamar didn't mean to slow her pace, but she must have, because Mariana cast a questioning look her way.

She couldn't bring herself to answer. All her life, Jerusalem had been home. Those walls and gates had represented safety, security, and belonging.

Suddenly they were something very different. They towered above her, a clear warning. Inside lay danger. Inside lay enemies who sought her life. Inside lay a ripped veil that had torn her world apart.

Her heart thudded painfully in her chest. How had this happened? *Why* had it happened? Why was she the one who stood to bear the punishment for something so beyond her control?

The walls offered no answers.

CHAPTER TEN

Sabbath days were always quieter than any other day of the week—the markets were empty, cook fires were unlit, businesses were closed. But today seemed abnormally subdued, even for a Sabbath. Especially for a Sabbath during Passover, when the week-long celebration usually meant an air of rejoicing in the city that was bursting with pilgrims.

All voices were hushed as they made their way to the temple compound, and the quiet finally drew her attention to something she hadn't considered as they'd walked through the garden of tombs.

She hadn't heard a single bird singing all morning. No insects whirring. No rustle of small animals in the grasses. Maybe that, even more than the feeling of not belonging in her own home, was what had made Tamar's shoulders go a little tauter with each step.

The world was out of balance today. Nature, it seemed, was holding its breath. Waiting.

A shiver coursed down her spine as the inevitable question followed: *Waiting for what?*

Mariana's arm was still looped through hers, Bithnia and Gaius still following behind them. The Jews gathered in the temple compound were more diverse than usual, many of them having traveled there from lands far and wide for Passover.

They looked less odd, she and Mariana, than they usually would have. Here, this week, there were Gentile women aplenty—Gentile by blood but part of families who had converted to Judaism in decades or centuries past. All manners of dress were represented, all manners of hairstyles.

Even so, the visitors still moved out of the way when Mariana and Tamar approached. Their clothes shouted not only "Roman" but "*rich* Roman"—the most dangerous kind. The only rich Romans in Judea were the ones with political power, after all.

Another wave of uneasiness swept over her. She was quite literally wearing the robes of the governor's wife. Pretending to be something she was so far from being that it seemed the entire swarm of pilgrims ought to have been able to see it in a glance.

Yet no one did. No one looked past her stola and vittae and palla to see the Jewish woman beneath them. Just as Mariana had said.

She'd lifted the palla over her intricately braided and bound hair, but it hadn't brought the comfort she'd hoped. The silk still felt strange against her skin—lovely, but in a way that was wrong. Unfamiliar.

Usually, she'd be able to leave the outer court reserved to Gentiles and at least enter the women's court, but today Mariana led her instead to a place still in the outermost court, but right beside the walkway where people passed to enter the inner ones and then exited again toward the city.

Every voice was a hush, a whisper. Where was the excited babble of a holy day? Where were the children laughing and chasing each other? Where were the heated arguments between the sects, debating whichever passage of Scripture had been read?

Mariana managed to convey with only her eyes that this was the best place to just stand and listen. With Bithnia and Gaius standing invisibly behind them, Tamar settled in to do so.

She spotted a man with a scroll unfurled, but his voice didn't reach them as he read the day's passage. Nor could she make out the questions he posed after reading. Whatever answers—or more questions—people offered seemed to be eaten up by the heaviness that pervaded the place.

After another minute, she gave up straining to hear the morning's teaching and instead focused on what she should have been paying attention to all along—listening to the passersby.

For the first twenty minutes, she heard nothing that could help her. All the talk was of the crucifixion. Some debated whether Jesus had been deserving of death. *"He was a heretic!"* said one and *"He was guiltless! It was only jealousy that condemned Him,"* said another. Others mused on whether Pilate would face any chastisement from Rome for releasing Barabbas. After all, the man had been involved in an uprising. Surely Caesar wouldn't appreciate an insurrectionist being set free.

Then, finally, she caught a phrase that had her straightening. "…in two, cleanly. As if a knife had sliced it."

The veil. What else could it be?

"What can it mean?" a second voice asked. "Is God so angry with us that He has removed His presence entirely?"

"I do not know. But Caiaphas is in a fury over it—or so he says. If you ask me, he has simply been biding his time and has finally found an excuse."

A chill swept up Tamar's spine. She wanted to look back to Bithnia but didn't dare. All she could do was glance over at Mariana, whose studied expression of indifference said that she was listening just as intently.

"An excuse for what?"

"To get rid of the head weaver so he can promote his niece."

His niece? Who was his niece? Heat suffused her, burning away the chill from earlier. It must be someone already in the workshop, if she would be promoted. But she didn't recall any of the women ever claiming an association with the high priest, and it was something that should have come up.

She felt Bithnia ease closer to her back. "Who?"

Tamar shook her head.

The men continued. "Does he really think he can get away with blaming this on a weaver? No fault in the veil could have resulted in a clean slice like that."

"He just got away with executing a teacher who preached nothing but love and forgiveness, did he not?"

The second man hissed out a breath. "That cannot bode well. Tamar is beloved by the weavers. If he dismisses or punishes her, the women will stand with her."

"If so, then I daresay any who object will face the same fate. You know Caiaphas. He will lobby to replace anyone who sides with Tamar, just as he is even now lobbying to have all of Jesus's disciples rounded up and punished for following Him."

The fire that had flashed through her veins settled in her stomach. Whoever these men were, they must know someone in her workshop well, to talk so knowledgeably and call her by name. She shifted, angling for a better view, and managed to get a look at the two men's faces.

One was unfamiliar, but the other… She had seen him before, on a visit to the home of one of her girls. She couldn't place him at first, but then his expression shifted, and recognition settled. Illana's brother. They had the same mouth, and worry settled over their brows in the same way.

That certainly explained his familiarity with the shop and with her.

The fire burned, making her stomach churn. It warmed her in a far different way to hear that her girls held her in such high esteem. It ought to give her a feeling of accomplishment, of peace. She ought to be able to smile at hearing that the care she took, the firm but loving hand she'd tried so hard to keep with them, accomplished what she'd always hoped.

Instead, their loyalty to her would be cause for punishment. If she was blamed, if she was punished, if she couldn't get out of this, then they'd *all* pay the price.

She had to convince them otherwise—not to stand beside her. She had to make certain each girl, each woman, knew that if they respected her, they would accept her replacement, whoever it was.

Turning to Mariana, she whispered, "I need to visit some of my weavers. Not all of them, but I know the ones who are likely to bear this punishment with me. I know my strongest supporters. I must speak with them and warn them not to stand with me."

Even as she said the names, even as Mariana nodded, Tamar's heart sank. They lived in different sectors of the city. Traveling through the crowded streets, even on the Sabbath when people wouldn't go far, would take hours. Visiting each of them would take all day.

But it must be done. What kind of leader would she be if she let her friends suffer because of their association with her? She knew well that the walk throughout Jerusalem, combined with coming from the tomb and returning to it, would make her guilty of breaking the Sabbath laws.

But perhaps Bithnia was right. Perhaps, when it was to save lives, it was not a sin.

"Shall we start now?" Mariana asked. "Or perhaps see if we hear more first while we are here?"

A new feeling surged, a new kind of guilt. "I cannot ask you to come with me, Mariana. You ought to go home to your husband and children. This will take all day."

There was no reason for this stranger to argue, but the argument sprang up immediately in her eyes. It firmed her mouth. It straightened her spine and made her shoulders roll back. "The children's nurse went straight home when we left the governor's palace. She will be there to help with Felix and Livia. Valerius will be sleeping. Gaius and I will stay with you."

"As will I," Bithnia promised, despite having heard the same words Tamar did.

Tamar shook her head. "Go home, Bithnia, please. Or—Illana is your friend, isn't she? Go to her, warn her against standing with me. I imagine her brother has cautioned her as well, but tell her it is my wish that she accept my replacement peaceably."

If Bithnia were truly the slave she was pretending to be, that spark in her eyes likely would have earned her a slap. "You cannot make us abandon you, Tamar. Did King Solomon not say, 'Two are better than one'?"

Tamar's lips twitched. It had only been a day ago that she said those same words to Bithnia after she'd found the frayed thread, but it seemed a lifetime had passed since then. To think that then, her biggest worry had been one damaged thread and the weeks of work it had lost them. Then, she'd never have believed that the veil in the temple could be cut so neatly in two.

"He did. But we also all know the dangers of lashing ourselves to a sinking ship. Caiaphas will not relent, especially if he has been looking for a reason to replace me. That does not mean you should suffer too. You were not even working there yet when that veil was made. Of all the weavers, you cannot be blamed. Your newness will protect you."

But the girl shook her head. "Perhaps I have only been there a few weeks, but in that time I have learned far more than weaving from you, Tamar. It was Illana's stories of you that made me want to work there, rather than in the merchant weaver's shop I had been in before."

"It is the work for the Lord that drew you, not me." Perhaps it was foolish to try to tell someone her own motivations, but that made far more sense than thinking that *she* had been a draw for anyone. She tried to be a good leader, yes. A teacher, helping the women to keep their eyes always on their purpose, not just the mechanical work of their hands. But she was far from the sort of teacher that gathered disciples. No one ought to follow her anywhere.

Rather than answer, Bithnia made a motion that caught the attention of Illana's brother. His name was Gideon, wasn't it? He must know Bithnia, given how close a friend she was to his sister, and indeed, recognition flashed immediately over his face. No, not just recognition. Affection clear enough that the concern that chased quickly after it made all the sense in the world.

He eased closer to them but quickly directed his face back to his companion. It wouldn't do for him to be seen talking to a woman in public. "Bithnia. What are you doing here? I thought we all agreed that you would stay out of sight."

"Circumstances changed," she whispered. "Were your words conjecture, or have you heard this from others?"

Gideon sighed. "It was the talk among the priests this morning. I intend to warn Illana, though we both know she will not listen. Last night she said that Tamar had been the only mother she has had in the last five years, since Imma died, and she will not abandon her."

Another swell of emotion crashed like an errant wave instead of carrying her away. She'd had no idea Illana thought of her like that. "Where is she? I will convince her."

Gideon jolted when he followed her voice to her figure, frowning and staring at her for a long moment before amazement crossed his face. "Tamar?" He barely whispered her name.

She nodded, knowing Illana's brother posed no threat to her, especially if she was promising to help keep his sister safe. "I will convince them to be wise. To accept with grace whatever Caiaphas does."

"You can try," Gideon said, his doubt clear. "But you will not succeed. If you know my sister at all, you know how stubborn she is."

She did, at that. It was what had made her such a good weaver. She refused to give up until she'd mastered each new skill. Someday she would be ready for Tamar's position, after another few years of work.

"Do you know who it is?" At his blank blink, Tamar clarified. "Who is Caiaphas's niece? No one has laid claim to that association."

Gideon shook his head. "The priests I heard talking didn't mention her by name. Presumably someone with considerable experience, if he thinks she could handle the responsibility."

It shouldn't be what mattered just now. She needed to focus on keeping her girls safe, not on identifying her replacement. Even so, the question wouldn't leave her mind.

She lifted her chin. "Is Illana at your family home?"

He shook his head. "A cousin's instead. Though when the temple guards stopped by last night, I told them I was uncertain where she had gone, that she said she was celebrating with a friend but I could not remember who."

The guards no doubt didn't believe that, but what could they do?

He told Tamar where to find Illana, made them swear they'd be careful, and then steered his unfamiliar friend away from them.

Her mind was already sketching out the most efficient route through the city, to reach all the women she wanted to reach before sundown. She'd brought with her the scroll with the records of her workers and their homes, tucked into the stola, but she didn't need to consult it.

She knew who her friends were. How hard could it be to convince them to save themselves?

Sarah stood tall in the main room of her house, afternoon light painting gold over her cheeks as she glowered down at Tamar. They'd known each other for sixteen years and had always gotten along well. They weren't the sort of friends that joked and jested, but they *were* the sort that brought food to each other when some-one had a sick family member, who often ate together when they paused their work in the weaving room, who would walk together through the markets, talking about whatever was on their hearts.

Sarah hadn't hesitated to begin frowning from the very moment Tamar launched into her explanation—right after she recovered from the shock of seeing Tamar dressed as she was. "And so," she finished now, though she felt tired and deflated after hours of this, "it is best if you stand with whomever Caiaphas appoints in my place. Do not defend me."

Sarah folded her arms over her chest and darted a look toward the doorway. Mariana and Gaius had been waiting outside each home, not wanting to offend any of her friends by entering, but Sarah had seen them when she opened to Tamar's knock and demanded an explanation of *that* and her clothing before she'd listen to anything else.

If she *had* listened to anything else. "Let me get this straight. You are asking me to break one of God's sacred commandments?"

"What?" Horror filled Tamar. "Of course not! Why would you—"

"You are asking me to bear false witness against you." Sarah's eyes flashed back to hers. "To say that I do not think you are the best woman for your job. That I believe anyone else could do as *good* a job."

"I..." She halted, huffed out a breath. "Sarah, that is not what I am asking you to do. I am simply asking you to be silent and protect your own position." She gestured to the room around her, tidy if small. Sarah had been widowed ages ago, and her only children were daughters. Were it not for her position as a weaver, she'd have nowhere to go, no way to support the youngest girl, Naomi, until she was of age to marry like her two elder sisters. "For Naomi's sake."

Sarah's eyes narrowed still more. "I would rather return to my father's house with my daughter, despite his cruelties, than let her see me deciding to save myself at the cost of my friend. That is not what the Lord would want of me, Tamar."

Tamar's shoulders sagged under the featherlight weight of the silk she wore. "You would rather put this burden on me? To know that I am the ruin of so many?"

"You are guilty of *nothing*." Sarah slashed a hand through the air. "Everyone knows it. So instead of wasting your time trying to convince us to abandon you, you should be trying instead to find a way to convince Caiaphas of this. You will save us by saving *yourself*, Tamar."

She'd visited five other women already today, and though none had been quite so forceful as Sarah, that was the bottom line they'd all reached, despite Tamar's best efforts to convince them otherwise.

More defeats that were twisted victories. She couldn't keep the tears from surging to her eyes. She could appreciate their loyalty, their friendship, their faith in her. Her heart ought to be uplifted by their support. Instead, she couldn't shake the gnawing fear that she'd only drag them all down with her, every one of them who refused to denounce her and promise their allegiance to her replacement. Would Caiaphas replace a quarter of the weavers? Half? Three-quarters?

Each of the five she'd talked to swore that the other girls they worked beside would stand where they did—beside Tamar.

Her only hope at this point, horrible as it was, was that they would change their minds when it came down to it. That they would melt away in the face of adversity, like the crowds who had welcomed Jesus a week ago.

Sarah reached out and settled her hand on Tamar's shoulder, making her newly aware of the exquisite fabric that covered it. "Tamar. I see how heavy this burden weighs on you, but please, my friend. Do not ask us to abandon you. I have nothing against Davorah, you know I have not. If you were not there at all, she would be a fine enough leader, I suppose. But she is not you. She does not have your talent at the looms, and she does not have your way with people."

Tamar's head snapped up. "Davorah?"

Sarah frowned. "Did you not know that is who it is? I suppose not. She does not... She is not fond of her uncle. I know she has made an effort to keep the association unknown so no one looks at her differently since his appointment all those years ago. But I thought you knew—it has been so long."

Davorah. Tamar shook her head, her mind flashing back to yesterday, when she'd returned from the temple. Davorah had been there. Davorah had asked where she was going. Had she already known Caiaphas's plan? Had they made some secret agreement that at the first mistake she made, they would pounce?

Her skin prickled. How fortunate that she hadn't known where she was going, to tell the woman she'd thought was a friend, if a vague one. Hadn't she thought even then about how little she knew the woman she'd served beside for longer than anyone else? Davorah was always so quiet, reserved.

Perhaps because, all along, she'd been harboring resentment. Bitterness. Hating Tamar for gaining the leadership role despite being the younger, just because she'd been brought on a bit earlier.

But with Tamar gone, Davorah would be the senior weaver. Caiaphas wouldn't need to pull any strings or rely on his position to give Tamar's to her. She was the logical choice. The heir apparent, so to speak.

Sarah squeezed her shoulder again and then dropped her hand away. "Fight this, Tamar. Fight, knowing we will all fight with you."

Feeling a bit dazed, Tamar found herself nodding. "I will. I will fight." She didn't know how to win, or if it was wise to try. But somehow, knowing the name and face of her adversary stoked the fires within her.

It had been one thing when Caiaphas was the only opponent she could name. It had been easy to see only his position and defer to it. But Davorah, she knew. Davorah, she had trusted. Davorah had *betrayed* her.

Her fingers curled into her palm. She glanced up at Sarah briefly and then spun toward the door. "Thank you, Sarah. I wish I had spoken to you first."

Her friend hurried to open the door for her, her frown just as intense as it had been before. "Tamar, do be careful. Do not confront anyone today. Caiaphas is still in a rage, waiting for that teacher's disciples to try something. He'll be better appeased tomorrow, when the third day has dawned and He is still dead in the tomb."

Tamar saw both Bithnia and Mariana wince at Sarah's words, but she couldn't dwell on that right now. She was sorry they were mourning, but what did they honestly expect to happen when they followed a teacher who claimed to be the equal of God?

He had been crucified. Buried. No amount of sorrow would change that, and though Sarah's words sounded harsh, they were still true. Not just for their teacher, but for Caiaphas, and hence her.

She nodded her agreement. "I will wait."

CHAPTER ELEVEN

B ithnia left them near the city's gate, pointing toward her family's home. "I would invite you to stay with us," she said in a hush, casting an anxious glance around her, "but I do not think my home is any safer than yours just now."

They'd drawn near enough to Tamar's home to verify that temple guards were lurking at the corners, waiting for her to appear. Even though she likely could have walked right past them in her current garb without earning a second glance, they'd take notice if she approached either of the doors. What business, after all, would a wealthy Roman matron have with Tamar's family?

But Bithnia's claim made her frown. Not that she was fishing for an invitation, but... "I cannot think why your family would be in any danger, Bithnia. I doubt Caiaphas even knows who you are, given how new you are."

"That is not why," Bithnia said softly. She glanced toward Mariana and Gaius, and then toward the home built into the wall. "My brother...he is one of the seventy."

Tamar frowned. "The seventy what?"

"Disciples. Of Jesus. There are thousands who follow Him, of course, and everyone knows of the Twelve—or Eleven now, I suppose. My brother said that Judas, the traitor, hanged himself last night."

Tamar *had* heard of the Twelve, now that Bithnia mentioned it. But not the seventy.

"A while back, Jesus chose seventy of the men who had been with Him the longest and sent them out into the towns He planned to visit, to prepare the way for Him. To preach the good news of salvation from sin. My brother Noam was one of them." Bithnia scanned the street, not seeming satisfied at the lack of guards. "He is concerned—they all are—that we will be rounded up. He said that as soon as the Sabbath is over at sundown, or perhaps at first light, we should expect them to move."

Tamar reached for Bithnia's hand. After all this girl had done to help Tamar, why was she resigning herself to this fate for herself? "Then you should not go home. You should come with me."

Bithnia gave a closed-lip smile. "No. If the followers are taken, I will be with them. I am not ashamed of where I have put my faith."

"In Jesus?" She squeezed the girl's hand. "Bithnia, He is gone. I am sorry, but it is true. There is no reason for anyone else to face prison or death for their loyalty to Him."

Bithnia squeezed her fingers in return but then pulled away. "I will not deny Him. Better to be thrown to the lions or cast into the furnace than to deny the Lord."

"That was different." The fact that Bithnia equated them made bands of worry tighten around Tamar's chest. "That was denying God. Not a teacher. Even if He was a prophet—"

"He is more than a teacher. More than a prophet." Bithnia sought Mariana's gaze, and she must have seen something in it that encouraged her. "He is the Son of God."

Tamar pulled back a step. That was the phrase Valerius had used, and one she'd heard rumors about Jesus claiming. But to hear

Bithnia speak it… She ought to know better. Valerius likely didn't, having been raised in a society that had so many stories about demigods and heroes with one immortal parent. But Bithnia should.

God was One. God was alone. God was all. He was not like Jupiter, descending to earth and dallying with human women. The very thought was abhorrent. God was perfection. The definition of morality. How could any Jew even suggest that God had a human—half-human?—son. It was ludicrous.

It was worse than ludicrous. It was heresy. The moment Jesus went from preaching repentance and love to claiming that *He* was the means to forgiveness, Bithnia ought to have known to run, just as Tamar's family had.

Perhaps her young friend read the disapproval on her face. Her expression shifted, not to apology but to resignation. She handed Tamar the sack she'd been carrying, which had the rest of the food she'd brought that morning. "You are welcome to stay in the tomb as long as you need. I will check on you again tomorrow and bring you more food."

"There is no need. I will return home tomorrow." She didn't know if she would, or if Levi would have another plan in place for her when she met him at noon at the market stall he'd named, but she suddenly didn't want Bithnia coming again. Even so, she owed the girl. She'd risked much to help her. "Thank you for all you have done, Bithnia."

"It is a privilege to help you. It is what Jesus would have advised me to do."

Tamar had no answer to that, so she said no more, just offered a tight smile and watched Bithnia dart off.

Mariana shifted closer. "This disturbs you—calling Jesus the Son of God."

It was a statement, an observation, not a question. Yet the pause waited for an explanation. Tamar sighed. "I imagine Roman inheritance laws are not *so* different from ours. When a man has a son, all that he owns belongs to that son. He is not just a servant, not just another worker, not just a child to love. He is the heir. When he travels on behalf of his father, he has his father's authority. He can give orders in his father's name. Even while the father still lives, while the wealth and land are his and he is the only one who can decide how to use it, the son can act on his behalf. He is the one person in the family who is equal to his father."

Mariana nodded, and understanding lit her eyes. "So if Jesus is the Son of God..."

"He is equal to God. He has the authority of God. And that cannot be."

"But what if it can?" Mariana leaned close, her eyes burning brighter than the sinking sun. "Has He not acted with the authority of God? He calmed the waves. Stilled the wind. Raised the dead."

"Nonsense." For what felt like the hundredth time that day, she bristled. "Just a story."

"It is not, and you know it. Lazarus lives only a few miles from here. You *know* he was four days in the grave, yet you have seen him walking in the city again. You cannot deny that!"

Tamar bit back a retort. She did know that Lazarus had been reported dead. His was a prominent family, owning a wide expanse of land in Bethany. Vineyards, farms, a villa to match none other. His sudden death had rocked the whole region, and though Tamar didn't know the family personally, she had felt so sorry for his two sisters, who were left with no one.

But then came the claims that Jesus had called Lazarus forth and, after four days in the grave, he emerged. Where there should have been rot and stink, there had been a man in perfect health.

Her eldest brother, Moshe, had refused to believe it. Her second-eldest, Jeremiah, had instead gotten a dark look on his face, muttering that if Lazarus had indeed been resurrected by Jesus, he would soon wish he hadn't been. That the high priest would seek to silence him in whatever way he could find. Her younger brother, Simon, had pressed his lips together and said nothing.

Mariana held her gaze. "He healed the sick. Gave sight to the blind. Opened the ears of the deaf. He healed Gaius when he was on the brink of death, from miles away, just by speaking a word."

"Coincidence."

"It was *not*." Mariana splayed a hand over her chest. "I saw it, Tamar. I saw him struggle for each breath. I saw him grow weaker and weaker. Then all at once, without warning, he simply sat up, healthy again. The fever hadn't just broken, he was *healthy*. Stronger than he'd been in years. No shadows under his eyes. Healthy color in his cheeks."

"My arthritic joints were young again," Gaius added from behind her. "All the aches and pains of age, gone. I remembered being so sick, wishing death would hurry. And then, it was like a flash of light was before my eyes, and I was…bright. Filled with light. Made anew."

She could see there was no point in arguing. And, to be honest, she didn't know how she would have. It was one thing to dismiss a story heard secondhand or to try to explain that sometimes things were coincidence, that people just got better.

But they didn't, not like that. Men blind from birth didn't simply begin seeing one afternoon. Men on the brink of death, who'd been wasting away for weeks, didn't sit up with strong muscles and revived joints.

God also didn't walk among men anymore though. He didn't have a son. He was *One*.

The incongruity made her head ache.

Mariana offered a sweet, guileless smile. "I will not try to convince you. But I will offer you what Bithnia could not—refuge for the night. Come to our home, please. Do not spend another night on the cave floor. Have a hot meal, sleep in a real bed."

"No." The refusal was out before she could stop it. But how could she have anyway? Pharisees didn't eat with Gentiles, and even if this woman and her husband really had cleansed their house of idols, they still were not Jews. They hadn't gone through the ritual of conversion. If she ate at their table and slept under their roof, she would be unclean.

Mariana blinked at her quick answer, hurt flashing in her eyes. But she covered it quickly. "Of course. Well then, will you at least accept a cushion and blankets?"

Why was she so kind? So generous? Tamar shook her head. "You have done so much already. I will be fine. And I will change back into my garments when I return to the cave and will leave these within it. Your husband can collect them tomorrow, perhaps?"

Mariana's smile went sad. "Very well."

There was nothing left to say other than farewell. She couldn't promise they'd see each other again. She couldn't apologize for all that separated them.

Well, there was one thing. "Thank you. For your help today." She still didn't know why a total stranger had done so much for her, but she was certain that she wouldn't have been able to walk through the city as she'd done without Mariana at her side, without her clothes, without the appearance they presented.

She was a sweet woman. Perhaps, in another world…or perhaps if they *did* go through the full conversion process…

But for now, this was how it must be. She said her goodbyes and then slipped through the gates.

Exhaustion hit her the moment she was outside the city. For the first time since she awoke, she was alone again, and she felt it. *Alone.* Each step she took toward the beautiful garden cemetery, it pummeled her. *Alone.*

Then, as she started up the garden path, an even worse sensation. *Not alone.*

She looked over her shoulder, trying to make out shapes in the gathering dusk. Who was that slipping out of the gates?

Men, without question. Men who seemed to carry something in their hands. Spears? Swords?

Guards? Perhaps her disguise hadn't been so convincing after all. Perhaps they'd been following her and were just waiting for a moment to pounce when she wasn't in the company of others.

No. She didn't know if it was fear or rage that fueled her, but she wouldn't give up now. She wouldn't let them take her so that Caiaphas and his sect could silence her the way they were seeking to do with Lazarus. She wasn't just going to let him steal from her everything she'd worked for all these many years.

She wouldn't go quietly. She wouldn't go at all.

Opting for speed over stealth, she ran up the path, sending pebbles dancing beneath her feet. She prayed that darkness would fall quickly, prayed for a burst of energy, prayed that somehow the guards' eyes would be blinded.

Halfway up the path, she tripped on a rock cloaked in shadow, tumbled forward onto her knees, and caught herself with her hands. Fire lit her palms, and a new horror seized her when she pushed herself up and saw the condition of her borrowed garment. "No," she breathed into the twilight. Was it only dirt, or had she ripped the fabric? She reached to investigate but stopped herself just in the nick of time. Her hands were bleeding, caked in dirt—if she touched the silk, she'd only make it worse.

Were those voices coming from farther down the path? Yes, masculine ones. She ignored her pulsing palms and stinging knees and took off again, running as quickly as she could.

By the time she gained the cave, her chest was heaving, her eyes stinging with tears as hot as her palms felt. She couldn't let them flow, though, couldn't make a sound. She'd spotted the Romans guarding the tomb of the Teacher as she crested the hill, but they'd been looking the other way. One thing, at least, that had gone right.

Hands trembling, she hurried to the back of the tomb and the chamber hidden in darkness. Her clothes waited there, but before she dared to change, she first reached for the full waterskin Bithnia had brought along with the food that morning. She splashed some of it onto her hands, hoping that she'd gotten the worst of the dirt and blood off.

She needed light, a basin, soap to bubble away the dirt. She needed to make certain every pebble was cleared from her skin. She needed honey and bandages to wrap them.

She had only water and darkness, pain and fear. She washed her palms again as best she could then felt around for the folded clothing she'd left and used the inside of her tunic to pat her stinging hands dry. By the time she slipped the silk off and her own wool on, her whole body was shaking. She tugged at the cloth bands of the vittae, desperate now to have the last of the Roman garments off.

She wanted her own things. Her own life. Her own family. She wanted the headscarf that Illana had taken, the cook fire in her family's kitchen, the comforting sound of her nieces and nephews laughing and playing. She wanted to know that when she went back to the weaving room after the festival concluded, she would still have a place there.

Davorah.

The pain seemed to spiral from her palms, up her arms, and to her heart. No, they'd never been close friends. But they had worked side by side for so long. How could Davorah do this to her? How could she plot against Tamar? Had it been there all along, all these years? Or had she only begun to think it her right when her uncle ascended to the high priesthood? But even if so, that was so long ago—nearly a decade. A decade for her to have resented Tamar, to have stewed, to have plotted.

She hadn't wanted anyone to know that she was of Caiaphas's family, Sarah had said. Because then her plotting would be obvious.

Male shouts came from outside, and Tamar pressed her back to the wall. It was utterly dark here. She needn't worry. Probably. Not unless they searched inside better than Valerius had done last night. Not unless they realized it wasn't merely a wall but a corridor to a second chamber.

Through the pounding of blood in her ears, she couldn't make out their words. Then, finally, she realized it wasn't only that. The words weren't Aramaic or Greek. They were Latin.

Her breath shuddered out. Not temple guards. Roman guards. The next shift to guard the other tomb, probably.

Weak with relief she knew she shouldn't indulge, she slid to the floor. They were still her enemy. But they weren't the enemy she feared most right now.

CHAPTER TWELVE

Valerius waved the three soldiers away and motioned Albus and Caeso into the same positions they'd had last night. He hadn't asked them to take another night shift, but when he'd announced that he would, they volunteered.

He hadn't argued. They were good company, they never struggled to stay awake for a night watch, and he wouldn't have to explain himself to them when he kept to the same routine he'd initiated before. He merely nodded at them and said, "I will do a circuit again."

"Do you want to eat first, sir?"

He'd done that last night, he supposed. But tonight, he had a more pressing concern. "You go ahead. Livia thinks she left something here this morning, and I promised her I would check."

His men smiled at that. Livia had them all wrapped around her sweet little finger. No one would question him looking for this "something" now, when barely any light remained in the sky, rather than tomorrow morning.

Since this "something" was in fact a someone, he hastened away, one of their torches in hand.

He'd intercepted Mariana just moments after she and Tamar parted ways, it seemed, and she'd had that look on her face that said she was trying not to be hurt, not to be disappointed. He guessed that she'd invited Tamar home and been refused. He knew that, intellectually, she understood.

That never stopped the sting.

But she'd perked up when he promised he would check in on Tamar and make certain she was settled, and showed her that he'd brought a blanket and pillow for Tamar, suspecting she would opt for another night in her proven hiding spot rather than finding a new one. If he was wrong, he'd simply set them aside and gather them back up in the morning.

He didn't do anything so obvious as glance over his shoulder to make certain his men weren't looking. He just walked into the cave that Bithnia's family owned. He'd lain awake longer than he should have that morning, marveling at how, hours after he'd prayed that God would send him someone to explain what would happen now that Jesus was gone, what it meant for those who loved Him, He'd sent a believer. A follower of Jesus.

Bithnia might not have had all the answers. But even so—she was a *follower*. She had spent the day with Mariana and Gaius, and they now knew where she lived. According to Gaius, she'd even whispered a time and place they could meet her family two days from now...assuming they hadn't been arrested.

God had answered. God had provided a means to get answers.

He stepped now into the dark of the cave, his torch casting its flickering orange light on an empty space. But he wasn't about to fall for that again. "Tamar?" he called quietly. "It is only me. Valerius."

A beat of silent stillness, and then she eased around the back wall. She wore her own clothes again, but she was holding her hands strangely. He frowned. "What is the matter?"

"Nothing." But as she drew closer, he could see blood on her palms that had him hissing out a sympathetic breath.

"It looks as though you slipped and caught yourself on rocks."

She shrugged, clearly trying to ignore it. But her hands trembled. Cold? Pain?

If only she'd accepted Mariana's invitation. He understood why she hadn't, of course, but sometimes he wished these people whose God he loved could put aside their pride and accept friendship without so many rules and regulations. He'd read the Scripture. God had never told them they couldn't so much as share a meal or a roof with other peoples. It was man who had devised those rules. Men who were afraid, after the last captivity, of falling away again. Men who were so keen on making sure that didn't recur that they overcompensated.

He removed the bag he'd been carrying slung over his shoulder, disguised by his cloak, and dropped it to the ground as he fitted the torch into a hole in the wall that seemed designed for it. "I brought you a few things."

"Oh, you needn't have—"

"Perhaps instead of arguing, you simply ought to thank the Lord for His provision?" He lifted a brow and crouched down to open the bag. "It isn't much. I knew you wouldn't eat or drink anything I brought, but there are no stipulations about blankets, are there? We can cut a few strips off to bind your hands too."

He pulled his knife from his belt and got to work, trying not to count the seconds until she lowered herself to the floor several feet away from him. Twenty-three.

"You and your wife are too kind."

"I do not think one can be *too* kind. We are simply trying to live a life that will please the Lord."

She nodded, and her hair fell forward, into her face. It had a wave and curl he recognized—the same sort Mariana's always had after she'd worn her hair up all day in its twists and braids and finally took it down at night. She had the yellow and blue headscarf again, but it wasn't quite in place. No doubt her hands hurt enough that she couldn't be precise with them.

"I fear…when I fell. Your wife's fine silk… I will take it home with me tomorrow and wash it. I pray it is not ripped. There is no way I could ever replace it if it is damaged."

His knife sliced through the wool of the blanket as she said it, and he had to breathe a short laugh. "Tamar, Mariana will not care if it is ruined. She does not like silk. She says it is too decadent. She only accepts such gifts to keep from offending her friend. But I assure you, if it is ruined, she will not mourn its loss."

A glance showed him that Tamar's jaw was set. "I care though."

He studied her face for a moment. More than its only vaguely familiar lines and features, he saw bits and pieces he knew far better. His sister in the flair of her nostrils. His mother in the straightness of her spine. Mariana in the glint in her eye.

She didn't want to be in anyone's debt, he would imagine, especially not theirs. But she was right that there was no way she could replace the silk. He could count on one hand the number of Jews he'd spotted wearing the rare imported fabric, and they'd all been at Herod's court, not living ordinary lives in Jerusalem. Frankly, he couldn't afford to dress his wife regularly in silk either. It was only due to Claudia's generosity that Mariana even knew she didn't like to wear it.

"If you find it needs replacing, then I know my wife would treasure something you wove yourself. You must be talented, to have earned your position."

Tamar measured him for a long moment, no doubt trying to discern if he spoke the truth or offered a comforting lie. He finished slicing off the long strip of cloth from the blanket, folded it in half, and made another slice in the middle to create two bandages of more manageable length.

Perhaps she believed him. Or perhaps she was too weary to argue. Either way, she nodded. "Thank you."

The words sounded as though they cost her far more than a breath and a few sounds. He held out the cloth. "May I assist you, or would you be more comfortable doing it yourself?"

"I...do not know. I imagine I can do the left, but I may need some help on my right."

Were she one of his men, he simply would have issued a command to let him help so that it would be accomplished more quickly and with more speed. Had she been one of the women in his family, she'd have known she could trust him with so simple a task and would have accepted his help eagerly.

As it was, he told himself to be patient. She was neither a soldier nor a sister, and a single day's acquaintance wasn't enough to prove to her that he meant her no harm.

Her hands continued to tremble as she wrapped the first strip around her left palm, and he winced again as he saw the raw flesh better in the torchlight as she held it up. It needed a more thorough cleaning too, but he didn't have the means available to him to offer. That would have to wait until she returned home tomorrow.

She got it wrapped well enough but had trouble securing the end and, after an exasperated huff, held it out to him. He gently tucked the end under the other strips and then reached for her other, dominant hand. "Let me know if it is too tight." He'd bound plenty of wounds on his men over the years, but he'd discovered with his wife and daughter that the same amount of pressure was too much for them.

She made no objection though, so he concentrated on wrapping the cloth in even circles and avoiding so much as a graze of his fingertips on her flesh, knowing it would make her uncomfortable. In half the time it had taken her, he was finished. He turned away, pulling forward the cushion he'd brought and handing it to her. "If you need anything else through the night, make the call of a nightjar."

She blinked at him. "I have not imitated birdcalls since I was a child."

"It will return to you, if you need it." Offering her a smile, he pushed to his feet and reached for his torch. "Would you like to get situated while you have the light?"

She shook her head, but then she paused, drew in a breath, and nodded. It took her only a moment to spread out the blanket and position the pillow at one end of it. "Thank you."

He nodded, and once she'd settled again onto her makeshift bed, he turned toward the exit. Albus and Caeso were talking quietly at the other tomb, no doubt enjoying their dinners. He did a quick patrol of the rest of the garden and then joined them, putting his torch in its spot.

"Did you find Livia's missing toy, sir?" Albus asked.

"No toys in evidence." He settled onto the same rock he'd used as a chair last night and drew out his rations. "I will look again before we leave in the morning."

He debated whether to simply tell his men about Tamar and instruct them to stay quiet about it and help protect her, but his lips wouldn't form the words. They were good men, yes. But mostly they were good Romans. While they wouldn't mind pulling one over on the temple guards, he was sure, they wouldn't understand why they should protect a strange Jewish woman.

For that matter, Caeso had a bit of a reputation when it came to women, and while Valerius doubted he would do anything questionable, he would quite likely crack a few off-color jokes or look at Tamar in a way that would send her running toward Jerusalem, risks be hanged.

No, he would trust that the Lord had led his family instead of his men to her for a purpose, and he would respect that. Honor it. Trust it.

Much like last night, as soon as they were all done eating, they fell into their positions with comfortable silence, senses on alert and yet relaxed. Tonight, Valerius found his thoughts pounding against the stone at his back.

Jesus was in there.

He hadn't let himself think about it too much last night, but tonight the thoughts wouldn't leave him. Just a few feet away, separated by a thick stone slab and the immeasurable chasm between life and death, lay his Master.

In the morning, he knew, women would come to anoint the body properly. He and his men would have to roll away the stone, after officially recording that the seal had been unbroken, that no one had entered the tomb. He'd dismiss his men from this assignment, and they'd likely never set foot in this garden again.

He would have no cause to, either. Maybe that was why his feet felt rooted to the rocky ground beneath him now.

Jesus was here. The man he'd been too ashamed to bring under his roof before, even though Jesus did what no other rabbi ever would—He dined with sinners, with Gentiles, with outcasts. He healed not only the children of Israel but anyone with faith enough to ask.

This was the closest Valerius had ever been to Him, other than when He'd hung on the cross, and that pierced him as surely as Longinus's spear had pierced the Master's side at Golgotha. *I missed my chance.* He could have pushed closer in a crowd. He could have gone to beg the Lord for Gaius's life himself instead of sending his Jewish friends from Capernaum.

When he looked out into the night, he saw again the unnatural darkness that had gathered the moment they pierced Jesus's wrists and feet and hoisted the cross into its hole. When he blinked, he saw his Lord's chest heaving, struggling to draw air into His lungs.

He saw Gaius's chest, struggling in the same way, yet without a cross to blame it on. He saw the sweat on his beloved servant's brows, the hollows under his eyes, the way each bone had protruded after two weeks of growing weaker and weaker.

The wind whipped through the garden, and in it he heard the rumbling of the earth as Jesus cried out to His Father. His feet remembered the feeling.

He recalled the way he'd shaken every bit as much, with gratitude instead of fear, when Gaius suddenly opened his eyes and sat up. Light in his eyes. Health flushing his cheeks. Hollows gone, flesh plump with a youth he hadn't had in decades.

Yet the tomb behind him was cold and dark and silent. The earth that had ripped itself apart at this man's death now rested just as His body did, silent and still.

Albus shifted, and Valerius remembered the sneer on the face of one of the criminals crucified with him. The taunt that the man had found it necessary to make, even though doing so would have been agony. What had made that man want so much to torment Him that he had put weight on his staked feet and hoisted himself up so he could fill his lungs with air? All that, only to challenge Jesus to call down the angels and save them, if He was truly the Son of God.

When this was over, he would report to Pilate. With a bit of luck, he'd catch his old friend in a lull and be able to have more of a conversation than a simple report demanded. He would ask Pilate what he'd seen in Him, that he'd put that sign above the cross. He'd ask him—and for that matter, Mariana—what Claudia had dreamed about Him. He'd sit down with Longinus and ask what had changed his mind about Him as he watched Him die.

He craved the stories, the accounts. He needed them like he needed his next breath, his next meal. The man he'd followed was now just a lifeless body sealed behind a rock behind him…but his wife was right.

Dying hadn't made Moses or Elijah, Elisha or Ezekiel, Daniel or Isaiah any less a chosen instrument of God.

Jesus had been something none of those prophets had been.

Valerius repositioned his spear, looked out into the full darkness that had fallen, and remembered the story he'd heard about Jesus striding across the Sea of Galilee to meet His disciples' boat. When he'd first heard the story, the soldiers he'd been with had laughed, scoffed—Longinus among them. A ridiculous tale, they'd said. Even Aeneas and Achilles and Heracles of old hadn't been able to master nature.

But Valerius's heart had pounded, faith unfurling. Because if someone was only making up the story, they would have left it at that. They wouldn't have added the part about Peter challenging Him. "Lord, if it is You, command me to come to You."

Plenty of prophets had done the impossible—but none had been able to give that same power to others, not that he'd read.

Shifting slowly, he pressed his hand against the cool stone separating him from Jesus. The Lord he followed hadn't merely given sight to the blind and healed the sick—He'd empowered His disciples to do the same. He'd sent them out ahead of Him to do the same work. He'd promised they would do greater works than what they'd seen Him do.

Was that promise void now, just because He lay in this tomb? *No.* It couldn't be. Moses's word, the Law of God, was no less potent because Moses died. Elisha's bones had still contained such power that a corpse lowered onto them sprang back to life. Isaiah's prophecies still guided a nation, and Daniel was remembered the world over as being one of the wisest men ever to live, centuries after his body came to rest in Babylon.

Death was far from the end for a true man of God. Or even of a true man of knowledge, of philosophy, of political influence. Often, death was the purifying furnace of the ideas those leaders had proposed. If they stood the test, if they could stand when the Teacher was gone, then they went on to shape cities, nations, the world.

If not, if they withered away without the charisma of the leader shouting them out, then you would realize it had never been the ideas at all. It had just been charm, blinding and deceptive.

The cold seeped into his palm, and the world seemed to hold its breath. There were still no animals scurrying about, no birds singing their mournful night songs. The only creatures who continued to move as if nothing had changed were people.

But he knew something had changed. Creation had been robbed of a key part of itself. He didn't understand how it all worked, but he remembered frowning over the very first words of Scripture, asking the rabbi why God said, "Let *us* make..." Who, he had asked, was this plural, if God was One?

God and His Spirit, the rabbi had said. *The same Spirit that descended upon the prophets.* Jesus had spoken of the Spirit too. He had called it *His* Spirit and promised to send Him to dwell with His followers. Not to move now and then, to descend and later depart. To dwell.

The same Spirit, Valerius was sure. God's...Jesus's. Which meant that Jesus was one with God, just as He'd claimed. '*I and the Father are one.*' He, then, was part of that "us" in Creation.

Creation knew it now. It knew that something had shifted.

Valerius shuddered as the chill from the rock worked its way up his arm, into his core. The first time creation had shifted was when Adam sinned, when a curse fell on the whole world. When roses grew thorns and wheat fields grew weeds and animals began to kill and to die. When pain entered the world and had never again let it go.

That had just been when the first man disobeyed a command and ate the forbidden fruit. What would happen now, when men had crucified the very Son of God? What curse would the Father pour out on them?

His gaze shifted toward the neighboring tomb and the woman hidden within it. The veil had torn. The presence of God, protected behind it, had surely departed.

The world would see, through the test of Jesus's death, that He had been all He said.

Valerius feared they would see it through a curse like none other. The end of days had surely begun. God had left them, just as He had left the garden where He'd once walked with Adam and Eve.

The wind curled around him, a cold finger that drew itself over his neck, up his cheek. Jesus had promised they would continue to do His work.

But what would that look like in a dying world?

CHAPTER THIRTEEN

Anger chased Tamar into her sleep, tinting her dreams with red edges. She kept startling awake, the images of her sleeping mind taunting her. Davorah, again and again. Some were memories of their years working beside each other. Others could have been, or just as easily could have been imagination, as normal as they were.

Davorah's quiet face. Her hands, always busy. The dim, subdued smiles they'd exchanged.

Then suddenly they would shift, and Davorah would be sneering, snarling, turning her back to work on something Tamar could never see no matter how desperately she tried to shift. Was it the veil she was working on? Which one?

The one that had torn? Had Davorah somehow sabotaged the work, so that Tamar would be blamed when it failed under its own weight?

Even her dream-mind knew that was ridiculous. There could be no such duplicity, no such deception. The very nature of the work forbade it.

So the dream shifted, and it was her own fingers at the loom. More often than not these days, she wasn't one of the weavers in the workshop, not unless someone was sick and unable to join them— which, granted, happened regularly. But she had no particular seat, no position that was hers alone, no rod, no shuttle she alone used.

Yet now she did. She sat on a stool that her dream self knew was hers, and she had been working so long at it already that she knew her neck and back screamed in pain. But pausing, stretching wasn't an option. With an urgency pressing ever harder upon her, she worked faster, fingers flying.

But instead of growing, the cloth seemed to shrink under her fingers. Her throat wanted to protest, but no sound came out, and she turned to shoot an accusing gaze at the women to her right, to her left.

No one was there.

Where were they? Where were Bithnia, Illana, Hinda, Sarah? Where was Davorah?

She'd lured them away. Tamar felt the certainty in her stomach, and black hatred surged up like tar, like pitch, bubbling up from the ground beneath her and climbing up her legs, staining every inch of the silk she wore until she knew it was ruined.

Faster, she must weave faster. Her hands ached, pulsed with the effort, but the more quickly she wove, the more the cloth unraveled.

Her hands shook with pain, and she stumbled back, suddenly viewing the veil as she knew she never had. It was complete, hanging in its place. Surrounding and protecting the Holy of Holies, where her feet were never permitted to tread. She shouldn't even be here in this court, but the ground didn't open up to consume her, lightning didn't fork down to strike her dead. She just stood on the cold stone floor, no one else nearby, and admired the work of her hands.

Such an intricate tapestry, worthy of hanging before the presence of God. Perfection in every thread. She let her gaze caress each bold color—scarlet, purple, blue, and gold. She traced them as they drew the images meant to remind the priests of the God they served. The God who had created the garden, who had put man in it. The God who had punished man by exiling him into a fallen world, who had placed guardians at the gates of Eden to keep him from returning, to keep him from tasting of the Tree of Life now that he had stained himself with sin.

It is a mercy to die, some unfamiliar voice said, slick and oily and dark in her ear. *Would you not rather die and escape the torment of a world without God than live, knowing He is not here?*

But He was. He was there in that Most Holy Place. Just behind the veil. A presence so pure, so precious, that man's sin must never draw near. That was why she labored day in and day out. That was why they created veil after masterful veil. God must be guarded. God must be protected.

Yet even as she found her favorite cherubim in the tapestry, she watched the threads fray. "No!" The word fell silently from paralyzed lips, making the threads unravel all the faster. The cherubim vanished in snapped threads, and then the sword it held in front of the gate, the trees behind it, the blue of the sky.

Everything she looked at, every representation of creation, vanished. Dissolved. The curtain was falling, and no matter how she stretched, she couldn't reach it. When she finally did, she couldn't lift it. Couldn't put it back on its rods. Couldn't hold up its impossible weight.

But she had to. She *had* to! She couldn't let the veil fail again, couldn't let God be exposed to the sins of man.

The earth shook, shooting pain into her palms as she tried to hold everything in place, where it should be.

It crashed down around her, crushing her, and she squeezed her eyes shut and let it bury her. Yes, it was a tomb, but that was safe. Death was an escape from the panic. Only, it kept gnawing at her. Ripping at her flesh. Slicing through her soul as it had done to the veil.

Everything was a ruin. They had failed God completely. All their hard work, the centuries of studying Scripture and finding new ways to enforce it, to make certain that every child of Abraham had the Law written on their heads and their hearts, as He had commanded them—gone. A puff of smoke. Filthy rags.

Filthy, filthy rags. The tar-blackened silk clung to her legs, sin that ate at the flesh beneath. She could feel it rotting her from the inside out. Sin. Hatred. Bitterness.

Davorah. This is Davorah's fault.

Thinking it made the stain creep higher, higher, higher. Her breath came in gasps, quicker with every inch the stain rose. It was going to consume her. Despite all her care, all her attention to the Law, all the work she'd done for God, sin was overwhelming her.

Did you think you were worthy of protecting Him? Did you think you were pure enough to touch something that would be so near to His presence? You are a sinner! Filthy. Unworthy.

She tried to swipe away the grime, but that only spread the growing black to her bleeding palms. She tried to pull the ruined silk away, but it only sank deeper into her skin. Everything she tried only made it worse. The sin increased, stained her darker, and the weight of the tomb, the shattered veil, pressed down upon her.

Death is what you deserve. Death is the wage of your sin.

She whimpered, forcing syllables out in a breath between her teeth. "Lord, have mercy."

The weight pressed harder, crushing her. Then a different voice whispered in her ear. *You must let go of it, Daughter.*

Confusion swirled in the darkness, the words making no sense. She tried to push her way, swim her way, out of the suffocating veil... then realized that she wasn't really pushing it. She had her fingers knotted in it. Every shove moved only *her*, not the cloth.

You are not strong enough to bear that weight. You must let go. You must let Me shoulder it.

Her fingers curled tighter, more deliberately. This was her work. This was her creation. This was what she had spent her life doing, working for God. This was her offering, her sacrifice!

I do not desire sacrifice; a burnt offering I would refuse. The sacrifice I desire is a contrite heart. A broken, contrite spirit I will not spurn.

The more tightly she clung to that frayed, ruined, collapsed fabric, the more her palms burned. The more she tried to run from that ever-growing stain, the faster it crept up her legs, over her hips, toward her heart.

The voice was right. She wasn't strong enough. All her work, a lifetime of effort, hadn't meant a thing. One thing went wrong, one betrayal pierced her, and hatred and bitterness had filled her heart. What, then, did that say about the nature of that heart? What did it say, that she refused help when it was offered, even though she knew she couldn't do it, do anything, on her own?

She looked around again for her weavers, but if they were there, the darkness concealed them. If they were there, they could offer no assistance. Her only help lay with God.

I will take it. I will rescue you. You have only to let go, Daughter. Let go of the sin. Let go of the burden. Cling to Me instead.

Tears blurred the darkness, shuddered through her. She'd wanted to do it herself. She'd wanted to prove she was worthy. She'd wanted to know that her work had helped God.

Did I need your help when I laid the foundations of the earth? You count the threads of the veil as if all of creation will crumble if you do not, but do you know the measure of My creation? Have you stretched the measuring line across it?

She uncurled her forefinger from its hold. "I have not, Lord," she breathed. She could measure only the threads of a tapestry. Create only a flat, lifeless version of what God had made. She could not breathe into it and make it move, make it feel, make it think and love and multiply.

You lead your charges in a hymn each morning, but did you make the stars to sing in the heavens? Do you make mankind shout for joy?

"No, Lord." She uncurled another finger, felt the weight of the veil slip away a little more. She always took such care to choose a hymn, a psalm to start their day. But they were only echoes of something far greater. Shadows of the song the Lord wrote in their hearts.

You decide when to drink, but do you shut up the seas behind their doors? Do you make the clouds spread out like a garment upon the shoulders of the world?

"Only You can do that, Lord." She drew in a long breath. Straightened another finger.

You think you know when morning will come, when evening will come. You command your weavers when to arrive and when to depart. But who can cast night over noonday?

"You, Lord."

Who can shake the wicked from the earth like dust from a cloth?

"You, Lord."

Who protects whom?

She stared at her hand in the darkness, still clutching the cloth, though her left had let it go. Her life's work. Her worthiness. Her offering to God—to protect His purity, to...

Light seared her eyes, pain and joy all at once, and she understood. The veil had never been meant to protect God from man.

The veil was to protect man from God. From His terrible, beautiful light. It had never been about the work of their hands—it had been about the work of His.

There is a time to laugh, but there is also a time to weep. There is a time to weave, but also a time to rend. A time to build walls...a time to tear them down.

She was a sinful creature, quick to judge, quick to sink into bitterness, quick to cling to her pride...but all of her sin, all of humanity's sin, wasn't enough to break down the wall between man and God—the very thing the veil had been.

How foolish Caiaphas had been, that *she* had been, to ever think they could. Sin could never tear down that wall. Sin couldn't bridge the distance. Sin couldn't stain God. The intensity of His light would scour it white as snow again.

Only God could tear down the wall. Only God could remove the divide. Only God could decide that He would walk among man again. The more they tried to accomplish it on their own, with their added rituals, their added rules, their added righteousness, the heavier they made the burden.

It was a burden mankind had never been intended to carry. A stain they could never scrub out. Only the purifying fire of the Lord could make them clean again. Only His hands could draw them closer to heaven, out from under the horrible burden they'd created for themselves.

"Forgive me, Lord." Her lips formed the words as she levered her eyes open, expecting darkness but seeing instead a strange, faint gray that she couldn't place. "Save me. Restore me."

Come to Me. Words she'd heard before, in a voice that sounded so very like the one that had been adapting Job and Ecclesiastes for her as she slept. *Come to Me, you who are weary and burdened. I will give you rest.*

Though it was her heart that heard the words and not her ears, still it sounded as though the voice came from wherever that strange light was coming from. She sat up, panicking briefly as the veil seemed to wrap itself around her again, to tangle once more in her fingers.

But no. Only a blanket. Only bandages on her hands.

She reached out for the wall, expecting the smooth, even ones of her home and finding damp, cool stone instead. She stood, toes reaching out for the edge of the carpet she and her brothers' wives had woven, but the same stone met her there too.

The light brightened. Not gray now. Golden. White. The sunrise? Her body tried to tell her that it wasn't quite dawn, no matter what her eyes said, but her body was no doubt confused by the restless— yet so very restful—night.

Ears straining for the next notes of comfort, she stepped out of the cave, wincing at the onslaught of light.

CHAPTER FOURTEEN

His muscles were stiff from standing so long in one place, but Valerius wasn't about to declare he'd take another round of scouting the garden. Night had given way to the first soft gray of pre-dawn, and soon enough they'd be released from their duties altogether.

The women who followed Jesus would arrive with their jars of ointments and oils. Valerius and his men would open the tomb. They'd go and make their report.

He repeated the litany as he'd been doing all night—a silent reminder that the night would end, heavy and strange as it had felt. The world's silence would surely break. Even if it broke in the raining down of fire and brimstone, the stillness that had his every nerve on edge would be over.

Albus and Caeso felt the strangeness too, he could tell. The calm attention they'd had at the beginning of the night, the one they always had, had given way to hunched shoulders and jerking motions as they sought out sounds that simply weren't there but should have been. He knew they would be eager to be done with this assignment.

He wasn't sure he'd ever be done with it though. Something about standing here, outside his master's tomb, made him think that the heavy sorrow had sunk into his very bones. He'd carry it around with him forever, missing the face he'd only ever seen at a great distance or twisted in agony. He would always strain for the words that had resonated so deeply in his heart. He would walk through this life wondering how to cling to the light that had been stolen from it.

Then real sound met his ears—a shuffling of feet, sandals on stone. He turned his head to the right just as Albus and Caeso did, sucking in a breath of alarm when he saw the figure stumble from the tomb's opening.

"Halt!" Albus shouted, his spear at the ready.

Tamar froze.

Uncountable thoughts skipped through Valerius's mind. He would tell Albus to stand down. He would say she had every right to be in that cave, however odd it might seem. If only she'd still been in the Roman clothes! But that would have looked even stranger. Yet now, dressed in the garments the temple guard had described to them, more or less, his men would know exactly who she was. Would they care? Would they disobey him? Would his authority crumble because of this stranger his family had decided to befriend?

Before any of those thoughts could turn into words, before Tamar could do more than turn her head their way, before Albus could move, light flashed around them. Settled.

It wasn't the sun—the sun hadn't quite crested the horizon. Besides, this light was brighter than the sun. Closer. More focused. It came from behind him, or perhaps above him, from all around him.

It felt like fire, not on his skin but in his soul.

He tried to move, to shout, to spin around when the earth seemed to heave under him, but he couldn't. Every limb had locked into place, and he couldn't decide if he felt too heavy or too light—disconnected from his body or too mired in it. His eyes could still see though. His ears could still hear.

The fire didn't consume him. Didn't burn him up. It…lit him. Restored him, parts of him he hadn't known were withered. He felt it at work in every bone, every sinew, every thought.

Ancient hurts, grudges against his siblings, spats with his childhood friends—gone. Regrets over things done or not done—gone. Fears that he'd fail as a father, as a husband—gone. Memories of words he shouldn't have spoken, hurts he gave to others—gone. None could withstand the light of the fire, not while it blazed over him and in him and through him.

Gradually, either his eyes adjusted to the light or it faded enough to let him see through it. He saw Tamar, locked into place like a statue, just as he was. He saw Albus, at the edge of his vision, every inch as still. Caeso must be too. He could have sworn he sensed his men's thoughts—or perhaps his own echoed too loudly in his mind. *What is this?*

He knew. It was the Lord. What he didn't know was whether this was the end of the world or something else. Would this flash travel over the whole earth? Would it consume Mariana, Livia, Felix, Gaius? Would it shoot across the Mediterranean and find his siblings, his parents, in Rome?

Would it merely cleanse them all, or would it consume them?

The light focused, solidified, dimmed, and he realized he was looking not at a column of fire or brilliance, but at a man. He stood in a white garment, still radiating light, walking past Valerius and between Albus and Caeso, as if he'd come from the tomb.

Another moment, and he could see the man's profile as he turned onto the garden path. It was familiar...yet not. No human face had ever radiated like that. But when the man smiled into the early morning, Valerius knew Him.

Jesus.

He would have shouted it, but his throat was still paralyzed. He would have wept, but his eyes couldn't form tears.

Cool air blew against his neck as the rumbling increased. The shaking beneath his feet intensified, and he couldn't brace against it. He watched as Albus and Caeso tumbled like statues in an earthquake, watched it from the strange perspective of falling with them—they remained always upright in his view, but the earth went sideways. He felt no pain as he struck the ground. Instead, it seemed to welcome him, cradle him.

The thudding of his heart told him that it was the stone that had moved, that had shaken them down—the stone that had sealed the tomb. It was rolling, even though the only three men who had been here and capable of moving it were all turned to rock themselves. He heard a soft *whoosh*, caught another glimmer of light in his periphery, and could have sworn this new light had wings.

An angel? He'd heard the stories of them, of course, and read the description of the ones carved into the ark, with their wings arched over the mercy seat. But just as many stories in Scripture described them as men, awesome but still sometimes mistaken as human.

Was he seeing one now, with his own eyes? Was that arm, lit from within, the arm of one of God's own messengers?

The tomb's stone creaked to a halt, and Jesus paused on the path, turning His head as if listening.

Had he been capable of it, Valerius would have frowned. Jesus had somehow gotten out of the tomb while the stone was still in place. Why, then, had the angel moved the stone afterward?

Even as he thought about the question, Jesus vanished from view. Valerius sensed the angel moving but couldn't tell where he went. He waited, expecting the paralysis to release him, expecting control over his muscles to return.

It didn't.

Panic tried to chase away the peace, but it was like raindrops battering a stone wall. Nothing could penetrate the wall of light that had encased him, it seemed. He waited, his ears picking up new sounds from the path.

Footsteps. Several sets of them, the light sound signaling women as clearly as the quiet voices did. He couldn't make out the words yet, but he could tell that tears clogged the throat of at least one speaker, and more quiet weeping underscored the voices. At least three women, then. He had a feeling they would be some of those who had gathered beneath the cross on Friday, the women who hadn't abandoned their Lord even when His disciples scattered.

Valerius strained against the light. He couldn't see it anymore, but still he *felt* it, felt it cradling him, holding him like a swaddling blanket. He wanted to move though, to greet the women, to shout that Jesus wasn't there.

He could only hold his place, still as a statue. From his sideways vantage point, he could see one set of feet break away from the others and run toward the tomb. If he strained his eyes, he could make out a feminine garment, coming into better focus as she skidded into view, stopping there before the open tomb.

The first rays of the sun finally shot over the landscape, and it must have pierced her. She gasped, desperation saturating the sound, and then she spun around. "He is gone! Someone has—someone has stolen Him away!"

Something crashed to the ground, and the scent of oil wafted to his nose—a lamp. These women would have set out well before daylight to be arriving here now, and they'd have needed a lamp to guide their way.

Another female voice, sounding older than the first, said, "Quick, Magdalene. You run to Jerusalem to tell Peter and John. We will tell the others at your family's home. Someone will know what to do." Urgency laced her words.

"Yes. Yes, I...I will." He heard her footsteps, far faster than before, running back down the path.

The other steps didn't retreat again though. He watched as several pairs of feet moved toward him, past him, clearly skirting him in confusion. They passed into the cave and came to a halt. He could imagine them looking around, searching for some explanation. What did they see? Was the angel still there? Visible?

A moment later, he had his answer. A voice rang out, deep but clear as a bell, and it could belong to no one but the one whose shining arm he'd seen before. "Do not be afraid," he said, and the greeting settled like a comforting touch on Valerius's heart. The women must have been frightened—how could they not be? The stone was rolled away, the tomb empty, their Lord gone, and then a brilliant figure greeted them.

"I know that you are seeking Jesus, who was crucified," the voice continued. "But why would you seek the living among the dead? He is not here. He is risen."

Gasps echoed out of the tomb. Valerius would have smiled had he been able.

"Look, here is the place where He was laid. There are His burial clothes. Do you not remember what He said to you while He was still in Galilee, that the Son of Man must be delivered into the hands of sinful men to be crucified? Do you not remember that He promised He would rise again on the third day?"

Valerius couldn't close his eyes, but he wanted to, to savor the words. He hadn't heard that promise. He hadn't known his Lord had said death wouldn't defeat Him.

If he had, would he have understood as he stood beneath the cross? As he felt the whole world buck and weep and rebel at His passing?

Even as he wanted to think so, he knew better. If these women, if His own disciples, forgot that, if they gave up all hope and thought Him truly dead and gone, then how would he have done any differently?

Even faith, even knowledge, withered in the face of the cruelties of life. Even when one had already witnessed a miracle, one couldn't always cling to the hope of another when one was parched in the desert, one's children dying. He'd learned that from the Scriptures well before these last few days of despair.

But Jesus had triumphed over despair. He had triumphed over the tomb. He had triumphed over the sin He'd known would be fatal.

Fatal, but fleeting. How strange and beautiful that was. How strange to think that a God who was Spirit had taken on flesh, and valued that flesh enough to take it up again even after relinquishing it to death.

Something he would have to ponder later, when those women's feet weren't rushing by him again.

Time meant nothing as he lay there in that peaceful stillness, staring up at clouds that skidded across the sky, changing from pink to gold to white. Apart from his open eyes, it felt like the most restful sleep. Every muscle at ease. No discomfort at all, despite the rocks and uneven ground he knew were beneath him.

He knew it the moment the paralysis released him. He felt it in the return of the need to blink, the way his muscles suddenly felt the ground beneath him. He leaped to his feet as Albus and Caeso did the same, their eyes both grazing him for a shocked split second before moving to the tomb.

Valerius didn't turn around to see it, not yet. He turned instead toward Tamar as his men entered the empty cave.

She too had fallen. She wouldn't even have been visible when the women came upon them. Had she heard the angel's words?

He couldn't tell, to look at her bemused face. He didn't know her well enough to read what that set of her mouth meant, or that quirk of her brow. But he knew she understood him when he nodded toward the path away from this tomb, his command unspoken but clear. She ought to leave. Now, before his men came back out.

She obeyed, darting into the tomb but emerging again a scant moment later, yesterday's silk in her arms. She disappeared from sight a second before Albus and Caeso stepped out.

"I do not understand it." Caeso stopped beside Valerius but kept his face turned toward the tomb. "We saw the body in there. We rolled the stone into place ourselves. We checked the seal when we arrived last night, and it had not been disturbed."

"How did the stone move?" Albus settled his gaze on Valerius. "You were the nearest, my lord. Did you see? I could hear it rolling, but I could see nothing but the sky."

Valerius shifted his gaze from Albus to Caeso. "Did neither of you see anything at all?"

They both shook their heads, brows drawing into different versions of the same frown. "Not until the women ran up," Caeso said. "I could see them when they drew near and passed between us."

"But you did not see Jesus walking out of the tomb?"

They stared at him, dumbfounded.

He didn't know whether to smile or sigh. "Light? Did you see a bright light?"

They hesitated, looked at each other, and then each gave a slow, hesitant nod.

That was something at least. "First I found the light blinding, but then it focused. Into the form of a man. It was Jesus. I recognized Him from the cross. As He was walking away, I felt the stone begin to roll. I could just make out an arm and a...wing, it looked like." At their frowns, he drew in a breath. "It matches the Hebrew descriptions of angels. Some of them, anyway. God's messengers."

Their frowns didn't lessen. "If the dead man had already risen and was walking away," Albus said, "why did the angel roll away the stone?"

He had wondered the same thing, of course. But now he felt certain he had the answer. "So they could see—the women. So they could see at a glance that the tomb was empty. He rolled it away not to let the Lord out, but to let us in."

Caeso rubbed a hand over his face and then let it fall. It didn't make it far though. Just to his chest, where it splayed over his heart.

"The governor will never believe us. We will be killed for this. And yet, if I am going to die, I am glad I felt this first. I am glad I..." He trailed off, his eyes shifting to the empty tomb again. "I do not even know what all those things you have explained mean. Who this God is, who His Son is. But I know I saw a corpse in that tomb, and now it is empty. I saw a light that made me aware of every wrong thing I have ever done, a light that burned it all away."

"I thought it was just me." Albus rubbed at his chest too. "I do not even want to do those things anymore. I do not want that life." He looked to Valerius. "What life does that leave us? We know nothing of the ways of the Jews."

Valerius clapped a hand on each man's shoulder. "I will share all I have learned with you, most gladly. But first things first, my friends. We need to go make our report to Pilate."

Albus's face darkened. "Right. The question of what life to live will be irrelevant."

He squeezed each man's shoulder. "I do not believe we were struck but left alive, only to be killed for what we witnessed. But if so, then I will go to the grave bearing that witness anyway. Though He was dead, He lives again. Jesus is the Son of God."

Pivoting on his heel, he led his men away.

CHAPTER FIFTEEN

The world outside the tomb made no sense. Tamar raced down the garden path and then toward the city, but she couldn't have described what she saw or felt or smelled. Her senses were still consumed by what had just happened.

First the dream, with its startling clarity, with the voices vying for a place in her head and in her heart. That first one, all sticky darkness and despair. Then the second. The one that had reminded her of who God really is. The one that had beckoned her out of the darkness and into the light.

She'd expected dawn, grays and purples, the soft light of early morning. But that flash had been so brilliant, it rendered her useless.

But she'd known it. She'd known it as somehow the same as that second voice, just seen with her eyes instead of heard with her ears. She'd known it as the voice that spoke through the Scriptures. She'd known it as the One who made all and held all in His hands.

God had stepped down into the garden that morning—a garden of tombs instead of the Eden lost to mankind. He'd stepped down, and He'd walked out of that tomb. She hadn't seen Him, exactly—who could look on the face of God in all His glory and live?—but she'd seen parts of Him. She recognized Him.

But not just God, the unknowable, unfathomable Creator. God had been *man*. It was a man who'd been sealed in that tomb.

It was a man who'd walked out of it.

"Jesus." She whispered the name as she flew toward the opening gates, a name that suddenly tasted like honey on her lips.

A heretic, she'd thought, because He'd made Himself equal to God. But she saw now. She understood. It wasn't heresy if it was *true*. If it was true, then denying it was the heresy. If it was true, He'd be a madman to deny it, not to admit it.

Of its truth she had no doubt, not now. Mere mortals didn't walk out of sealed tombs days after they'd been killed. The light of their glory didn't so stupefy everyone around that they fell to the ground like corpses themselves.

But she wasn't dead. She was more alive than she'd ever felt before. She felt like the bush at Moses's bare feet, burned but not consumed. Purified. Vibrant. Too alive now to ever die.

As she gained the city gate and sped through it, she gave only the most fleeting of thoughts to whether the temple guards would be there, looking for her. She gave no thought to anything other than finding her family and telling them what she'd witnessed. To finding Bithnia and sharing the same good news.

She didn't even have the words for it—and did she deserve to do the telling? She was no dedicated disciple. She hadn't been, anyway. This wasn't a gift she deserved to share. Yet her chest was bursting with it. How could she see such a thing as a resurrected man and not proclaim it?

A warning slithered up her spine as she turned a corner she'd walked yesterday beside Mariana. What was it the Roman woman had pointed out?

That Lazarus too had been resurrected. Those who couldn't deny it, as they wanted to do, had sought to silence him for it instead.

Those people would simply ignore her. Wouldn't they?

No. Perhaps, had she been anyone else. But Caiaphas, high priest and member of the sect of the Sadducees, wouldn't let her get away with spreading such a tale when he already sought to strip her of all she'd worked for.

Her steps slowed. By rights, the warning ought to dim the light inside her. It ought to bring fear and panic and resentment back to her spirit.

None of it came. Instead, caution felt like a hand on her shoulder, gentle and sure. It sounded like a whisper in her ear, the same volume as the voice in the Lord's tomb that she'd just been able to make out. *Do not be afraid.*

The God who tore the veil in two, the God who raised Jesus from the dead, would not be silenced by Caiaphas. Even if she, Tamar, was, what did it matter? The truth would still be known. That was the most important thing. With or without her words, the truth would be made known.

She took another turn, down a street she rarely traveled, simply because she felt that light, beckoning pressure on her back, the same one that had propelled her out of the cave that morning. What would have happened had she not obeyed it then? True, the Roman guards wouldn't have spotted her—but then she wouldn't have seen the light. She wouldn't have just caught the voice of the angel. She wouldn't know this thing that she could now claim from the depth of her being.

At the next corner, she turned again, walked a ways, made another turn. Not until she was staring at the back door of her cousin Levi's house did she realize that it had been her destination. Not just going, though. *Led.* She couldn't have said how or why or what exactly had been guiding her, but she lifted her hand and rapped softly on the door then slipped inside as she always did.

Levi's wife, Hannah, dropped her spoon in her pot when Tamar entered. She rushed forward with arms outstretched. "Tamar!" Even as Tamar pulled the door closed behind her and shoved her bundle of silk onto a bench, Hannah had her arms around her. "We have been so worried. Levi felt horrible for sending you out with only a few coins. He had not paused to think that there would be no rooms. He has been prowling the city every daylight hour since, searching for you."

Tamar found herself grinning, though she wouldn't have thought it possible. "Well, if he could not find me, then no wonder the guards could not either."

"Not for their lack of trying." Hannah pulled away, bracing Tamar there with her hands on her shoulders. "They have stopped by three times already. When he has not been out looking you for, Levi has been in conference with your brothers, trying to devise a defense to present to Caiaphas. They have an appointment with him tomorrow."

Tomorrow. That surely meant that, even if the guards found her, they would do nothing more than detain her until then.

Which in turn meant that there was still time to talk to her cousin, to her brothers, to her family. To tell them what she'd learned. What she'd seen. What she'd experienced. "Is he at home now?"

Hannah shook her head. "He thought perhaps you had found a family of pilgrims to camp with and was resuming his search among them."

"I am blessed to have such a cousin."

Giving her a warm smile, Hannah turned back to her cook fire. "You must be famished! Please tell me you found food somewhere."

"I have had some, yes. But I would not argue with breakfast. May I help?"

Hannah nodded toward the oven where its small flat loaves, unleavened for Pesach, were baking. "You can keep an eye on the bread and get out a few clusters of raisins for the children. And tell me where you have been."

Tamar fell into the familiar work of the kitchen, helping her cousin prepare the morning meal for her four little ones while she summarized what had passed since the Sabbath began. Hannah was as horrified as one might expect, overhearing that Bithnia had lent her a tomb, and she nearly dropped the entire pot of porridge when Tamar told her about Mariana, motioning toward the silk.

The bread was out of the oven by then, so Tamar moved to the bundle and shook it out. She could see at a glance where her knees had struck the ground—dirt and a bit of blood stained the twin spots. But there were no rips, thankfully.

Hannah slid the bowl onto another workbench and moved forward, eyes as wide as the full moon. "Silk?" She breathed the word like a prayer and reached a tentative finger out to touch it. "I have only ever seen it at the back of the best stalls. The merchants guard it like gold."

For good reason. It took so very long to travel the Silk Road, and there were so many dangers along the way. But at the moment, she wished she or one of her relatives had at least *some* experience with it. "How do I wash it, do you think? I do not want to ruin it."

Hannah only blinked at her. "I have no idea. Lye may be too harsh, I suppose. Perhaps you should return it to the Roman as it is. Her laundress will know."

As sensible as that advice was, Tamar pursed her lips rather than granting the point. She didn't want to return it dirty and stained, a visual reminder of how she'd felt last night. A small hint of that horrible part of the dream.

She brushed at the dirt, dislodging some of it with her fingers. It was simple dirt, not the black tar of her sin. It would come out. A brush, water, perhaps some sort of soap. It was fabric, not a soul.

Her eyes slid shut. She could still see the images from the dream, feel the panic as the stain climbed higher. She could recall with detail every fault she'd become aware of as she stood in the imagined temple before the place where God was said to dwell.

She'd stood there, in reality, on Friday. She'd stood before the Holy of Holies, and she'd lived. Not because God wasn't present, not because she'd been righteous. But because He was so merciful. He was so merciful that He'd torn down the divide between Himself and mankind. He'd made a way to approach Him. A way of light. A way of forgiveness. A way of love and hope. While Tamar's cousin had been slaughtering the Passover lambs for the pilgrims, as Jesus died on the cross, God had torn down the divide.

"Children! Your food is ready!"

Tamar's eyes flew open at Hannah's call, and moments later the stampede of little feet pushed more serious thoughts aside. She would tell Hannah the rest later, and Levi. She would find a way to slip unseen into her own home and tell her brothers.

But after she'd finished eating with her happy, oblivious little cousins, a new urgency settled in her chest. "Can I leave the silk with you for now? I need to check on Bithnia. She risked so much to help me."

Hannah nodded as she held out a hand to her. "You had better change your clothes first." She flashed a dimpled grin. "I do not have silk to offer you, but you can wear my pink set."

Tamar changed her clothes, brushed her hair, washed her face, and felt more awake and rejuvenated than she had any business feeling after two nights on the floor of a tomb.

Before leaving, she checked the scroll that she still had with her to be sure she remembered where Bithnia lived, and then she set out, confident in where she was going, even as questions and phrases swirled through her head.

He was dead, but now He lives.

My sins were black as pitch, so how do I now feel white as snow?

He made a way to the Father—how do I follow Him?

Jerusalem was a different city from the one she'd seen yesterday. The streets were bustling again, full of chatter and movement and life. It seemed that every street she turned down was not only filled with people, but that those people were talking about the Teacher who'd been crucified.

So many of the men talking wore dark expressions, fear and sorrow underscoring the snippets of words she caught. "If we can now be handed over to Rome and executed for disagreeing with the Sadducees on the resurrection, then I hate to see what Judea will become," one said.

A street over, another was musing, "We only made the pilgrimage this year to see the Teacher. We had hoped he would heal Abba. But we arrived not only to be gouged by the temple inspectors—which we expected—but to learn that they had turned Him over to Rome out of jealousy."

"And broke the law concerning witnesses to do it," another replied.

Tamar skirted them, at once wanting to shout what she knew and knowing she couldn't. She didn't dare. But she tucked away all she heard.

At last she arrived at the neighborhood where Bithnia lived. Here she saw no temple guards lurking, so she walked boldly to the front door and knocked on it. A woman around her age answered, her features proclaiming that she was related to Bithnia, perhaps her mother. She smiled a welcome and ushered Tamar inside before even asking who she was. The moment she said her name, the woman's eyes went wide and she reached for Tamar's hands. "I am so glad you found us! Bithnia was worried for you."

Tamar squeezed the woman's hand. "And I for her. She mentioned yesterday that she feared your family would be arrested. I saw no guards though."

The woman acknowledged both aspects with a tilt of her head. "Only I and the younger children have stayed here. Bithnia is with her brother and father and the other disciples, in the upper room of our cousin's home. You can find her there if you like. Or I can simply assure her that you are well, if you prefer."

She didn't have to ask whose disciples Bithnia was with, not now. Yesterday, the thought of joining them, the risk of being caught with them, would have made her grateful for the easy refusal Bithnia's mother had provided for her. But this morning, everything was different.

She wanted to be among these people. She wanted to observe how they prayed to God, she wanted to witness the fellowship. Did they know yet what had happened at the tomb that morning? She hoped so. She felt inadequate to carry such news.

"I will join them, if you can direct me."

"Of course."

A moment later, Tamar was on the street again, though this time her journey was short. The home in question was only a two-minute walk away, and as Bithnia's mother had promised, she knew it when she saw it. It was large, and it had an exterior staircase leading up to a rooftop that had been enclosed for gatherings.

Her heart pounded from nerves rather than exertion by the time she reached the top and knocked. Would they even let her in?

Her knock was answered quickly, though the stranger's face regarded her with suspicion, even after she murmured, "I am looking for Bithnia. Her mother sent me here."

His lips flattened. "I will send her out. Wait below."

Disappointment settled on her shoulders. She wanted to see Bithnia, yes. But only now did she realize that she'd also wanted to experience a gathering of Jesus's followers.

"Tamar?"

She jolted at the familiar voice, her eyes going wide when a far more familiar face moved into view behind the stranger's. "Levi?"

Her cousin elbowed the first man aside and opened the door wide, a joyful smile on his face. "All my searching for you, and *you* find *me*!" He gestured her inside, pulling her into a quick embrace.

She hugged him back, but she felt as though she'd been stung by a torpedo fish. Not paralyzed as she'd been that morning, but her limbs weren't responding as they should. They felt distant, as if on strings controlled by a puppeteer. "Levi, what are you doing here?"

Her cousin pulled away, somehow sheepish when he regarded her, yet anything but when he shifted his gaze toward the assembly gathered here.

She looked beyond him for the first time, her mouth falling open in shock when she saw the number of people swarming this large upper room. She'd expected the eleven primary disciples, perhaps the women who had been at the tomb that morning, their families. Twenty, perhaps as many as forty people. Bithnia had mentioned the seventy who had been sent out, among whom her brother was numbered, so perhaps even that many.

But there were well over a hundred people here, perhaps closer to two hundred. The space was big enough to welcome them all without it feeling overly crowded, but this was no gathering of strangers, surely, with each standing to himself. People stood or sat in clusters, some talking quietly, others praying. Just looking at them made her aware of the holy feel of the place, as if hope and sorrow mingled here.

She found herself searching the crowd for the women whose faces she'd never even seen, listening for their voices. Would she know them? If she told these people what she'd heard that morning, the light she'd seen, the encounter with God that she'd had in her own heart and mind last night, would they believe her or dismiss her?

"These are the followers of Jesus," she said softly, moving her eyes back to her cousin. "*You* are a follower of Jesus. Why did you never say so?"

Levi wet his lips. "Abba forbade me to speak of it with anyone in the family. Hannah knows, of course, and is always eager to hear more. And…"

She raised her brows. "And?"

"One of your brothers follows Him too."

The floor might as well have dropped out from under her. But rather than send her plummeting, it left her floating. "What? Which one?" How had he kept it a secret from the rest of the family? But then she remembered the conversation they'd had about Lazarus being raised from the dead. She remembered Moshe's disbelief, Jeremiah's dark predictions—and the way Simon had refused to say a word.

"Simon," she said even as Levi said the same.

His eyes twinkled. "You noticed?"

"I did not realize I had. But yes." She scanned the room again. "Is he here?"

Levi shook his head. "He left at first light with his friend Cleopas. I think he intends to stay a few days with him at his home in Emmaus. He will be sorry he left though. They had scarcely gone when some of the women came with the oddest story."

If her heart had sunk when she realized her brother wasn't here, it lifted again now. Those women must be the ones she'd heard at the tomb. Their odd story must be the one she'd witnessed too.

Levi offered no more explanation for it, and she could hardly blame him for that. As far as he knew, she'd never made a decision to follow Jesus. She'd heard that one sermon, yes, along with the whole family. She, along with most of them, had welcomed Him into the city a week ago. But then the bickering had begun at home, and she'd found herself taking the side of Moshe, who insisted they would pay the price if they aligned themselves with a heretic. He'd forbade any of them from having anything more to do with the Teacher, and as the head of the family, all were expected to obey.

Simon clearly hadn't. Perhaps that was why he'd left Jerusalem with Cleopas. Honestly, she'd seen little of her youngest brother in the last two years. He was the most gregarious of her brothers, so was the one who traveled through the region representing the family's wares. She wondered now what friends he had made as he traveled. How many times *he* had heard the Teacher speak. What lessons he had learned and then had kept to himself when Moshe forbade him to talk about them.

She wished he'd spoken when he was home. Even as she doubted that she'd have understood.

"Tamar?" Bithnia slipped in beside them, looking curiously between her and Levi.

Tamar smiled and motioned to him. "My cousin. It seems my brother is among the group too."

Her young friend's eyes lit. "I did not realize."

Tamar's smile grew. "Neither did I. But I am glad to learn it."

CHAPTER SIXTEEN

Valerius stood yet again in the governor's court, listening yet again to the high priest rage. This time, Valerius wasn't against the wall, observing unobserved. This time, he stood in front of his men before Pilate, posture perfect, expression stoic as stone, just as he'd been trained to do in the face of opposition.

Pilate wasn't the opposition here though. Pilate had listened to his report with interest, something akin to wonder in his eyes. Pilate wanted to believe him, Valerius realized as he spoke. He didn't know if he could believe Valerius—but he wanted to. When Pilate went home tonight, when he told Claudia what Valerius had reported, *she* would believe. She would remember the dreams that had apparently disturbed her so—he'd yet to hear the full story of them—and she would grip her husband's arm and look into his eyes. "I knew there was something special about Him," she would say. "Did I not warn you not to be guilty of that righteous man's death?"

Pilate's education had been the same as Valerius's. He had been taught to question. To doubt. To examine. To consider. He had been instructed in how to make decisions based on logic rather than emotion. How to detach himself from what he wanted so that he could determine what he ought to want.

Even so, the more Caiaphas sputtered and spewed and demanded, the more Pilate inclined away from the high priest he'd worked so well with for so many years and toward Valerius.

"They ought to be executed for such brazen and blatant neglect of their duties!"

Valerius had lost track of the man's tirade minutes ago, but he focused his attention on him again, now that he'd concluded his argument. Behind him, he heard the slightest shift. Either Albus or Caeso shifting his weight from one foot to the other.

Pontius let out a long sigh. "I have known Valerius Marius since we were children," he said, voice even. "He is as honest a man as they come. Not given to flights of fancy, and his many years of service to Rome have shown only the most exemplary of conduct. Your accusations against him and his soldiers are insulting to Caesar and his men."

Caiaphas looked as though he might spit in his rage. "His *men* let those heretics steal the body of their teacher away! Exactly the thing this guard was to prevent."

Words bubbled up, but they had no chance of making it past Valerius's lips. Not now, when he was representing his men before the governor officially.

Pilate lifted his chin. "I have heard the reports from each of these men, independently of one another. Their stories are consistent, even as each is unique. No one went into that tomb, not before the women who came to anoint the body and found it missing. The only movement was someone coming *out* of the tomb, and then the stone rolling away."

"Preposterous!" Caiaphas bellowed. But his face had gone pale under the flush of rage. It wasn't just anger fueling him. It was fear, and the hatred that sprang up so easily in the wake of it.

If Jesus rose from the dead, then Caiphas's machinations had been for nothing. If Jesus was alive, then his sect's claims about the impossibility of resurrection had been rendered moot. If Jesus was alive, then everything he believed had been proven a lie.

Valerius had been where the priest was. The tipping point, when he had to decide either to refuse to believe and cling to what he'd always known, despite all evidence to the contrary, or to abandon everything familiar, everything that had defined him, and risk it all for something new and uncertain.

He'd stood on that precipice shortly after arriving in Judea, when he first heard the words of the Baptizer calling him to repent. When he'd first heard the words "the kingdom of God is near."

He hadn't known who this God was, or what His kingdom was supposed to be. But John's warnings about a life of sin and selfishness had resonated deep in his soul. The life he'd described was the very one that Valerius had witnessed in Rome. The very one he'd been chasing because it was all he'd known to do.

He'd been raised a Stoic, taught to push his emotions aside and focus on logic. He'd been taught to identify what was in his sphere of influence and make no reach outside it, lest he open himself to frustration. He'd been taught to take pleasure when and where he could but to protect his heart from soft feelings at all cost, lest he let those feelings make *him* soft. He'd been taught, in essence, to keep himself and his concerns always at the center of his attention, to grow his authority as he could but to keep other people's concerns from swaying him.

Then came that moment on the banks of the Jordan, that call to something different. The charge to live for God first, to put his neighbors before himself, to focus on love instead of greed. That moment when he realized that his sphere of influence would never extend beyond a sliver of the world, and that a heart guarded from any feeling soon turned to stone.

He'd known that if he continued on that path, he'd end up just like his father, and his father's father. In Rome, that had seemed fine. But that was before he'd suddenly seen the cost of his choices. How many people he'd hurt. How many lives he'd been willing to ruin to pursue his own interests. How empty he felt inside.

He'd known, when he stepped in that river to be baptized, that he was stepping away from his upbringing, from his heritage, from his parents and siblings. He'd known that they would never forgive him for his choices. He'd known that he'd be happier alone with God than surrounded by people who cared only for themselves.

Well, not alone. God had ensured that by blessing him with a wife whose heart was ready to receive the Lord too. They had made those choices together, he and Mariana. Stepped into the river together. But that only meant that their choices risked fracturing two families, not just one. Hers too would be shaken and rocked by their decisions when they realized the implications. He wouldn't be surprised if they tried to insist upon a divorce when they realized where he'd led their daughter.

They had been married less than a year when they made that choice together. He hadn't been at all convinced, when he felt the stirring of the Baptist's words, that his pretty young wife would have any interest in the God of the Jews. She could have insisted then and there that he return her to her family in Rome.

Instead, she'd gazed deep into his eyes and said that if this God had earned Valerius's regard, then she would learn of Him too.

Caiaphas would be looking over that precipice now too. Seeing beyond the edge only a fall to his death, the unknown full of vicious crags and threats. Behind him, he would see the life he'd built behind him, the one founded on argument and the gathering of power, on working not only to be secure but to be *right*.

Here stood three Romans, enemies of his people, telling him he was wrong. Telling him that his worst fears were realized. Telling him that everything he'd founded his life on was a lie, proven so by the man he'd wanted so badly to execute that he twisted the Law, the very Law he'd sworn to preserve, to do so.

As Valerius watched the priest's face, he prayed that he would see the Lord's hand in it, that he would make the same decision other priests had made—the decision to embrace a hard truth instead of an easy half truth. That he would risk it all to believe.

Yet he wasn't surprised when he saw instead Caiaphas's expression close off. He watched the fear solidify into hatred once more. He saw the hatred rise and lash out, a whip ready to tear the flesh from his enemies.

Pilate leaned back in his chair, the projected air of relaxation no doubt meant to do exactly what it was doing—infuriate Caiaphas even more, by pointing out that in this court, *he* was the one in control. The one with the higher power. The one who had the right to be relaxed while others were on edge. "Preposterous things happen all the time. Is your entire religion not founded on it? Is it not preposterous for Moses to have parted the sea with an outraised arm? Preposterous that your people would eat for forty years of a strange substance sent like the dew each morning? Is it not preposterous that your prophet Elijah would hold back the rain for three years with his prayer? That Daniel would survive a den of hungry lions, or his friends a furnace made hot enough to kill the guards who delivered them to it? Is it not preposterous that Judas Maccabeus and his ragtag group of men would fight off one of the fiercest armies of the world?"

With each bit of Jewish history Pilate spouted off—most of them stories Valerius had told him about just in the last year—Caiaphas's fists clenched tighter. "You would compare this blasphemer and His scheming, body-snatching followers to our most revered prophets?"

Pilate blinked. "I am comparing nothing. I am merely reminding you that this God you claim earned His fame among the nations by making the impossible possible. Or would you disagree with that assertion? Is He in fact no more capable of raising the dead than Apollo or Jupiter?"

"He did *not* raise the dead!"

"Interesting that you would say so." Pilate craned his head and met Valerius's eyes. "Didn't you say there was a prophet of old who raised the only son of the woman who offered him housing? And I have received several reports of this Jesus doing the same in His few short years of ministry. The daughter of one of your own priests...that widow whose only son had died...and of course, Lazarus of Bethany."

"Lies."

The glance Pilate sent to Caiaphas was condescending enough to deserve the fury sparking in the priest's eyes. "So your theory about what happened this morning is...?"

Caiaphas jerked up his chin. "Your men fell asleep. The Teacher's disciples snuck in and stole away the body."

Another lazy, provocative blink from the governor. "My men fell asleep? Are you aware this is a crime punishable by death in the Roman legion, and hence a crime so rare we only have to prosecute it once every several years? Yet you claim this crime was committed by not just one of my well-trained soldiers but by all three of them. And not only did they doze off, they slept so soundly that these disciples were able to roll away that enormous stone without waking them and then to carry a body past them?"

Caiaphas's jaw ticked, he clenched his teeth so tightly. He nodded.

Pilate smirked. "That, my friend, is a far more preposterous theory than stories of angels and the dead rising. You are clearly not well acquainted with the training of a Roman legionary."

Valerius had to press his lips against a smile. Leave it to Pontius to somehow acknowledge that God could work such wonders but insist in the same breath that the miracle was less impressive than Roman military might.

Pilate waved his fingers in a dismissal that had the priest's face flushing redder still. "I cannot stop you from spreading this interpretation among your people, but I will not participate in the lie and thereby sentence three good men, three excellent soldiers, to death. I take them at their word."

Caiaphas surged forward a step. "My lord, you *must* report their crime! If you do not, then this dangerous deception will spread far and wide!"

Pontius motioned at the guards standing against the walls. "You had better get to work making your story more believable then, hadn't you? Do show yourself out, Caiaphas. Unless you would prefer an escort."

His eyes flashing between the governor and soldiers striding toward him, Caiaphas straightened his spine, nodded once in something that was certainly not acquiescence, and spun on his heel.

Only once Caiaphas had left the court did Pilate straighten again and turn to Valerius, motioning him forward. His face shifted from an expression meant to annoy the priest to one that could only be called worry.

Valerius took a knee beside the governor's chair so that his head was closer to Pilate's. "Yes, my lord?"

Pilate leaned close. "This is a dangerous tale you claim—and a dangerous counter tale Caiaphas has devised. I meant what I said, that I will not accept a report that all three of you fell asleep. But be honest with me, Valerius. How did this happen?"

Valerius met Pilate's gaze. "Exactly as I said, my lord. A strange paralysis fell upon us all that we can only attribute to the hand of God. None of us could move. We were like dead men, except that we could move our eyes and breathe."

Pilate's eyes went unfocused. "I do not understand this God of the Jews. But it seems He isn't to be trifled with. I do not want to be guilty of angering Him any more than I already have done." He dropped his voice to a whisper. "Claudia will be relieved at this report. Relieved to know that my inability to stop His death was, somehow, not irreversible."

"Mariana will be relieved as well."

His wife's name made Pilate sit upright again. "Of course. You will want to get home to her and tell her the news. Dismiss your men to their rest and find your own. I will send a message directly to your commander, alerting him to these accusations but assuring him I have examined you all and found you to be without deception or fault."

"Thank you, Governor." Valerius didn't think that his commander would doubt his word, even given how difficult a story it was to believe. Pilate wasn't wrong. It was inconceivable to think all three of them would have fallen into such a deep sleep. Such things simply didn't happen. Even so, having the governor's official backing could only help the report be accepted.

"I have known you many years, Valerius. What I said to the priest was the truth. You are a man of honesty and conviction, with nothing to gain by this story and everything to lose. But I know you to be clever too. If you were going to lie, you would have come up with a more convincing one. You would have claimed to have been overwhelmed by a larger force, you would have knocked each other over the head to fabricate evidence of it. No one in his right mind would claim such an act of God unless it was true."

At Pilate's wave of instruction, Valerius stood again. He had to wonder whether another governor would have believed him so readily. One who didn't know him so well, one whose wife hadn't become so fond of his own. But then, a God who positioned each star just so in the heavens could also position men where He wanted them.

This particular governor for this moment in Judea's history. This particular centurion to be guarding His Son's tomb. What a humbling and heady thing it was, all at once, to be a tool in the hand of the Master Creator. To be part of a story so miraculous.

They said their farewells, and a moment later he was leading his men out of the palace and saying goodbye to them at the barracks. He didn't know what story they would tell their ninety-eight comrades, or if they would say anything at all about what they witnessed that morning. But they would know that they could speak to him about it any time they needed to. They had already arranged a time in a few days when they would join his family for dinner to learn more about God and Jesus.

For his own part, he hastened home, greeting the young doorkeeper with a nod and a smile but not pausing for conversation as he usually did. Mariana ought to be waking now. The children likely had been up for an hour or more already, given their breakfast by their nurse and taken up to the roof to enjoy playing in the cool of the morning. They would make their way down once they spotted him, and he would take them in his arms with that surge of love he'd been so surprised to find he could feel, the first time he'd held Livia. But he would have a few moments alone with Mariana first, and he would relish those too.

He found her in her outer chamber, still bleary-eyed from sleep but dressed for the day, a cup of steaming chamomile tea in her hand. She rose when he entered, sliding the cup onto a table and holding out her arms.

He walked into them, closed his around her, and held her tight against his chest. Her hair smelled of flowers, and her arms felt of comfort. He buried his nose in her hair and whispered, "He lives, beloved. He lives. Even death could not defeat our Lord."

CHAPTER SEVENTEEN

Tamar sat beside Bithnia in the upper room, against the back wall. Levi had left at one point to go home and assure Hannah that he and Tamar had been reunited. When he returned, he reported that Hannah would have liked to join them here, but the children were in a boisterous mood. She'd opted instead to take them to play with Tamar's nieces and nephews at the larger family home, and there to speak with Tamar's sisters-in-law.

Tamar didn't know what either of them would say about all this. More, she didn't know what Moshe and Jeremiah would say. Simon's stance she could guess at, but he had no wife yet to take their side in the family home, and he'd apparently given no clue as to when he intended to return from Emmaus.

Soon, she hoped. Perhaps tomorrow or the next day. As much as she didn't want to leave this gathering and the way she felt here among these people, she craved her younger brother's company. She wanted to tell him that she understood now. That she believed as he did.

The word the women had brought earlier that morning hadn't been much believed by most, it seemed. Tamar suspected that it sounded too good to be true. They must have dismissed it as something they merely *wished* were true. But not long after she arrived, two of the Twelve, Peter and young John, had burst into the room, their own words bearing witness to the empty tomb. Then another woman, one of the voices she'd heard, flew inside, saying she had seen Jesus Himself. That He had called her by name, had told her to come and tell the disciples that He lived, and that He would go before them into Galilee.

All had been amazed. Well, not all. Another woman had joined them in the upper room in time to hear this testimony from the young beauty she greeted as Magdalene, and Bithnia had whispered that it was Mary, mother of the Lord. Tamar sat at the opposite end of the large chamber, but even from the distance, she had seen the peace on the woman's countenance. "My Son keeps His promises," she'd said, her voice ringing out over the assembly. She'd looked out over them all—did she know everyone? She certainly wouldn't have recognized Tamar, and yet when her gaze paused for a second on Tamar's face, she saw only welcome within it. "Come, my friends. Let us pray for strength for what comes next for us. Jesus did not defeat death so that we could huddle here in this room forever. The time will come when we will need to go forth. We must be prepared for that day."

Tamar had never prayed in the way that this Mary guided them in doing, beseeching God as Father. In her house, God had been too big, too far, too austere to be Father. To call oneself His child would be to presume too much. They dared only to be children of Abraham.

Yet this woman's familiar words matched the Lord, the One Tamar had met last night in her dreams. The One who spoke directly to her. Who revealed to her the sins that darkened her deepest heart and then promised salvation from their consequences, forgiveness for their existence. She remembered one of the stories Moshe had quoted as a reason to steer clear of Jesus—when a paralytic had been lowered through a roof to be healed, Jesus had first told him, "Your sins are forgiven." Only when Moshe and his companions questioned His authority had He said also, "Rise and walk."

The young man had walked—her brother didn't contest that. But he had balked at the audacity of a man claiming the authority to forgive sins. Only God, he claimed, could do that.

God certainly could. She had felt that forgiveness flowing through her as she wrestled with her own demons last night. But she had offered no sacrifice at the temple for forgiveness. She had followed no prescribed rules to earn it. She had made no offering.

Yet as the light enveloped her that morning, she knew without doubt she was clean. Cleansed. Made pure, made whole. Through God's power, yes—but not through a sacrifice *she* made.

He'd made the sacrifice for her. He'd let Jesus be slain. Let Him die. Knowing He would rise again.

As she sat among the believers, she listened to each whispered story in turn. Listened to them agree that this Man, among all men, had never committed a sin. She balked at first too, just as Moshe would have done. How could she not? They had all sinned.

They all could bear witness to each other's sins. Her brothers would certainly be the first to point out her imperfections. The weavers could attest to the times over the years she'd lost her temper when something went wrong, even if it was through no fault of any one individual. Friends knew she had lied. Just as she knew her parents' sins, and those of her uncles and aunts, her cousins and siblings and friends.

Yet everyone here who knew Jesus said the same thing. He rarely acted in the expected way, He frequently did things they couldn't understand...but never had He sinned. The Father, they said, was always His first priority. He was perfect. A lamb without blemish, young John had said. Worthy to be slain on their behalf. The One capable of taking away the sins of the world, of any who would look upon Him.

"Like the bronze serpent Moses was told to make in the wilderness," John said. "Any who looked upon it could be healed of the serpents' bites. But they had to *look*. They had to come. They had to have the faith to accept the salvation. It is the same for us, with our Lord Jesus."

Tamar let the words seep into her soul, closing her eyes to better absorb them. They fit so well with her realizations of the night and the morning. She hadn't just been stained with sin, bitten by its poison—she'd been clinging to it. Clinging to her determination to earn righteousness. To serve God how *she* wanted, to protect Him.

How had she ever thought that even possible? How had she ever dared to think that she, sinful human that she was, could protect God's holiness?

He in His mercy had known that. He had torn down the divide. He'd done it through this sacrifice, lifted up before His children. His own Son.

At some point, someone passed around some bread and dried fish, and she ate a few bites without really tasting it. Bithnia studied her face as she ate her own bread. "You look anxious."

Tamar drew in a long breath. "I ought to get home soon. I need to talk to my brothers and their wives."

Her young friend frowned. "What will they say?"

The very question plaguing her. If she told them what she'd experienced, would they believe her?

Did it matter?

She let that question roll around her tongue along with the bite she chewed. It did, in that it could affect her life from now on. "I do not know. If Moshe, my eldest brother, gets into one of his stubborn moods, he could tell me I am not welcome under the family roof anymore if I insist on following Jesus. He could tell Simon the same."

"Where would you go? To Levi's?"

Tamar could only shrug. She'd never had to give such a question a moment's thought. Until now, she had no real fear of angering her siblings—first because she had no argument with them, but second because she was one of the few women in the city who earned a wage sufficient to live on.

That was uncertain now too. Even thinking about it made the peace she'd felt draw a few steps away.

She grasped at it, willing it back. Pushing thoughts of her work aside. But then looking at them again, because she couldn't just ignore it. Tomorrow, her brothers would meet with Caiaphas to discuss the charges against her. Not thinking about it today would help nothing.

Bithnia leaned closer until their shoulders touched. "I am sorry. I did not mean to upset you."

Tamar drew in a long breath and turned the piece of bread in her fingers this way and that. "It is hardly your fault. I am only thinking about my position. I have worked so hard to earn it. I am not guilty of what Caiaphas is blaming me for. And yet when I think those thoughts…" She splayed her free hand over her chest. "I do not know what to do."

Bithnia nodded. "I know you have been wronged in this, and I have no specific advice. But it brings to mind one of Jesus's teachings. That we are to forgive as we want to be forgiven." She looked over, her brown eyes deep with something Tamar was only beginning to recognize as a faith more profound than any she'd known before. "He told us to pray for our enemies also."

A pang coursed through Tamar's chest. Such advice went against her every instinct. She had warred between fighting back or flying to safety—but never had she considered forgiving Caiaphas or praying for him.

"What was the Lord's instruction?" Tamar asked quietly.

Bithnia smiled. "He told one of His disciples that if someone continues to sin against us, we are to continue to forgive—even up to seventy times seven."

Tamar lowered the piece of bread to her lap.

"He told us to love our enemies. To pray for those who hurt us. Not to pray that they stop for our own sakes but to pray for *them*. For their souls. For their salvation."

Tamar closed her eyes again. "This is a hard teaching."

"It is. But Jesus did it. He let Himself be crucified, to suffer and die. At any moment, He could have chosen to stop it. But instead, He paid the ultimate penalty for sin. For *our* sin. Like the Pesach lamb."

As prayers rose around her, Tamar pondered how she could obey those lessons. Could she truly forgive Caiaphas and those who had made her life so difficult these last few days? She bowed her head as realization of her own self-centeredness washed over her.

Forgive my pride, Lord. Even as she had insisted that this impossible thing had nothing to do with her, her only focus had been on herself and her team. Never once had she thought about the high priest with anything but bitterness.

Now she did. Now she wondered what fears must haunt him, taunt him, to spur him into the actions he had taken in these last days and weeks and months. He had heard the stories of Jesus and seen not a savior, not a way to God, but a rival. Someone who challenged his beliefs and inspired people to follow Him instead of Caiaphas. Jesus had chided the religious leaders openly for seeking their own benefit above the ways of God, for adorning the Law with their own rules, for caring more about the exterior than the interior.

So many had followed Him. So many had gone out to hear His sermons. That impromptu welcome last week? That must have lit a new explosion of fear in Caiaphas.

He had been the high priest for fifteen years, longer than any other man in recent history. His political career had been one of great success. Did it seem now that everything was disintegrating? Did he see all he'd been working for unraveling like a tapestry, sliced in two like the veil?

She put the last bite of bread into her mouth and let it dissolve on her tongue. Fifteen years...the same length of time she'd been in her position. She hadn't paused to think about that before now. It hadn't mattered.

But it helped her understand him. Jesus must seem to him as threatening as Caiaphas was to her.

"When He was hanging on the cross," came a woman's voice from somewhere in the crowd, "do you know what He prayed? He asked God to forgive those who put Him there. He said, 'Forgive them, Father. They do not know what they are doing.'"

Forgive them. That "them" certainly included Caiaphas. Caiaphas, who thought he was eliminating a political opponent. Who thought he was ridding Israel of a heretic who would lead them astray. He didn't know he was killing God's anointed. If he knew, if that's how he'd thought of Him, he couldn't have done it.

Much like David, hidden in the cave when Saul came in. Had he been thinking of him as his enemy, perhaps he'd have taken the opportunity to kill him. But he'd seen Saul through different eyes. The eyes of the Spirit. He'd seen the anointing that could not be reversed even by Saul's sin.

People so rarely did what they thought was wrong. They almost always did what they believed was right. It was only that they were so very bad at differentiating, even when they had rules and laws to guide them.

Yet Jesus had forgiven those who put Him on the cross, while He was hanging there in agony. Even then, He was concerned not for Himself, but for the souls of others. Even then, He was interceding with the Father for them.

Tamar twisted her fingers in the end of the dark pink headscarf she'd woven for Hannah three years ago. The veil had torn when the earth shook...the earth had shaken when Jesus died...Jesus had died as the paschal lambs were being sacrificed for the pilgrims. What did that mean?

Father, forgive them.

In all their history, so very few had dared to approach God. Moses, of course. A few of the prophets had visions of being in His courtroom.

David had danced before the ark. But the whole point of the veil was to separate sinful man from sinless God, lest their sins convict them before His face and they die. That the veil was gone, that God had made a way to welcome them into His presence again, like in Eden…

That divide could only be bridged by atonement. And that was what Jesus had offered. His was the blood spilled to pay that sin debt. He, in the moment of His death, had provided a way back to the Father.

She remembered the voice in her dreams, the one that called her His daughter. She remembered the call of that light, to go out and bear witness to the impossible. She remembered the way she felt when she realized God loved her enough to meet her there, in the cold of a borrowed tomb.

What was she? A weaver. A woman. A sister, a friend. No one special. Even so, He loved her. He called her.

Her next breath tasted of peace again. If God loved her so, he loved Caiaphas just as much. He offered forgiveness to him too. He wanted him to embrace the way back into His presence, not refuse to look at the promise of healing.

Leaning her head against the wall, she let her eyes slide closed, and she prayed for her enemy.

She didn't know how long she'd been sitting like that before commotion rose on the stairs outside and everyone stirred, coming to alertness. Guards? No. There were only two sets of footsteps, and if they were going to be arrested, more than two would be sent to accomplish it.

The door burst open a moment later, and when Tamar spotted her brother Simon running through it, she pushed quickly to her feet.

"We saw Him!" he shouted for the whole assembly to hear. "On the road to Emmaus. He walked with us the whole way, did He not, Cleopas?"

Tamar had met Cleopas several times but didn't know him well. Even so, there was no disguising the light on his face as he nodded. "He opened the Scriptures to us, explaining how the Son of Man must suffer and die in order to fulfill the Scriptures."

"We didn't recognize Him. Not then." Simon's gaze locked on his friend's face, a bit of bemusement on his own. "I still do not know how our eyes were so blinded. But we invited Him in to eat with us, and when He broke the bread, we knew Him."

Cleopas's smile beamed over his face as he nodded. "We did. It was like the Passover meal, when He told us the bread was His body—the moment He broke the loaf, we knew."

"We *knew*. Our eyes were opened, and we saw Him truly—but then He vanished from the room!" Simon turned, no doubt looking for one of the faces he knew best from this group of disciples—this group to which she hadn't realized he belonged so fully.

His gaze snagged on hers. His eyes went wide.

Tamar could only smile. They both, today, it seemed, had encountered the risen Lord. Whatever change that brought, she wouldn't just endure it. She would embrace it.

She would walk the second mile.

CHAPTER EIGHTEEN

Never in her life had Tamar stood in the court of the high priest—never had she imagined she would. It wasn't a place where women were welcome for day-to-day business. They came only when they were bringing a case before him...or when a case was brought against them.

That, she supposed, was her current situation, but it didn't feel like it anymore. She strode into the beautiful chamber surrounded by all three of her brothers and Levi too, all of them determined to speak on her behalf.

She could appreciate their love. Their loyalty. Their willingness to stand beside her, even Moshe and Jeremiah, who had shaken their heads when she and Simon went home last night and told them about Jesus's resurrection. That, they said, was a different matter from this. This was a leader looking for someone to blame, and they weren't about to let their sister be the scapegoat.

The scapegoat was an important part of the Law, though. A symbol of how God removed the sins from His people. She wasn't one in any true sense. She couldn't take those sins and remove them from anyone...but still it seemed important to remember the purpose of the animal. Not that it was cast out—but that it was sent out for a reason.

Jesus did not defeat death so that we could huddle in this room forever, Mary had said. She was certainly right. They needed to go out. First to their families. Then to their neighbors. If those in Jerusalem wouldn't hear them, then they would go farther, then farther still. Tamar didn't know from where the strength would come to do so, but she trusted that come it would.

Because here she stood, in the court of Israel's highest official, filled with the same calm she'd known when the light of the risen Christ had washed over her. Then, her every muscle had gone still. Now, the stillness was inward instead.

The fear, still. The ambition, frozen. The yearning for justice, shifted.

Justice was, of course, what God wanted for all people. But Jesus's sacrifice had proven that God had a view of justice well beyond Tamar's limited understanding. She would trust that He would see it done, in the next life if not in this one.

Caiaphas sat in his chair, scribes at desks on either side of him. The room was large, austere, proclaiming with a single glance that the man holding court within it was important. Though there were Roman officials technically over him—the governor, Herod— Caiaphas was the highest-ranking Jew in Judea, and by all accounts, he had served their people well in his many years of service, hence why he'd held the position so long.

She'd never expected to be brought before him like this. She'd thought that living her life as best as she could, doing her job with a dedication to the Lord, would guarantee that life would go according to plan.

Praise God that she'd been wrong. Her plan never could have foreseen Jesus. Her plan never would have taken her on such an unexpected journey. But she wouldn't wish the last days undone, not for anything. So she would accept this trial as part of that journey. Unforeseen by her, but not beyond God's hand. He had led her here, and He would guide her now, and into whatever steps came next.

The case before theirs finished, and another official waved them forward. She went, two of her closest relatives on either side of her. She was keenly aware of the garment she had donned for the occasion—borrowed again, but made by her own hand with all the love she felt for her cousin's wife. It would proclaim her skill to any who knew to look, but that was beside the point. She'd already proven her skill as a weaver, years and years ago. It was how she'd gotten her first position as a woman at the seventy-two rods. It was how she'd been promoted. Perhaps that skill was what Caiaphas thought was on trial today.

She knew better. Today, she didn't stand before the high priest as the head weaver. She stood before God as a woman, a person, her hands still, her talents stripped away. This wasn't about her skills. It was about how she would react as a follower of Christ. This borrowed garment, as it moved with her, represented something different to her. It reminded her of the love of her family; of the concern of a stranger who had lent her a very different garment.

Her every pulse seemed to fill her whole chest, her whole body. She didn't know what to do now, with all of that. She didn't know how to respond. She could only trust that He would show her.

At Caiaphas's command, one of the scribes stood, a scroll unrolled in his hands. His voice, when he read, sounded nearly bored. "The woman Tamar, head weaver of the temple weaving room, is accused of creating a defective veil and sending it for use in the temple, to guard the Holy of Holies. Evidence against her is the failure of said veil during the earthquake on Friday last, at which point the entire veil was torn asunder, ripped in two from top to bottom, as was witnessed by dozens of priests who have signed their testimony accordingly. This is an affront against the holiness of Adonai, and the woman must be punished. Her fault has allowed sinful man to sully the Most Holy Place."

Moshe stepped forward, his face a mask just as hard as the priest's. "As Tamar's eldest brother and head of the household to which she belongs, I beg my lord to consider the circumstances of this truly shocking event. We do not question the event itself, but the testimony of the priests records only the ripping—no one could possibly have witnessed my sister being the agent of this destruction. She was, of course, nowhere near it at the time. So I invite my lord to consider. The veil in question was relatively new to service, we all know—it was hung only a month ago, correct?"

Caiaphas answered only with a movement of his brows.

Moshe clearly expected nothing less. "In which case, the procedure for the veil being accepted, approved, and put in place ought to be fresh on your mind and easily accessible in the court records, if necessary. I would invite my lord to recall that my sister was by no means the final voice approving this veil. She was the leader of the seventy-two women who wove it, yes, and she went over every thread—a task that took weeks, beyond the many years the weaving itself took, which was continually inspected—to ensure perfection. But she was far from the only person to do so. Is it not true that my lord sent a team of priests to inspect it just as thoroughly?"

Another twitch of Caiaphas's face—his lips, this time.

Moshe clearly took it as acknowledgment. "And did any of them report a flaw?"

Caiaphas looked to the scribe, though he knew the answer. The scribe consulted another scroll and replied, tone still bored, "They did not."

"In which case, surely my lord is not suggesting that such a flaw was then present, while the veil was yet in the weaving room? Surely my sister could not have introduced such a fault, yet your hand-chosen priests missed it?"

Caiaphas's jaw clenched.

So did Tamar's hands. Was her brother *trying* to put him on the defensive? How could that possibly help?

But Moshe paced before the priest's chair now, all confidence in his argument. "So then, the veil was perfect while it was under my sister's authority—this has been agreed upon by your own men, and then by you yourself, is this not correct? Is one of the duties of your office not to give the final approval of any veil before it is hung?"

Tamar's eyes slid shut. Casting the blame on Caiaphas surely wouldn't go well.

Moshe pushed on. "Three hundred men carried the veil to its place after it was approved for hanging. Who is to say that, if a fault was introduced, it was not by one of them? My cousin Levi was present while it was hung and gave testimony to me on the procedure, explaining how difficult it is. Who is to say the flaw was not caused by fumbling hands then?"

"You dare to accuse my priests?"

Moshe paused, and when Tamar opened her eyes again, she found him standing with his shoulders back, his chin up. "Which is more likely, my lord? That the flaw was present in the weaving room yet missed by so many trained, careful eyes—including those of my sister, who is the most revered weaver in all of Israel—or that the damage was done by untrained hands after it left the room?"

He made a broad motion with his hands. "The tear took place in an earthquake, witnessed by you and by your own priests. I posit that this is proof that it was an act of God and God alone, not one caused by any human, be it my sister or another. Therefore, no man or woman ought to be held accountable for the tragedy."

"Are you quite finished?" Caiaphas tapped his fingertips against the wide metal arm of his chair, the frustration that had flared in his eyes as her brother spoke reduced to a smolder. He looked at her not with hatred, exactly, but with a flat, dark gaze that said he didn't care what was said. His mind had been made up the moment he saw the torn veil on Friday.

Moshe sucked in a breath, let it out again. "Yes, my lord. I daresay the evidence is clear, and I trust in your just judgment." The right words—the wrong tone. They were a challenge, and she nearly winced as they rang throughout the courtroom.

Caiaphas settled his gaze on her. It should have unnerved her. Should have traced a shiver down her spine. It did neither. It only filled her with a strange compassion. As her brother's words faded to echo and then into nothingness, she felt strangely as though only she and Caiaphas were left. She saw him as she never had before.

He was so afraid. So afraid of losing it all. He couldn't see that salvation would come only when he let go of the burden suffocating him. His fingers were still digging into that ruined veil, clinging to what he knew. What he understood. What had served him well thus far in life. He held in his hands the image of the world as he perceived it, the rules he knew to obey, the power and might he had so carefully hewn for himself over decades of planning and maneuvering, politics and service.

To his mind, letting go of it—letting anyone else force it from his hands—would be the end of everything he'd worked for. It would be, in his eyes, his own destruction.

He blinked and lifted his brows. "And you, woman? What have you to say for yourself?"

She had debated all night, as she'd lain awake in the bed Levi and Hannah had given her, what she would say to that question. She had known what Moshe intended to say in her defense, more or less, but also knew that she'd be given a chance to speak. How could she respond? What would turning the other cheek or walking the second mile look like? She hadn't known last night as darkness fell. She hadn't known as she stared up at the black ceiling, seeing nothing with her physical eyes but playing out the preceding days over and over in her mind. She hadn't known as dawn turned the room pink and gold and her heart raced with a memory of yesterday's very different, more-than-physical light.

She hadn't known until right now, as she stood here. Not until this very moment.

She stepped forward, her heart light and steady and bright. She offered the high priest a small but sincere smile and bowed her head. He was striking at her skill as a weaver—she would offer him her very humanity. He was asking her to bear an unjust punishment—she would offer to bear even more. "I submit myself to your censure. And I ask that all the blame be put solely on me and that you do not extend it to the other weavers, nor to any of the priests who carried the veil or installed it."

Her brothers clamored behind her. That, she suspected, was why the high priest narrowed his eyes. "You admit your guilt?"

Sarah's words filled her mind, about bearing false witness. She couldn't lie. She knew very well that the veil had not torn through anything she had done. It had been God and God alone who took down the divide between heaven and earth. She tilted her head. "No. I do not believe it was the work or failure of any man or woman that resulted in the veil tearing. I believe only God Himself could have rent the curtain in that way. But I will accept the punishment. And I forgive you for it, my lord."

His face flushed red. "You *forgive* me?"

She met his gaze, as she never would have dared to do had she just met him in the street. But she didn't fear him. Not because there was nothing more he could do, no other blame he could cast her way that would be any worse than what he already was casting, but because she wanted him to *see*. She wanted him to experience the freedom of releasing the burden of sin, the burden of planning his own destiny, the burden of thinking *he* was responsible for God, rather than the other way around.

She wanted him to taste true freedom. "Yes. I forgive you. These last several days, people have told me what they suspect your motivations are for blaming me—me personally, no one else. Perhaps their suspicions are true...perhaps they are not. Only you know that. But I dare to stand before you now and tell you that I understand your choices. I understand why this has angered you so much. I understand the weight of that veil and all it represents, the responsibility its very existence puts on your shoulders, as perhaps no one else in Israel can. And I am praying that God gives you His comfort and endows you with strength to serve our people well. I forgive you for the pain you have caused my family. I forgive you for blaming me. I will take that blame willingly."

"No!"

Tamar spun at the unexpected voice—not one of her brothers or cousin, not one of the women she could nearly imagine charging in here to defend her—Sarah, Bithnia, even Illana. It was none of them. It was Davorah who ran forward, falling to her knees at Tamar's side.

"I bear witness in this woman's favor," she cried out, face turned up to Caiaphas. Horror etched her every feature, horror and pleading and a desperation that Tamar knew only too well.

He stood, thunder in his brows. "Davorah! What are you doing here?"

Davorah clasped her hands in front of her, the perfect image of a supplicant. "Begging you not to make such a mistake as to dismiss the best weaver in Israel from the position she deserves. She allowed no mistake in that veil, my lord. She permits no fault in the weaving room. And she leads us by the best example, inviting us to examine our hearts and dwell on the Lord as we work. She reminds us, each and every day, that our work is holy, and so we are to be holy. We need her."

Caiaphas's expression shifted to one she'd never seen on his face before. "You are just as capable of such leadership."

"I am not." Tears glimmered in Davorah's eyes, making pressure band about Tamar's chest. The woman's clasped hands trembled visibly. "Nor do I want to be a leader at all. I want only to serve at the loom, doing what I know I can."

Tamar dropped to her knees beside Davorah and slid a steady arm around her quaking shoulders. The memory of the bitterness, the hatred she had felt the other night shamed her anew.

This woman was no conniver. No betrayer. Her uncle's ambitions were not her own. How had Tamar let her own fears lead her into such thoughts? She knew Davorah. If not as well as others, only because she was quiet and kept her own counsel. But that was part of who she was. It gave Tamar no valid excuse to heap condemnation and accusation upon her unsuspecting head.

She was more than a quiet, circumspect woman though. She was a woman who would run uninvited into the high priest's court. That took courage. Never mind that he was her uncle. That would make it no less intimidating, especially given that she'd taken such care over the last decades to keep the relationship a secret, indicating a desire for humility. That would be dashed to pieces by this action too. But a woman who would defend a friend like this was a woman capable of more than she gave herself credit for.

Tamar rubbed a hand over her arm. "You are a woman of strength and conviction," she said to her friend. "You are a woman of talent and skill. You are a woman who will lead with her actions but who will speak exactly when she needs to."

"No." Tears streaming down her cheeks, Davorah leaned into Tamar's shoulder. "I cannot. I do not want to leave my seat at the loom. It is what I know, what I am good at. I do not want to leave it."

"We are all called to new things, new challenges. We never know if we can do them, but the Lord equips us." She gave Davorah a squeeze. "You will be exactly the leader those women need in this time. I know you will be. You are selfless and loyal, brave and true. You can do this."

Davorah wrapped her arms around Tamar and clung. Focusing solely on her, Tamar didn't realize Caiaphas had left his seat and approached them until he crouched down and rested a hand on his niece's head. It didn't seem to faze Davorah, but Tamar looked up, surprised.

Hers was the face he was studying. His wore a far different expression than it had before. "It seems my niece is right. You have demonstrated exactly who you are in this moment. A leader."

For a moment, she paused. Had this been a test? Part of his examination? Had he told his niece to come, to see how Tamar would respond? But no, Davorah's distress was very real—and the high priest's distaste for Tamar had been too clear.

She rubbed a hand over her friend's back. This was no plan—just a heartfelt disruption of one. To Caiaphas's plan, but not to God's. His plan was already woven. She had only to follow the threads. And right now, that meant encouraging Davorah. "She will be a fine leader too."

"She will. And perhaps she will have her day. But not this one. Your position remains your own, Tamar."

It should have filled her with joy, shouldn't it have? Victory. She'd won.

But she didn't want to win. She didn't want to take, to be released from the first mile that was asked of her. Not that she thought the

Lord wanted her to suffer, exactly, but He had made His will known over these last few days. He had changed the old ways. How could she continue to work for them? To serve every day creating something she no longer believed was necessary?

She gave the high priest a small smile and hoped he saw in her eyes what made her say, "I thank you, my lord, for your faith in me. But I request that you allow me to retire from my service to the temple."

Behind her, her brothers and cousins murmured, shifted, clearly wanting to shout out that Caiaphas should ignore her.

His brows furrowed, and a strange sort of regret colored his eyes. "Why? Has this episode made you lose your desire to serve the Lord?"

"On the contrary." She urged Davorah away, smoothing back the woman's damp, dark locks from her face. "But I do truly believe God Himself took that veil down, and I believe it was for a purpose, not just an accident of the earthquake. Far be it from me to try to replace it. If the Lord wishes to show His face again to His people, then I will stand in its light and praise Him for it. I will not seek to cover it again."

For a long moment, Caiaphas said nothing. He merely held her gaze, measuring her as she would a skein. He was a weaver too, she realized. Of people and policy rather than of thread and yarn. He had heard more cases than she could possibly know. He had tried and succeeded at keeping the peace between their people and Rome. He had worked diligently for years to uphold the Law of God under the scrutiny of Pilate. But in his eyes, she saw respect. Acknowledgment. And yes, still that shimmer of fear. Because the Lord's face was a fearsome thing. Nothing man ever did could make him worthy of seeing it.

But God could choose to make them worthy. God could send the means. God could bridge the divide.

Caiaphas nodded and wrapped an arm around his niece's shoulders, urging her to her feet. Tamar rose with them.

He looked past her, to her relatives. His lips turned up in a tired smile. "This woman is a credit to your family."

In unison, they all said, "We know."

She shook her head. Perhaps a week ago, that mattered. Now, she only wanted to be a credit to her Lord.

He nudged Davorah toward Tamar, nodded once more to her brothers and cousin, and then strode back to his seat. It took only a moment to dismiss their case officially and call forward the next.

Tamar wove her arm through Davorah's and led her outward until they reached the light of the spring day, not saying another word until sunlight caressed them.

Even then, Davorah beat her to it. "I did not know, Tamar. I promise you. I did not know he had such intentions. I thought he knew I liked things exactly as they were. When Sarah pounded on my door last night and told me what was going on, what he was trying to do..." She shook her head.

Tamar smiled. "You have nothing to apologize for. And truly, my friend, you will rise to this occasion. You will do a wonderful job."

Davorah looked none too sure. But then, perhaps it wasn't only her abilities she was questioning. "What did you mean, about the veil? Why do you not want to work on it anymore?"

Ignoring the warning glance Moshe sent her, she drew Davorah onward. "Let me tell you about the last few days. It has been... miraculous."

CHAPTER NINETEEN

Valerius moved through the marketplace, scanning the stalls for an appropriate gift for Livia. They'd be celebrating the day of her birth in just a few days, but his senses were on alert for far more than that.

He hadn't slept yesterday when he returned home—he hadn't needed to. He'd felt more refreshed than he ever had after a full shift, whether at night or day. Instead, he and Mariana had spent the day talking, snatches here and there as they played with the children and shared their meals.

She had told him about her time with Tamar and Bithnia the day before. He had told her about the silent night and the brilliant dawn. About the Man who would not be held captive by death. They had wondered together, praised together.

Today, they'd both awakened with questions in their eyes.

The greatest miracle in the history of the world had just happened, right before their eyes. But what were they to do about it, other than believe?

"We need to find the others," Mariana had whispered, weaving her fingers into his. "Bithnia told me where to find them. She said to come today." Yet a question lingered in her eyes.

A question he understood all too well. The gathering Bithnia had mentioned was of believers, followers of Jesus, yes. But those followers were no friendlier to Romans than any other Jews were. Hadn't they run into that time and again already? Hadn't they heard the stories of Gentiles who approached the Lord, only for His disciples to try to send them away?

What made them think this would be any different? Jesus had always made room for them. But Jesus was no longer among their number. They had only the disciples, still bound by old prejudices, to whom they could appeal.

Which brought them to the more relevant question still. Could their hearts withstand another rebuff right now, when what they desperately needed was someone to come alongside them?

A step behind him, Mariana moved toward one of the stalls, reaching for an intricately carved wooden top. She righted it, gave it a spin, and smiled at the pattern that whirled to life as it twirled.

"She would love that," Valerius said in Latin. He hadn't even seen it as he walked by. His mind was already on the streets they'd walk when they left the marketplace. Assuming they didn't decide along the way that it wasn't worth the risk of being turned away.

"Mm." Ordinarily, Mariana—haggler that she was—would have sent him a scowl for saying such a thing out loud, even in the language least likely to be understood by the merchant. Today, she just shrugged and put the top down again. "I do not know. It does not seem quite right."

He wasn't going to argue. Even though he knew it wasn't the top that seemed not quite right. It was this uncertainty they both felt.

What if Bithnia wasn't there to welcome them? Or, more likely still, what if her family rebuked her for inviting them? What if their presence upset everyone and created chaos? How could they assure them that they posed no threat? He wasn't wearing his centurion uniform just now, but his toga would do nothing to reassure them.

They moved on from that stall, bypassed all the others without even slowing to glance at anything, and then found themselves at the corner, looking down the street but not striding toward it.

"Is this the right thing?" Mariana whispered, twisting her fingers in her stola. "I want it so badly—to find fellowship with others like us—that I wonder if it is my own desire pulling me along rather than the will of God."

He chuckled, but he understood the question perfectly. "Wanting to worship God in communion with others cannot be bad, can it?"

They turned to the right, still ambling more than striding. He had a feeling his wife was offering silent prayers to heaven, just as he was doing. Even though he didn't know what the answer to those prayers would look like, he kept his eyes searching for it.

He smiled when Mariana, despite her lack of military training, proved the better scout. She halted him with a hand on his arm a few minutes later, her eyes locked on a group at the next corner. His own gaze had skittered over them, given how ordinary they looked. Four men in the lead, talking, their faces all similar enough to say they were brothers, or perhaps cousins. Behind them trailed two women, heads bent close together as they talked between themselves.

An ordinary family, but the fact that Mariana drew his attention to them made him realize that one of the two women was Tamar.

An odd feeling, almost like nostalgia, washed over him. How many times had he walked past her in this city before without even knowing it? How many times had he strode past her brothers? They'd likely passed him by in the temple each Sabbath as he and Mariana came for instruction in the Court of the Gentiles. No doubt they'd all detoured to the other side of a street to avoid each other at some point in the past.

Before meeting at the tomb, they were just…strangers. Romans and Jews. Men and women, even, which meant they couldn't simply speak in public. So many rules meant to keep them in their separate spheres. So many regulations designed to keep them from ever seeing how they were alike.

Why did society, *all* society, his and theirs both, focus only on the differences? Why did their leaders try to dictate with whom they could be friends?

He answered his own question even as he mentally asked it. Because differences created fear, and fear made room for power. Because it was only by standing on the backs of others that most leaders attained their heights, so first they must find someone to stand on. Because the best way to unite one people was to convince them they were better than, superior to, the natural rulers over, another.

Egyptians and Hebrews. Spartans and Helots. Rome and… everyone else they encountered, honestly. When taught that your civilization was the pinnacle of *all* human civilization, it stood to reason that every other culture deserved to be subjugated and any individual could be forced to serve you.

Understanding that now made him ache. This wasn't the world God had wanted for His creation. He had not created them to hate each other, to rule each other like this. He had made them of *one* family. One blood. It was only because of their pride and ambition, their desire to rival God, that He had scattered them.

So then, didn't it make sense that what could unite them again was coming together to worship Him?

His pulse pounded. Yes, he'd been trained to make decisions based solely on logic and reason, but this *felt* right. It felt true. It felt noble enough to be worthy of seeking after. But they were only half of the equation. The others had to feel the same way, for any unity to be found.

Perhaps their stares caught the attention of the group, or perhaps the others just spotted them in their own perusal, and Valerius's and Mariana's focused attention arrested theirs. Whichever the cause, the men stopped, conferred, frowns on their brows. Then, in turn, their sudden shift caused Tamar to halt her conversation with the unfamiliar woman and look up.

A smile lit her face.

Mariana gripped his arm more tightly. He knew that the smile would have sent a shaft of hope through her spirit, just as it had his. He covered her hand with his. "Let us wait. See if she comes to us. I fear we will scare off the whole crowd if we approach them."

Mariana nodded, keeping her face set toward Tamar. Keeping her smile bright and inviting.

Tamar said something to the woman—a sister-in-law? Cousin? Friend?—and then moved up to speak to the men. With their faces together like that, he had no question that this was Tamar's family, if any doubts had remained. The resemblance was unmistakable.

But it seemed that her family was no more harmonious than any other he knew. As she spoke, gesturing at them, two of the men sent a scowl their way dark enough to eclipse the sun. The other two listened with interest, one of them sending a far different look toward them—a contemplative, receptive look.

Please, God. Please make a way. Make a way for us to find fellowship. Make a way for unity among Your children again.

Even as he prayed it, he remembered some of the words Jesus had spoken. Of a sorrowful promise that He would divide. Turn mothers against daughters, fathers against sons. If families split over faith in Him, what hope did strangers have?

Two of the men stalked off a moment later, their hand gestures making it look as though they were resigning the rest of their family to their fate. The other two flanked Tamar, who craned her neck around to speak to the other woman. When they stood like that, a knot of three and then one lone woman, he had to think the other was just an acquaintance or friend. She hesitated for a moment at whatever Tamar said, nodded, and hurried off in the same direction the men had gone. Tamar faced forward again, and the trio started toward them.

Mariana's fingers dug into his arm. He gave them a squeeze that he had to make an effort to keep gentle. Each step they advanced felt like a decade, like an ocean, like an infinity crossed over.

He waited, pulse pounding as if he were running, though his feet held their spot. At last, the trio stopped just before them. Tamar was still smiling, and in her face he saw the echo of the light that had felled them both yesterday morning. The two men weren't exactly beaming at them, but their expressions were open. Welcoming?

The taller of the two nodded a greeting. "I am Levi—Tamar's cousin."

"The one who helped me escape the temple on Friday," Tamar added softly.

"And I am Simon, her younger brother."

Tamar's smile went even brighter. "He too saw our risen Lord yesterday—Jesus walked with him and his friend to Emmaus."

Hope bubbled up and spilled over in Valerius's chest. "You are followers of Jesus?"

Both men nodded, exchanging a glance over Tamar's head, grins playing at the corners of their mouths. "I, openly," Simon said. "Much to our older brothers' dismay."

"I hadn't proclaimed it, for fear of losing my position in the temple," Levi admitted. A sheepish look flitted over his face, but it swiftly dissolved. "No more. Now I know He is no mere teacher, no simple rabbi. He is the Son of God."

Simon eased forward a step. "Tamar has told us all that happened to her since Friday—and the roles both of you played in helping her. We owe you a debt of gratitude."

"You owe us nothing," Mariana said, her voice at once meek but sure. "It was our privilege to help your sister."

"But," Valerius added, squeezing her hand again, "there *is* something we crave, if it is at all within your power to grant it." He looked down at his wife, who looked up at him in the same moment. When he shifted his gaze back to Tamar's family, he saw that a question had entered their eyes, but no caution. "Fellowship. With other believers."

"Bithnia invited us to a gathering." Mariana leaned into his side. "We want to go but weren't certain we would truly be welcome."

Tamar renewed her smile. "We are headed there now. Join us, please."

"Truly?" His wife's excitement thrummed through her, traveling from her fingers to his and up his arms as well.

"Truly." Tamar held out a hand toward Mariana, and in the second it took for his wife to release his arm and take Tamar's hand, the enormity of it hit him. Two days ago, Tamar had recoiled from touching her. Two days ago, there had been disgust on her face as she considered entering a house, much less breaking bread, with Romans. Today, no clouds marred the welcome in her eyes. The light of the Son had burned them all away.

Neither Simon nor Levi went so far as to offer a hand to clasp, but their faces were bright. Even so, Valerius leaned closer to them and asked in a hush, "Are you certain? We do not want to cause any discord. I know this is a frightening time."

"We cannot live in fear forever," Levi said. The look on his face was more determination than anything. "We are waiting for the Lord's next instruction, but in the meantime, we must do what He taught already. We must live as He lived. My cousin told me that Jesus praised your faith. He healed your servant. He welcomed you. So how can we do otherwise?"

They were the right words, the words he needed. "I pray the others will feel the same. But if not, please know we will not be offended." Disappointed but not offended. "I am quite aware that life is rarely about what *ought* to be. We are all ruled by frailty and failure and fear."

They began moving, and Simon offered him a warm smile. "It is too true. So I suppose this, too, is a step of faith. Trusting that the fellowship will act as our Master wished and not on our fears."

Valerius breathed a laugh. "An act of faith as great as sending that message to Jesus, I think."

"I want to thank you," Simon said in an undertone after a few steps of contemplative silence. "You could have turned her in. You could have ignored her. Instead, your family went far out of your way to help her. You had no reason to do that."

"We had every reason." Mariana and Tamar had ended up ahead of them, and Valerius watched the way they walked together. Not so different from how they had on the Sabbath, except that now one could see at a glance how different they were. Yet the memory of that other image, of his wife and Tamar both dressed in Roman finery, just served to make him more aware of why this was so important.

"Perhaps our clothes are different, our cultures," Valerius said. "But if you change your garments, the style or cut of your hair, if you put your feet on a new street, in a different house, a different situation…are we really so different? When we find what we have in common, like our love for the Lord, what do other differences really matter?"

They were bold words, words that challenged the way the world worked. They were a risk, those words, perhaps even a test. Would these men keep walking beside him, or would the thought of being *alike* be too difficult for them to swallow?

Silence walked with them for another few steps, and then Levi gave a slow, thoughtful nod. "I think the opposite is often true too. That the people who by rights ought to be most like us—our families, our neighbors—can be strangers." He moved his gaze to his cousin. "Jesus foretold that He would come between families. That is no small thing, to break the bonds of blood."

Simon sighed. "He promised new families though. Families built by *His* blood."

The very thought filled Valerius with awe. God had shaken the earth on Friday. In the moment His Son died, all of creation had reacted. The sky had gone dark. The rocks had split. The veil had torn. The divide between heaven and earth, obliterated.

Had He taken down the divide between people too? Male and female? Slave and free? Roman and Jew? Was this a new era they were walking into, one that would allow them to look beyond social status, beyond culture, beyond citizenship?

He shook his head. "I want to believe it is possible. Want to believe God has worked this miracle already too. But…" He motioned to a few Jews who moved to the opposite side of the street to avoid them and cast dark looks their way when they realized their group mixed Jew and Roman.

This time, Simon's sigh crossed with a humorless laugh. "How sad it would be, if it were easier for a man to be resurrected after days in the tomb, than for beating hearts to accept as friend someone society said should be an enemy."

The thought resonated deep in Valerius's spirit. How horrible to think that God could open up a path to His arms, a path to heaven, and yet mankind would dedicate their time to pushing others from the path, saying they were unworthy.

May it not be so.

Levi mustered a smile. "God can make a way. He can make it possible. I know He gives us each the freedom to choose, but He is paving the road for us. We only have to have faith enough to step onto it."

That, Valerius supposed, was why each step felt like a leap of faith. He and Mariana had made their choice. They'd taken the steps onto the path. But it was yet to be seen who beyond these three would join them on it.

CHAPTER TWENTY

When they arrived, they discovered that the Eleven had moved to another room somewhere, leaving the larger group of believers in the upper room. Tamar wished the Eleven were there to offer their guidance but wondered if perhaps this was part of God's plan, allowing Valerius and Mariana to slip into the gathering virtually unnoticed, unchallenged. Bithnia welcomed them warmly and made no objection when they found a corner where they could pray, out of sight of most of the assembly.

"The Eleven are still convinced that there is danger," Bithnia whispered to them, settling on the floor between Tamar and Mariana, "and that they are the most likely targets, so it is safer for the rest of us if they are not among us. I think they mean to travel back to Galilee soon, as the Lord instructed them to do. Who is to say if perhaps that is to keep them safe?" She shrugged, somehow looking both tired and radiant. "We are praying for them. And for Imma Mary and a few of the other women who went with them."

"Galilee." Tamar had never traveled more than a few miles from Jerusalem, but she'd heard plenty of sneering comments over the years about the various regions. "Nothing good can come out of Nazareth" was a prime example.

Yet the Lord had lived there for years. He had been born, so Bithnia had informed her, in the hamlet of Bethlehem, then grown up in another small, inconsequential town. Not in Jerusalem, not in Athens, not in Rome. The King of all Ages had chosen obscurity. How strange a choice. Even stranger, He'd chosen as His disciples men at home in fishing boats and sheepfolds, not scribes and men of law.

The whole order of things, turned on its head. No wonder it left them reeling. Yet it was a delicious sort of dizziness. It reminded her of a time when she was a child, when the family had gone out of the city for an afternoon. She'd stood up too fast, her head had gone light, and rather than sit back down, she'd run. Arms out, laughter spilling from her lips, feet flying over the wildflower-dotted meadow. She'd felt, for the seconds the lightheadedness had lasted, like a bird. Like her feet didn't touch the ground for those moments. As if she was soaring with the angels.

The same sort of feeling possessed her now. Nothing looked quite like it used to, and her head was still spinning from all the rapid changes to both the cosmos and her own heart. But it was a good sort of spin. Freeing. Flying. She waited with bated breath to see where the Lord would guide her as she ran, arms outstretched.

Her gaze swept over the assembly. More were gathered here than yesterday, even with the core disciples having separated themselves. She sensed in all of them that same expectancy. No one knew exactly what they were waiting for, but they were ready to receive it.

"We will gather here every day," Bithnia whispered. "We will pray. All hours, as long as it takes. Days, weeks, months…until Jesus gives us instructions, we will pray."

Tamar nodded. "I am glad I have no further duties to pull me away. I can be here, praying and praising." The weaving room would continue its work without her.

Bithnia offered her a knowing smile and nodded toward her lap. Tamar wasn't certain why until she spoke. "Your fingers twitch at the mere thought of your looms. I imagine your ears strain for the familiar sounds of the shuttle. You will miss it."

Tamar granted that with a tilt of her head. "I will, yes." The work, and the women who made up so much of her world. She drew in a long breath and leaned back against the wall. "That work gave me purpose. I imagine when I close my eyes, I will always see the colors that brought scenes to life, that created art from strands of wool."

Bithnia reached for her hand. "My first day there, you said, 'We were made in the image of the Creator, and so we are creative. When we create, when we make something from these pieces He created first—wool and wood and dye from plants—we honor Him. We praise Him with our hands. We bring Him glory as we imitate His creative work.'"

Tamar smiled. "Lessons first imparted to me by my grandmother. When I was just a tiny girl, she drew me her into her lap, positioned my fingers on the loom, and taught me how individual strands must come together to create something new. 'One thread,' she said, 'is nothing on its own. We are nothing on our own. That is why God put us in families, why those families meet others to form tribes, why our tribes need one another to be a nation."

Bithnia and Mariana both smiled with her. Mariana murmured, "A beautiful lesson."

But that was only the start of it. "She reminded me that cloth is one of the most basic things, something everyone needs. But she taught me that it is even more important for the reminder it provides. She told me that I was but one thread. She was another. My parents, brothers, sisters, cousins…each just one strand. But together…together we are something more than twelve threads in a tangle. Together we are a tapestry."

She could all but hear her grandmother's sweet voice in her ear, all but feel her knowledgeable hands steadying Tamar's uncertain ones. All but see the threads of her life and family, stretched out before her on life's loom.

Bithnia's gaze went distant, her nod slow. It looked as though she was digesting the words, making them a part of her. "That is a perfect analogy. For so long, my own family had been only the expected colors, running in straight lines. Yes, there were always the surprises of deaths and births, of business that didn't go according to plan, of arguments between siblings and cousins who had once been the closest friends. But those were the expected pattern, as random as each moment might seem. That was what every life looked like—long stretches of a single color, broken here and there by another. When just traveling in a straight line, I cannot always see the pattern."

Mariana took Bithnia's other hand and squeezed it. "But step back, take a broader view, look beyond our own thread, and the beauty of the design emerges. I met the two of you. You brought us here. To *this*."

Tamar let her gaze wander around the gathering. "I wonder if it is even more than that. I think the very fabric has shifted. God rent the veil in two. I think all of history must note this as a turning point—that future generations will mark the time before Jesus came and then after. Because this is not the same tapestry any longer. We are part of a new picture. A new tapestry."

Mariana's nod was decisive. "One in which death does not mean the end of life."

Bithnia smiled. "One in which ordinary fishermen are called to be fishers of men. Where the first become last and the last become first. Where the greatest Man ever to walk the earth came as a servant."

A new tapestry. A new fabric. But some of the same principles would apply too. They were still individual threads, every person in this room. It was just that God was weaving them into His veil in new and unexpected ways. Dyeing raw wool with royal purple. Refining bulky thread into the finest web. Then using them to weave a picture never seen before.

As she looked out over the gathering, she wondered how many tribes were represented in this room. How many regions. How many sects. In some of the faces, she saw evidence of other peoples. Egyptian features, Greek ones, Persian. Because the Jews had already been dispersed among the nations before, and when they returned to the land promised to them, they never returned alone. They brought with them those who had seen the power of God through their witness. God raised children of Abraham from the scattered sands.

God had chosen to let His Son be killed, to rip the veil in two, at the very hour when the Passover lambs were being sacrificed for *them*. Not for the Jews of Jerusalem—but for the scattered children who had come home to Him.

Her gaze drifted to Mariana and then past her to Valerius. He was bowed in prayer beside her brother and cousin, lips moving in murmurs too quiet for her to hear, but his sincerity was as obvious as the sun. Tamar smiled. "You and your husband are new and unexpected threads, Mariana, but chosen by God. Colored by His masterful touch. And now you must be woven into the greater cloth."

Mariana blinked back tears, smiled, nodded. Then she bowed her head, clearly so overwhelmed that there was no recourse but prayer.

God had put their threads together, for reasons Tamar couldn't know yet. She could see how these two had helped her, of course, and she could hope that perhaps this was how she could help them in turn, by guiding their threads into the fabric of followers. Standing beside them. Claiming a new sister and brother in these two Romans—and perhaps mourning the ones who would not accept either them or her, now that she'd declared herself a follower of Jesus.

"Our home will not be associated with that heretic." Moshe had bit out the words when she'd spotted Valerius and Mariana, when she'd explained as succinctly as she could that they had saved her life and that they were disciples of the Messiah as she now was. "If you insist upon this path, then you are no longer part of our family."

He'd looked at her, at Simon. No room for discussion in his gaze.

Neither she nor her brother had wavered, and it wasn't just because Levi had said they were welcome in *his* home. It was because turning away from the risen Lord was inconceivable. Once one had been filled with that light, the thought of the sticky darkness couldn't be borne.

Perhaps he would relent. Perhaps he would experience the glory of the Lord for himself—he and his whole household. She prayed so, prayed that her brothers and their wives, their children, could know this joy.

But even if they didn't, she would rejoice. She would never stop praying, but she also wouldn't miss out on what new things God gave her.

Her fingers knotted in the fabric of the tunic she'd borrowed again from Hannah. She'd woven this cloth herself. Had dyed it until it was the perfect shade to complement her cousin's smile. It was the thing she was best at in life. The skill she had honed, the talent she had tended.

It would be useful, here as it was anywhere. Because cloth, as her grandmother had said, was one of the most basic things of life. Everyone needed it. Everyone wore it.

Her fingers remembered the feel of the silk too—an offering of friendship from Claudia to Mariana. An offer of help from Mariana to Tamar. She'd scrubbed it clean last night and had it dried and folded and ready to return.

But just giving back a borrowed garment wasn't enough. It was nothing but a thank-you. Nothing but an even return.

She wanted to add something to it.

So she studied her new friend. Noted the shade of *her* smile, the green-gold of her eyes, the pink of her cheeks. She planned what dyes she would use on the dried and processed flax she had stored in Moshe's house, ready to be spun into linen. She planned how fine she would make the thread. She designed the pattern she would create as she wove it into fabric.

Linen would never be as expensive as silk. But she would give her the work of her hands—the work of her heart.

She would welcome Mariana and her family into the tapestry of her life. Together, they would walk the newly created path from earth to heaven.

FROM THE AUTHOR

Dear Reader,

I have always loved those few words nestled into the crucifixion narrative: *and the veil of the temple was torn in two, from top to bottom.* It appears in Matthew, Mark, and Luke, along with the mention of the earth shaking and rocks splitting. Just a few words, a single sentence, yet so important a sentence that each of these Gospel writers made sure to include it.

Why? Biblical scholars have been explaining the wonder of this sign for millennia, and it is no less meaningful today than it was then. Because the temple veil served one purpose: to separate sinful man from holy God. Only one man dared to cross beyond that veil, once a year, and only after making certain his heart was cleansed of sin, so that he could offer atonement for the whole nation.

When God tore the veil in two, He sent a message to Israel that the old ways were done. That no longer did man have to stay removed from God, because there was a new High Priest who had offered atonement once and for all.

I loved getting to explore that theme in this book, as well as those that touch on our own creativity, the value of our work, and our often-misguided assumption that God needs us to defend Him.

Of course, I took some creative liberties with my characters, especially with Valerius. We don't know the names of the centurions who stood at the foot of the cross and guarded the tomb, or the one who asked Jesus from a distance to heal his servant. There is absolutely no reason to think they were all one person, but I thought it would be fun if they were, so I wrapped them all into my one character. Early church tradition gave the name Longinus to the one who pierced Jesus's side after He died, but modern scholars suspect that was less a name than a designation—the name literally means "shaft," like the shaft of the spear he used. Even so, I smiled at the thought of giving this early church centurion a cameo appearance as well. Those same early traditions ascribe a backstory to him—that he was going blind, but that when he pierced Christ's side, the water and blood flowed down onto him, got in his eyes, and healed his growing blindness.

Of course, another theme I thought this story provided the perfect means to explore was one that became a huge point of contention in the early Church, as told to us by Acts and the Epistles—the mixing of Jews and Gentiles. Prejudice has been part of the human story as long as history was recorded, and the hatred and distrust went deep and was very much mutual in Jesus's day. Yet He set a critical example for us to follow. Before His ascension, He left us with a clear instruction to go to all people and all nations—even the ones we don't like. The gospel is for all.

I hope you enjoyed the story of Tamar, Valerius, Mariana, and Bithnia, the symbols of death and rebirth, and the reminder that it isn't until we let go of our burdens that God can deliver us from them. May we embrace that truth with our hearts and come before Him unveiled, ready to receive the light of His face.

Roseanna

KEEPING THE FAITH

FILTHY RAGS

In today's church, most of us have heard countless sermons or read devotionals expounding on the passage in the Epistles where Paul names our righteousness as filthy rags. There's nothing we can do to earn salvation or make ourselves worthy. Yet even knowing that, we're often fueled to push our opinions, understandings, and perception of goodness on others. We are, in effect, trying to protect God (or our understanding of Him) just as Tamar was trying to do. She had to come to the realization that God doesn't need her to protect Him. That nothing we do or fail to do can achieve anything beyond His will.

Have you struggled with this in your life? Are you struggling with it now? Do you find yourself arguing with others about the "right way" to believe? How does it hearken back to the sects of religious leaders in Jesus's day?

GUIDED BY FEAR

As readers removed from the biblical narrative by thousands of years, it's sometimes easy to see certain historical figures as merely good or bad, hero or villain. Caiaphas the high priest is one such example—many Christians today see him, as well as the Pharisees, as villains in Christ's story. Jesus Himself, however, saw them as something different—people to be forgiven, people to be challenged so they might be saved.

Have you ever paused to wonder *why* Caiaphas was so opposed to Jesus? It is easy to forget how revolutionary His teachings of resurrection and His claims of being one with the Father really were. Caiaphas served as high priest longer than any other man in that era, and he was by all accounts a successful politician, keeping his people on good terms with their Roman rulers. Do you think fear played a role in his reaction to Jesus? When in your own life do you find yourself reacting out of fear? Are you afraid of new technology? Or ideas that don't agree with your own? Are you afraid of the differences you see between your generation and others?

GUARDING THE FAITH

Between the Old Testament and the New, hundreds of years went by, and readers are plunged into the life of Jesus without a lot of context. In the Old Testament, there were no mentions of Pharisees or Sadducees, for instance. How did these sects arise? What was their purpose?

Many of us today equate the word "Pharisee" with "hypocrite," thanks to Jesus rightfully calling them out...but in fact, the Pharisees arose as people who wanted to safeguard the faith. They wanted to make sure that the Jewish people never again forsook God, and so they took Scripture and turned it into rules to govern every aspect of daily life...though of course, as time went by, they also twisted those rules and Scriptures, as people tend to do, to suit their own needs. Jesus often called them out about ways they'd done this. What do you think He would call us out for today? In what ways do we let our ideas about how faith should be lived out get in the way of helping others learn the Truth?

THREADS IN THE TAPESTRY

At the end of *Unveiled*, Tamar reflects on life and people from her perspective as a weaver, seeing each of us as a thread in God's tapestry. If you follow a single thread in a woven fabric, it looks like a straight line—sometimes boring, sometimes crossed by only its match, sometimes with unexpected intersections with colors it wouldn't recognize. That thread cannot see the whole...but the weaver can.

How do you think your own life fits into the greater tapestry? Has it been full of surprises or mostly the expected complications and changes? Has there ever been a point in your life where it feels as though your life's tapestry has been ripped, torn, or cut? How have you reacted or how would you react to that? Have you ever looked back on history and been able to see a bit of the Master's plan in it, though people at the time wouldn't have been able to?

DIFFERENT AND THE SAME

Through the eyes of Jewish and Roman characters, this story explores one of the biggest challenges of the early Church—merging cultures. We know from Acts and the Epistles that the idea of letting

Gentiles into the faith without first converting to Judaism proved an enormous hurdle for many Jewish Christians.

We don't have that exact situation today, perhaps, but how does the same idea still challenge us? Do we judge fellow believers on how they're different? Do we struggle to accept those who look different, sound different, act different, or don't quite conform to all our traditions? Why do you think we seek the comfort of similarity? What can we learn if we see beyond it?

Jesus promised to be a cause of division between families, separating those who seemingly ought to be the same and believe the same. Have you seen faith in Christ do this? Have you ever found true friendship with someone the world says is nothing like you?

EVERY SKILLED WOMAN: WEAVING IN BIBLICAL TIMES

By Reverend Jane Willan, MS, MDiv

In ancient Jewish culture, women were tasked with the creation of sacred textiles. Although they did not participate in religious leadership or rituals to the same extent as men in ancient times, their influence and involvement were significant. This is evident in the creation of essential religious items. One example is the tallit, a prayer shawl expertly crafted by skilled female weavers and worn by men during prayer and religious rituals. The religious items created by women left an indelible mark on the spiritual and cultural tapestry of Jewish society.

Women created textiles for the tabernacle, a portable earthly dwelling place for the divine presence. Constructed by the Israelites during their exodus from Egypt under Moses's command, it served as the center of worship and sacrificial ceremonies until the construction of the first temple in Jerusalem. The role of women and the tabernacle is explicitly described in Exodus: "Every skilled woman spun with her hands and brought what she had spun—blue, purple or scarlet yarn or fine linen. And all the women who were willing and had the skill spun the goat hair" (Exodus 35:25–26).

Weaving was the final stage in creating these sacred textiles. But long before weaving could start, women were diligently at work in the fields harvesting flax and tending to sheep. Weaving required an abundance of flax and wool. The production of these materials, crucial for textile creation, often fell to women. Wool underwent meticulous cleaning and carding processes to disentangle and align the fibers before being spun into yarn using spindles. While men typically took care of the sheep, women played a pivotal role in the subsequent shearing, cleaning, and processing of wool.

Flax, one of the earliest domesticated crops, is essential for linen production. In regions such as the Fertile Crescent, in the modern-day Middle East, flax flourished along the riverbanks. The timing of its harvest, just before full maturity to ensure high-quality fibers, was crucial. Both men and women were involved in various stages of production, ranging from planting the seeds to harvesting the stalks.

Following the harvest, flax underwent a meticulous process, including retting (using water to dissolve cellular tissues), drying, breaking, and heckling (straightening and combing the fibers to remove the core and impurities). This process rendered it into fibers ready to be spun. Spinning flax into linen thread or yarn is done using a spindle or spinning wheel. The spinner twists the flax fibers together to form a continuous thread. The thickness of the thread can vary depending on the desired end use.

Women wove the temple veil, the most significant sacred textile, which divided the Holy of Holies, which housed the Ark of the Covenant, from the rest of the temple. The veil symbolized the divide between God and humanity, and the women's role in creating the veil underscored their contribution to the spiritual fabric of their community.

The writings of Josephus, a first-century Jewish historian, offer valuable insights into the temple and its sacred vestments. In his works, particularly *The Antiquities of the Jews* and *The Jewish War*, Josephus described the temple veil as an intricate masterpiece made of fine linen and adorned with symbolic colors, including blue, purple, and scarlet. Josephus drew a vivid parallel between the colors of the veil and the elements of the world: blue represented the air, scarlet signified fire, and purple mirrored the sea.

The intricate process of weaving and dyeing these special fabrics, especially the veil, not only showcased skilled craftsmanship but also imbued these materials with profound symbolic meaning. The use of expensive and hard-to-obtain dyes in the colors of blue, purple, and scarlet added significant value and symbolism, reflecting the deep spiritual investment in creating a space for the divine.

Blue dye, known as *tekhelet*, was likely derived from the secretions of the murex snail, found in the Mediterranean Sea. This dyeing process was both expensive and labor-intensive, requiring a substantial number of snails to produce even a small amount of dye. The color blue symbolized divinity and the heavens, serving as a reminder to the Israelites of the vast sky above and their deep connection to God.

Purple dye, known as *argaman* or Tyrian purple, was also sourced from the murex snail but through a slightly different process, resulting in a rich and deep purple hue. Like blue, purple was associated with wealth and status due to the difficulty and cost of its production.

In the context of the tabernacle, purple symbolized royalty and sovereignty, pointing to God's supreme kingship.

Scarlet, also known as *shani*, was crafted from the dried bodies of the crimson worm indigenous to the region. The process of obtaining and processing this dye was intricate, involving the collection of minuscule insects and extracting the dye from their bodies. Scarlet represented sacrifice and redemption, echoing the significance of blood in sacrificial rituals and the cost of atoning for sin.

These special and expensive dyes used in the weaving of textiles for the tabernacle, and later the temple, would likely have been procured through a collective effort supported by donations and offerings from the community, possibly supplemented by the temple treasury itself. The acquisition of such valuable materials underscored the collective commitment to worship and the construction of a sacred space.

The symbolic meanings attributed to these colors converged to convey an important spiritual message. They collectively formed a visual representation of God's character and the intricate relationship between God and the Israelites. It was skilled women who brought these elements to life, enabling the tabernacle's curtains to serve as visual expressions of faith. Their expertise and dedication turned these textiles into a vital part of the communal space for worship, showcasing their critical role in nurturing and expressing the community's spiritual life.

Although the labor of women was essential to the production of the veil, the actual design of the veil for the tabernacle likely saw limited involvement from women due to the prevailing cultural and religious context of ancient Israel. In this patriarchal society, tasks adhered to established traditions and hierarchies. While skilled women are acknowledged in the construction of textiles, their specific role in designing the veil remains uncertain. Men, including religious leaders, probably played a more significant role in shaping its design. Nevertheless, it is undeniable that the skills and dedication of women were indispensable in the creation of the veil.

In Christian theology, the rending or tearing of the temple veil at the moment of Christ's death assumed additional significance. It symbolized the end of the old covenant and the dawn of a new era, marking a pivotal shift in theological perspectives and altering the dynamics of the divine-human relationship.

The role of women in weaving and producing textiles for the tabernacle and temple in ancient Jewish culture was not only significant but also deeply intertwined with religious symbolism and communal dedication. These women, with their expertise in crafting materials such as linen and wool, as well as their mastery of intricate dyeing processes, played a vital part in creating sacred objects of great beauty and spiritual importance. The legacy of these female artisans endures as a testament to their craftsmanship, spirituality, and indispensable role in shaping the religious and cultural heritage of the Jewish people.

Fiction Author

ROSEANNA M. WHITE

Roseanna M. White is a bestselling, Christy Award–winning author who has long claimed that words are the air she breathes. When not writing fiction, she's homeschooling, editing, designing book covers, and pretending her house will clean itself. Roseanna is the author of a slew of historical novels whose stories span several continents and thousands of years. Spies and war and mayhem always seem to find their way into her books...to offset her real life, which is blessedly ordinary.

Nonfiction Author

REVEREND JANE WILLAN, MS, MDiv

Reverend Jane Willan writes contemporary women's fiction, mystery novels, church newsletters, and a weekly sermon.

Jane loves to set her novels amid church life. She believes that ecclesiology, liturgy, and church lady drama make for twisty plots and quirky characters. When not working at the church or creating new adventures for her characters, Jane relaxes at her favorite local bookstore, enjoying coffee and a variety of carbohydrates with frosting. Otherwise, you might catch her binge-watching a streaming series or hiking through the Connecticut woods with her husband and rescue dog, Ollie.

Jane earned a Bachelor of Arts degree from Hiram College, majoring in Religion and History, a Master of Science degree from Boston University, and a Master of Divinity from Vanderbilt University.

Read on for a sneak peek of another exciting story in the Mysteries & Wonders of the Bible series!

A LIFE RENEWED:
Shoshan's Story

BY GINGER GARRETT

From her deep sleep, Shoshan heard Him.

"Shoshan, wake up." At the sound of His voice, so rich and familiar, she tried to stir and open her eyes, but something pinned her arms to her sides. Besides, her eyelids were so heavy.

"The veil is torn," He whispered. "But wait for Me."

His palm rested lightly over the hollow of her throat. Warmth from His hand flooded over her cool skin. She sensed that He leaned down, His face inches from hers as He breathed the words of life. His breath was a soft breeze, like the first spring morning after a bitter winter.

She inhaled, a gasping sound, as His breath entered her body, sweeping away darkness, loosening stiff muscles. She struggled to open her eyes. She wanted only to say His name and look into His eyes again.

The bindings at her sides held fast. Shoshan fought against the bindings, and suddenly she was alone in the darkness. She sensed that He was not here with her anymore. He had gone somewhere, a deeper place, a more dreadful darkness. How she knew this, she could not say. He had left her here, but not forever. He would return.

She felt life returning to her limbs. Her chest rose and fell as breath moved in her body. It was good to lie here in the grave and wait.

Some time later, Shoshan awoke. How long she had dozed peacefully in the darkness, she did not know. When she still couldn't open her eyes, she realized her face was swathed in linen. There was a light near her feet. She could see the glow through the bindings around her head. Her body rested on a flat, hard rock, laid flat as if she had merely stretched out for a nap. The rock was uncomfortable, digging into her shoulder blades and hips. She wanted to stand up and rub her arms for warmth. Had the world always been this cold? She could not remember.

She inhaled deeply again, but this time a strip of fabric was sucked into her mouth. Spitting it out, she wiggled her head side to side then up and down to loosen the bindings. When the lower half of her face was free, she breathed in big, greedy inhalations, ignoring the brackish smell around her. There was another scent, too, a strong woodsy note, like…myrrh. Yes, it was myrrh. Myrrh and cassia, too, were heavy in the air, but just underneath was the sickening sweetness of rot.

Unnerved by that rotting scent, she worked to free her right hand. With that done, she tore at the linen strips around her face and body. They had been soaked in oil and easily tore away in her hand. She struggled to remember what she was doing or where she had just been. Had she woken from a dream, or was she in a dream? The light at the end of her feet beckoned her.

She was in a cold, dark cave, one where the dead were buried. But she was alive. Who had bandaged her like this and why? Had she been injured? Slowly, her mind pieced together little bits of memory, like mending tears in a garment, bringing jagged edges together, trying to make them fit.

Jesus had been here. She could feel something in the cave that could only be explained by His presence. He shifted the atmosphere in a way that no one could explain.

She remembered that now, how His presence changed a room. She had been with Him before, before waking like this, back when He taught people in the hills, and He had blessed a boy's fish and bread. It had mesmerized her, how He had blessed the meager portion before breaking it, and after He broke it, He gave it away. Somehow, that moment stayed with her above all the others. *Blessed, broken, given.* After that, those three words became a chant under her breath, the rhythm for her days.

Even when...

Her mind snapped shut, not wanting to show her its secrets. Not yet, not until she was free and standing in the sun.

The light at her feet told her there was an entrance not far, although it was partially covered by a stone or a door. If she could get her legs free, she could get out. Something told her she had to, that He was ready for her to walk out.

She wiggled and pushed her body until both arms were free. After ripping the remaining linens off her legs, she stood next to a wall in the shadows, panting from exertion. Something furry and warm scampered across her foot, and she shrieked, jumping back, one hand out to brace herself in case she stumbled. Her hand pressed against the wall, dislodging a pile of old dry bones. The bones rained down, covering her feet and calves.

She stared at the bones on the ground as her knees began to tremble. The myrrh was so strong, yet she never used it as a body oil or in her laundry. Lifting a strip of linen from her shoulder to her nose, she inhaled again the sharp spicy scent. Myrrh was used for the dead.

Now she knew she was right. She was standing in a grave, surrounded by the dead. *But no,* Shoshan corrected herself, *I am standing in my grave. Someone put me here, as if I was dead.*

I was dead.

An involuntary shudder ran through her.

The stone that stood at the entrance of the cave had a huge crack running through the center. Edging to it, feeling her legs move as they once did, marveling at the sensation of the cold dirt under her feet, she pressed her palms flat against the stone, inhaling sharply. It was cold and smooth to the touch. She ran her palms over it, feeling the surface, her arms tingling as if each sensation was a marvelous discovery.

She felt weightless, as though she could walk through the break in the stone if she wanted, walk right out.

Had she been dead? The thought was strange. That was impossible. She wasn't a ghost, was she? Every child in Rome was raised on mythical stories about ghosts and monsters. Those stories popped up in her mind, as if that was the explanation. Pressing harder against the stone, she felt her muscles flexing. She had always been told that ghosts had no physical body. But she had a body, so clearly she was more than a spirit.

From the other side she could hear voices. An argument had broken out. Their harsh tone made her step back, away from the light. She had forgotten how anger sounded, how it made her heart accelerate. But if one of them had peered into the grave, through the stone, maybe they were arguing out of fright. Neither knew what hid in the darkness.

"It is all right! I am alive!" she shouted, her voice echoing in the tomb. The voices went abruptly silent.

"Can you hear me?" she called again, louder. No reply came. Someone had been on the other side though, just a moment before. Someone must have heard her.

The stone groaned as it was pushed to one side. Someone pushed it for her. She would thank them. Eagerly, she stepped through the doorway into the open air. The light pierced her eyes, and she threw her arm over her face, her eyes watering. After blinking back the tears, she slowly lowered her arm and looked. She was alone.

She was on a hillside, just above a lovely city made from limestone bricks that glittered in the sun. Below, fruit trees were adorned in emerald green leaves and waving white blossoms.

She sat down beside the stone and breathed deeply. The air was fresh, and she drank it in, feeling the air whoosh in and out of her lungs, a delicious sensation. She could spend the whole day just sitting here breathing the cool garden air. Below her, the grass was brilliant green. The sun on her shoulders was tender.

Life was a miracle. But maybe this was all a dream? Surveying the city below, she felt recognition hit her with a jolt.

Jerusalem! Oh, I remember you!

It was spring, and she was in Jerusalem. She lived here, didn't she? Yes, she remembered that much now. She lived here with her husband, Antonius, and her...her hand fluttered over her abdomen. Her mind snapped shut again.

Do not panic. Think. Where am I?

She was on the north end of Jerusalem, on the other side of the hill where criminals were executed. The thought made her cold. Concentrating, she closed her eyes and inhaled again. It was there, yes, the faint but sharp odor of old blood. Someone had been crucified there recently, maybe days ago. She had to get home to her husband, Antonius. She had been raised to life, but everything else remained shrouded in her memory. He would remember though. Antonius was a shrewd man.

Below, to her far right, the temple was visible, and directly beneath her was the city wall. Everywhere around her were tombs. Some were sealed, as they had been for generations. Others, like hers, stood open, the stones rolled away. Many stones were cracked as if by violent force. The cracks split the rocks wide enough to illuminate the graves within. The graves were empty, and linen strips littered the garden path.

She needed to follow that path down the garden's hill, back into the city of Jerusalem. Someone had been just outside the grave, arguing. She had heard them. Something was terribly wrong, but she did not know what it was.

Putting her hands on the ground to stand, she caught sight of her left hand. Her marriage band, a solid gold band with a square ruby, was missing. She never took it off. Never. It was a symbol of her husband's devotion, which had waned of late. She remembered that with a groan. The band was a constant comfort, and she had polished it every afternoon before napping. She had been so tired since... Since...

Two young men dashed out from behind a stone below her on the path.

"Wait!" she called.

They did not look back but ran as if terrified. They had been the ones she'd heard fighting, she was sure of it. But what was scaring them? She was only a woman, unarmed and alone. They were young men in their prime. Looking around, she saw nothing that could intimidate them. Unless...had her appearance changed terribly? She touched her face, and examined her hands and arms, but she did not see or feel any deformities.

Then the events of her last day came rushing back. Pressing a hand to her forehead, as if she could stop them from crashing through her mind, she whimpered as each memory surfaced, one after the other. The young men were scared of her because her beating heart was a reversal of natural law. No one walked out of the grave.

She remembered that she had been in a bed, her head hurting so badly it was as if each stab of pain was a bolt of lightning. She had heard the voices of her husband and a woman. The woman's name was... The name was just out of reach.

She was sure there was something more. She had been in bed at that last moment of her life, but just before that, she remembered crouching on all fours, like an animal, panting and groaning. The thought horrified her. What had happened?

She had to get home. Everything felt wrong, and she sensed danger in the air. If the Romans were in a crucifying mood, she did not want to be alone on the streets. Only too recently, the Romans had crucified two thousand men at once for revolting against taxes. The terror, the smell, and the sounds… She had been afraid to leave her home for days afterward.

A woman hurrying over the hill saw her standing there and gasped in fright. Two men following behind shook their fists at Shoshan.

"They will find the body!" one of them yelled. "And the lot of you will be crucified for this! Jesus was just the beginning!"

Shoshan froze, her breath caught in her chest. How exactly did those men know she had been dead and come back to life? Had they seen her in the cemetery?

One of the men leered at her before he hurried away, and she realized she was dressed in only a thin linen tunic, nothing more than a sleeping gown. Instinctively her hand went to her hair. There was no veil covering her head.

She wore immodest bedclothes and had no veil to signify she was a married woman. Never would she dream of walking in public like this.

She found a length of discarded linen on the ground and wrapped it around her shoulders, then grabbed another, wider strip, trying to create a makeshift robe. More people came over the hill now, dazed and pale, as if in shock. Shoshan saw the scene as they did, a garden filled with broken graves. She watched as people looked inside the graves and shrieked in fright, then saw Shoshan and shrieked again.

Shoshan began to flee down the path, shocked to find her legs were strong and steady. Shouldn't her body be weaker? Her mind seized upon any evidence to refute the conclusion she had reached in the cave. Her resurrection was real. But that was hard to accept, even after experiencing it herself. Besides, she hadn't felt this good since...

What was it that nagged at her? So much of her memory was still gone.

There was no time to stop and think. Everywhere, she saw open graves, sealing stones lying on their sides, burial linens piled just outside the entrances. All around her, people were shouting. Some of the younger ones raced ahead of her, their eyes wild with fear or hope.

Shoshan now had only one thought: Antonius. She had to get home to her husband. He would know what had happened. He would know what to do next.

Staying close to the wall, Shoshan approached the north side of the city. The people running from the garden had dispersed back into the pilgrims and merchants entering Jerusalem. Scanning the crowds, she tried to spot anyone else wearing grave clothes. Other tombs had stood open. Where were those people? Wrapping her arms tightly around her chest, she shivered in the afternoon sun. The oil that had been rubbed onto her arms in the grave stung her nose. A few women cast sideways glances at her then grimaced at the sight of her, so poorly dressed and unveiled. None offered to help. Shoshan felt colder under their gaze. She just wanted to get home.

As she approached the Fish Gate, the smell hit her. Although her mother was a Jew, Shoshan had been raised in Rome, where there were no fresh fish markets. Everything there was imported, salted, and dried. The market here sold fish from the Mediterranean and the Sea of Galilee. The fish sat all day in the sun. They did not smell fresh by this time of day.

Then she noticed the noise, which was as overwhelming as the smell.

"Come and buy!"

"Over here!"

"Just for you!"

As she pressed through the gate, mingling with the crowd, several fishermen stopped, their mouths open midsentence, staring at her lack of clothing. It took a lot to shock a fisherman, she knew. She could feel warmth surging to her face with the embarrassment of a strange man staring at her body through the thin material of the grave linen.

A rough-looking elderly man, his face as craggy as the hills behind them, waved a shaking hand at her, beckoning her over. On the table in front of him was a display of fresh fish.

Something about him seemed familiar. Hesitating, she relented and approached him. Why did she know his face?

While she was still searching her memory, he removed his robe and handed it to her.

"Oh, I could not, sir," she protested, even as she quickly draped it across her shoulders and pushed her arms through. She would do anything to stop the stares, even borrow a man's robe that was threadbare and had dried fish scales stuck to it along the arms.

Out of the corner of her eye, she caught a group of young fisher-men counting their *denarii* and eyeing her. They thought she was a prostitute!

Quickly wrapping the tunic more tightly around her, she thanked the stranger for his robe. When her hand passed over her abdomen, a shock jolted her. She needed to remember something, something her body wanted her to know.

The man dug through the satchels at his feet. She watched, won-dering what he was looking for.

Not speaking, he frowned in concentration until his hand grasped a coin. As he straightened, his face was pinched, as if he was afraid too.

Why was everyone so afraid?

"Take this to Servia at the gate. She will sell you a veil."

She studied his face a moment longer, and then the memory came to her. "Oh! I do know you! I know your sons, Simon and Andrew."

His eyes cleared immediately, and he glared at her, lifting one finger to his lips to silence her. Leaning across the table, he motioned for her to lean toward him too.

"Have you seen them today?" he whispered.

"No," she admitted. "Were they in the cemetery too?"

"God forbid!" he gasped, jerking backward.

She raised her eyebrows and shook her head. "Did I offend you? I did not mean to. I just… I saw people running away from the cem-etery. I thought you meant they had been there too."

His glare softened, just barely. He moved closer, and his voice became soft. "If you walked with Jesus, get off the streets as fast as you can."

He turned away from her, shouting out for customers, ignoring her. He would not look at her again.

Shoshan felt as if every eye was upon her, and she did not know why. She had a robe on now, at least. But still, people stared. What was happening? Hurrying to buy a veil, Shoshan exhaled in relief as she whipped the thin fabric over her head and face. Now nothing would bring attention to her. She looked like any other respectable wife, out for the day's shopping.

Leaving the Fish Gate market, she hurried along the street toward the living district, where her modest home was. The very thought of home made her feet move more quickly. She would be home, and shut the door, and be in Antonius's arms in just a few more minutes.

All along the street, people stopped and slowly turned, staring at her before she even passed by. When they saw her, their eyes ran up and down, as if they were perplexed. Then their expressions turned to astonishment or terror. Mothers grabbed their children's hands and yanked them close. Men scowled, and their hands turned to fists, or else they crossed their arms, glaring at her. What was her crime? How was she offending them? She reached up to touch her face once more then looked at her fingers. They were pink and full, with no grime on them. Her face was clean. But something was scaring people, that was obvious.

Walking even more quickly, she passed a shop that sold mirrors and women's clothes, with the door propped open to encourage a breeze. She went inside to look at herself in the mirror. Studying her reflection, she could see no physical change, although her countenance had an otherworldly glow. Or was that just a trick of the light? Touching her face, she was relieved to find it warm and soft, the familiar face of a woman in her midtwenties, a bloom of health in her cheeks, her brown eyes bright and wide. Her hair cascaded down her shoulders, neatly combed and oiled.

What was so frightening about her? Maybe the strange combination of a radiant face with a grave tunic and the smell of myrrh unnerved people. Maybe something had happened in the city while she had been... She couldn't think of the appropriate word. *Dead? Sleeping?* She had no vocabulary for a temporary death.

The shopkeeper came from the back of the store and stopped. His nose wrinkled at something in the air. He was a tall man with a terribly curved spine, so that one shoulder sat much higher than the other. Shoshan's heart immediately went out to him. It looked like a painful malady to live with. Lifting a hand, she wanted to introduce herself, thinking she might come back and buy a mirror here. He needed the money for doctors, she was sure.

"By Jove!" Staring at her, he clutched the amulet on his chest. He was a Roman, then. Romans worshiped Jupiter, or Jove as he was also called, as the supreme god.

"I just wanted to—" Shoshan began.

"Get out before I call the guards!" the shopkeeper yelled.

People had gone mad. Was there poison in the water?

The shopkeeper lurched out of the store behind her.

"She is one of them!" he yelled, standing outside the shop, pointing back in at her. "She stinks of the grave!"

She pushed past him, exiting the shop. People parted from her, repelled away. Shoshan's mind whirled. She knew the myrrh had a strong fragrance, but how did these people know she was...what was she? She didn't even know!

A woman pointed to Shoshan and screamed in Aramaic. "*Koom!*"

One who stands up again, a resurrected one. But it also could mean one who intends to fight.

Shoshan threw up her hands in protest. "I just want to go home!"

A Roman guard turned the corner. His eyes locked on hers. The man was around her age, with light brown hair and brilliant green eyes. Handsome, except for a scar that ran across his left cheek and down through his jaw, from a sword, perhaps. The scar was raised and red, and it was hard not to stare at it. It must have happened when he was very young, and it must have hurt very badly. But she tore her gaze away from it as his hand raised to his sword. His breastplate caught the glare of the sun and blinded her, and she lifted her arm to shield her eyes.

"I do not want to fight," she called. Whatever rebellion was happening in these streets, she had no part in it. "I am on my way home!"

"Koom!" the woman yelled to the guard, still pointing at Shoshan.

The guard scowled and moved toward her, his hand still on his sword. Rome executed people for insurrection, she knew. The cries of "Koom!" did not stop, and the ground seemed to shake with every step the guard took toward her. Shoshan turned and ran with a speed that surprised her, shoving people aside, cutting around corners, taking stairs to streets that led to shops, and then cutting through the shops to new streets. People cursed her for knocking them down or out of the way, and no matter how fast she ran or which turns she took, she heard the calls. *Koom!* She heard the stomp of Roman boots, the clang of armor as more guards joined the first in pursuit of her.

Turning a corner, she dashed into a darkened shop that sold Roman codices. In the darkness, she fought to catch her breath.

Each shuddering gasp sounded so loud in her ears, and she clenched her jaw, willing herself to be quiet.

Would the guards think to look for a Jewish girl in a Roman shop? Hopefully not. The tread of boots drew closer.

In the darkness, a hand reached for her, landing on her arm. Before she could scream, another hand clasped over her mouth, and she was pulled backward into the shadows. She struggled to break the man's hold on her, but he was stronger.

When she was released, she was in a tiny room filled with about ten other people, all strangers to her. They sat around a table, hands folded in their laps, or eating flatbreads. They looked up at her with interest then looked at her captor as if he would explain.

No one here was afraid of her. Curious about her, yes, but not afraid. Slowly, she felt her muscles loosen, and she was able to breathe.

An oil lamp burned in the dark room, and flickering light cast dancing shadows on the walls, distorting the faces that huddled around it. Their faces seemed kind, though, as they squinted to look at her. Had it been even an hour since she stumbled out of her grave? So much had already happened. All she wanted was to go home, to see Antonius, to think that this was all a dream.

"Who are you?" she demanded, looking around the room.

The man who had grabbed and released her looked around at the others, his white bushy eyebrows jumping up and down as he chuckled.

"You are just in time," he replied then patted her lightly on her shoulder. "We were just about to make our introductions."

Was he crazy?

A woman who seemed familiar somehow to Shoshan, though Shoshan was sure she had never seen her before, shook her head.

"You owe her more of an explanation," she scolded the man. "Poor girl is scared." She peered across the jumping flame at Shoshan. "This man has been watching for us on the street, collecting us, one by one, pulling us to safety."

"It was smart thinking to hide in this shop." The shopkeeper smiled. "There are more guards on the streets every minute."

Shoshan stared at her, then at the shopkeeper, not understanding. She had only chosen this shop because it sold Roman codices. No one staging a rebellion against Rome would be shopping for those.

"Did you wake up in a grave?" the woman pressed.

Shoshan swallowed, the noise audible in the tiny room. How did this woman guess that?

"Do not worry," the woman replied, "we all did."

"I did not wake up in a grave," an elderly man said. "I woke up in a vegetable patch. A rabbit was tugging on a radish when up I popped. I do not think the poor thing will ever eat radishes again." He grunted, suddenly dismayed. "My grave was not tended to. Someone sold it for a garden. Such a thing should not be done."

"Let us all think," the woman said. "How long have you been dead? Does anyone know?"

No one spoke.

The woman tried again. "What is the last thing you remember?"

"David was dancing through the streets." The elderly man spoke first, his face transformed by the memory. "The Ark had come to Jerusalem. What joy! We feasted and sang until dawn. I was eighty years old. Glory to God."

His face cleared suddenly. "Where is the Ark now? Did David finish the temple he planned for it?"

"The Ark is not here," Shoshan murmured. Her mind was doing the math, trying to comprehend his statement. "And Solomon, David's son, is the one who built the temple. David was dead by then."

The man clicked his teeth. "I knew that, somehow. How did I know that?" His gaze fell to the floor, away to his right, as if searching his memories.

"Wait," one woman across from Shoshan interrupted. "I remember that I was bringing bread to the workers at the wall. King David had been gone for…well, you are right, he was dead. Had been for generations. Jerusalem had fallen. But we had no temple, no king."

Everyone fell silent, staring into the flickering light. Jerusalem without a temple? Without a king? No wall to protect it?

"The wall still stands," Shoshan said quickly, mentally going back through the stories she knew. "And the temple was rebuilt. Nehemiah led your people, yes?"

The woman nodded vigorously. "And a king?" she asked. "Who is the king?"

"There is a man called the King of the Jews. His name is Jesus." Shoshan took a deep breath. "He is the Messiah."

"Yes," everyone murmured, a sound of joy, like water in a fast-moving brook. It was as if Shoshan was reminding them of a name that had been on the tip of their tongue, just out of reach. But how could they know of Jesus? They had been dead when He was born!

Not Shoshan though. She had spent many afternoons following Him, listening to Him teach. Antonius was not interested in the new teacher roaming the countryside, especially because the teacher was a carpenter and construction worker like Antonius. They had probably worked on the same building projects together. Still, Antonius had never stopped her from leaving to hear Jesus, not even when she was...

Her hand flew to her abdomen. *Not even when I was pregnant and close to delivery.*

She leaped to her feet and lurched toward the door, but the older woman jumped up and caught her by the arms. Shoshan struggled and raised her voice until the shopkeeper placed his hand over her mouth again. Everyone looked stricken with fear now, their faces distorted, and she guessed they had been hunted too. She nodded, indicating that she would not scream, and he released her.

"I was pregnant," she gasped in the tiny room, trying to catch her breath as the memories crashed in. "I was in labor, and the midwife was yelling for someone, or something. That is the last thing I remember."

A different kind of silence fell over the room. No one would meet her eye. They guessed something she did not. She could see that in their eyes.

"What happened to your child?" asked the woman who brought bread to Nehemiah's workers.

Shoshan closed her eyes, thinking. "I do have one memory."

Opening her eyes, she looked around at their faces. They were all so beautiful, the joy radiating from them as if they carried a bit of heaven. Fear had looked so unnatural on them.

"I held her in my arms, and she laughed. Oh, she has dark lashes, so very long! And such delicate fingers. I think she might become an artist or a weaver. When she laughed, her eyes danced."

Shoshan shook her head lightly. "I was so happy that I thought my heart might burst, that I had no more room to contain so much joy. I have never felt anything like it."

The women in the room exchanged glances again then smiled at Shoshan.

"What is it?" Shoshan demanded.

The oldest woman spoke, her voice soft. "Newborns do not laugh. They cannot."

"I heard her laugh. I saw it," Shoshan responded, indignant.

"I know! I am not doubting you," the woman replied. "But it could not have happened. Not on earth."

Shoshan heard the shopkeeper clear his throat.

All her strength left her, and she slumped down, her hands pressing into her abdomen. Her memory was real, but it was a memory of another place. Jesus spoke of a place called paradise. Others called it heaven. She had been there with her daughter, hadn't she? The shattered pieces of her memory came together at once, the story making sense now.

"I died in childbirth," Shoshan said quietly. "I think my child did too." The women gathered around her, pushing the men aside, putting their arms and hands on her to comfort her. But Shoshan was confused more than stricken. She had seen her daughter, and her daughter was very much alive.

But had she seen a little body in the grave when she awoke? Shoshan tried to remember but couldn't remember anything past the little bedroom where she had been in labor. Antonius had been there, she remembered that, but did he know she was dying? Did he have a chance to say goodbye?

He must have been devastated. Utterly heartbroken. He lost his wife and daughter in the same day.

She knew that she must return home at once. Antonius needed to see her and to understand that miracles were happening.

He needed to know that anything was possible.

A NOTE FROM THE EDITORS

We hope you enjoyed the first book in the Mysteries & Wonders of the Bible series, published by Guideposts. For over seventy-five years, Guideposts, a nonprofit organization, has been driven by a vision of a world filled with hope. We aspire to be the voice of a trusted friend, a friend who makes you feel more hopeful and connected.

By making a purchase from Guideposts, you join our community in touching millions of lives, inspiring them to believe that all things are possible through faith, hope, and prayer. Your continued support allows us to provide uplifting resources to those in need. Whether through our communities, websites, apps, or publications, we inspire our audiences, bring them together, and comfort, uplift, entertain, and guide them. Visit us at guideposts.org to learn more.

We would love to hear from you. Write us at Guideposts, P.O. Box 5815, Harlan, Iowa 51593 or call us at (800) 932-2145. Did you love *Unveiled: Tamar's Story*? Leave a review for this product on guideposts.org/shop. Your feedback helps others in our community find relevant products.

Find inspiration, find faith, find Guideposts.
Shop our best sellers and favorites at
guideposts.org/shop
Or scan the QR code to go directly to our Shop

EXTRAORDINARY WOMEN OF THE BIBLE

There are many women in Scripture who do extraordinary things. Women whose lives and actions were pivotal in shaping their world as well as the world we know today. In each volume of Guideposts' Extraordinary Women of the Bible series, you'll meet these well-known women and learn their deepest thoughts, fears, joys, and secrets. Read their stories and discover the unexplored truths in their journeys of faith as they follow the paths God laid out for them.

Highly Favored: Mary's Story
Sins as Scarlet: Rahab's Story
A Harvest of Grace: Ruth and Naomi's Story
At His Feet: Mary Magdalene's Story
Tender Mercies: Elizabeth's Story
Woman of Redemption: Bathsheba's Story
Jewel of Persia: Esther's Story
A Heart Restored: Michal's Story

Beauty's Surrender: Sarah's Story
The Woman Warrior: Deborah's Story
The God Who Sees: Hagar's Story
The First Daughter: Eve's Story
The Ones Jesus Loved: Mary and Martha's Story
The Beginning of Wisdom: Bilqis's Story
The Shadow's Song: Mahlah and No'ah's Story
Days of Awe: Euodia and Syntyche's Story
Beloved Bride: Rachel's Story
A Promise Fulfilled: Hannah's Story

ORDINARY WOMEN OF THE BIBLE

From generation to generation and every walk of life, God seeks out women to do His will. Scripture offers us but fleeting, tantalizing glimpses into the lives of a number of everyday women in Bible times—many of whom are not even named in its pages. In each volume of Guideposts' Ordinary Women of the Bible series, you'll meet one of these unsung, ordinary women face-to-face and see how God used her to change the course of history.

Befitting Royalty: Lydia's Story
The Prophet's Songbird: Atarah's Story
Daughter of Light: Charilene's Story
The Reluctant Rival: Leah's Story
The Elder Sister: Miriam's Story
Where He Leads Me: Zipporah's Story
The Dream Weaver's Bride: Asenath's Story
Alone at the Well: Photine's Story
Raised for a Purpose: Talia's Story
Mother of Kings: Zemirah's Story
The Dearly Beloved: Apphia's Story

Find more inspiring stories in these best-loved Guideposts fiction series!

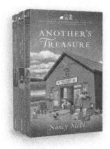

Mysteries of Lancaster County

Follow the Classen sisters as they unravel clues and uncover hidden secrets in Mysteries of Lancaster County. As you get to know these women and their friends, you'll see how God brings each of them together for a fresh start in life.

Secrets of Wayfarers Inn

Retired schoolteachers find themselves owners of an old warehouse-turned-inn that is filled with hidden passages, buried secrets, and stunning surprises that will set them on a course to puzzling mysteries from the Underground Railroad.

Tearoom Mysteries Series

Mix one stately Victorian home, a charming lakeside town in Maine, and two adventurous cousins with a passion for tea and hospitality. Add a large scoop of intriguing mystery, and sprinkle generously with faith, family, and friends, and you have the recipe for *Tearoom Mysteries*.

Ordinary Women of the Bible

Richly imagined stories—based on facts from the Bible—have all the plot twists and suspense of a great mystery, while bringing you fascinating insights on what it was like to be a woman living in the ancient world.

To learn more about these books, visit Guideposts.org/Shop